CAN THERE EVER TRULY BE AN *ENTERPRISE II*?

IS JAMES KIRK THE HORATIO HORNBLOWER OF THE FUTURE?

IS VULCAN RULED BY MALES, FEMALES—OR ANYONE WHO CAN EARN THE RIGHT?

These are just a few of the intriguing questions explored in this special anniversary issue of *The Best of Trek*®. In the twenty years since *Star Trek* first began, it has become far more than a television series—it has become a "real" universe to which its many loyal fans return again and again. And to commemorate the two decades of enjoyment and hope *Star Trek* has given so many people, we bring you this special collection about *Star Trek*, past, present, and yet to come.

THE BEST OF TREK® #10

THE BEST OF TREK® #10

FROM THE MAGAZINE FOR STAR TREK FANS

EDITED BY WALTER IRWIN & G. B. LOVE

A SIGNET BOOK

NEW AMERICAN LIBRARY

Copyright © 1986 by TREK®
Copyright © 1986 by Walter Irwin and G. B. Love

TREK® is a registered trademark of G. B. Love and Walter Irwin

 SIGNET TRADEMARK REG. U.S. PAT. OFF. AND FOREIGN COUNTRIES
REGISTERED TRADEMARK—MARCA REGISTRADA
HECHO EN CHICAGO. U.S.A.

SIGNET, SIGNET CLASSIC, MENTOR, PLUME, MERIDIAN AND NAL BOOKS
are published by New American Library,
1633 Broadway, New York, New York 10019

First Printing, June, 1986

1 2 3 4 5 6 7 8 9

PRINTED IN THE UNITED STATES OF AMERICA

We would like to dedicate this tenth volume of
The Best of Trek® to
Carolyn and DeForest Kelley
in appreciation of their kindness, courtesy,
and friendship

ACKNOWLEDGMENTS

Thanks are due, as always, to all of our writers, artists, correspondents, and—of course—readers who have helped make *Trek*® and *The Best of Trek*® a success over the past years.

Special thanks go to Earl Blair, Jim Houston, Leslie Thompson, and Janet Smith-Bozarth, all of whom gave us welcome and needed help during the early days. We also would like to thank our new editor at NAL, Karen Haas, whose experience with pocket Books' Star Trek fiction line helped prepare her for the wonderful and wacky world of *Trek*. Glad we didn't have to break in a rookie!

Very special thanks go to Sheila Gilbert, our former editor. Sheila worked with us from the very beginning, and we couldn't have asked for a more enthusiastic, understanding, and intelligent editor. We wish her the best of luck and much success in her new position at DAW Books. *Muchos gracias*, Sheila . . . you made it easy and fun.

CONTENTS

INTRODUCTION

Thank you for purchasing our tenth volume of articles and features collected from our magazine, *Trek*. We think you'll find that our writers have quite a bit to say about Star Trek and related ideas that you will find interesting and exciting. If you've seen our previous nine volumes, then you know what to expect. If you're a first-time reader: Welcome! You've got quite a treat in store!

This volume will be released in mid-1986, just a few short months before the twentieth anniversary of Star Trek's debut on national television. Just think of it! Star Trek is twenty years old! According to the results of the fan poll we took recently (you'll read the results in this volume), a goodly number of our readers weren't even *born* twenty years ago!

But we don't see this anniversary as a sign of age—we see it as a sign of youth. What other television series can boast an active and constantly growing fan base as loyal and as loving as Star Trek's? What other television series has gone through *three* different incarnations—four, if you count the ongoing fiction efforts of both professional and fan alike—each one unique and yet true to the original conception of Star Trek? And what other television series gains new fans each and every year it remains on the air, as new generations are born and grow to appreciate the series?

These questions answer themselves. Other television programs may promise to run forever (and some deserve to), but none of them has inspired the fan following and devotion that Star Trek has.

This is not the place to try to explain why. Indeed, a great deal of this ongoing *Best of Trek* series has dealt with trying to explain why, as have dozens of other books and articles. All we can say with assurance is that the prediction we made in the introduction to *Best of Trek #1* is definitely coming true: *There will always be a Star Trek*.

Even as you are reading this, the fourth Star Trek film should be soon reaching theaters. That there would ever be *any* Star Trek films was virtually unthinkable when we began *Trek* way back in 1974 . . . and now it's unthinkable that they should ever stop. Star Trek novels and other books (like this series) continue to sell in the hundreds of thousands. Star Trek fans still gather at conventions to watch episodes, trade memorabilia, meet the stars. Fanzines still flourish, giving amateur writers, artists, songwriters, and poets a place to perfect their craft and expose their dreams to the sympathetic eyes of other fans. Star Trek toys, games, storybooks, model kits, and the like continue to be manufactured and marketed to children of all ages. And it's virtually impossible to find anyone in this nation who cannot identify Captain Kirk, Mr. Spock, or the *Enterprise*.

Yes, Star Trek is here to stay. And so are we.

This tenth volume is also an anniversary for us. When we released our first *Best of Trek* volume back in April 1978, critics asked, "Just how much can you say about Star Trek?" Well, we think that first volume, and nine more after it, have pretty well answered *that* question. As long as we continue to have new readers, as long as we continue to receive articles and features (and ideas for them) from those readers, we won't have to worry about running out of things to say about Star Trek.

The nicest thing about these last ten volumes and last eight years has been all of the letters from you readers. We've heard from virtually every part of the globe, from people of every age, race, social class, political belief, religion, background, and personal taste. From them we've gained a wider perspective into the world around us and into the lives and beliefs of others, and, consequently, more insight into ourselves.

We've also been privileged to meet many of you in person. It's always a thrill to be recognized and praised for one's work, and you're always welcome to come right up and say "Hi!" But as pleased and flattered as we are to receive your praise, it is our contributors who truly deserve it. That bugaboo question "Just how much can you say about Star Trek?" would have been answered pretty quickly with "Not much" if we had had to do it on our own. We'd like to take this opportunity to offer heartfelt thanks to each and every one of you who ever contributed to *Trek*. Even if, for one reason or another, we did not choose to publish your contribution, we read, enjoyed, and learned from it.

We'd like to name all of our contributors, but space doesn't allow us to here. So, as this is our tenth volume, we decided to include a cumulative index.

We also thank those of you who continue to support us by subscribing to *Trek*. There is an ad elsewhere in this volume with more information, but if it is missing for some reason, our rates are as follows: $13 for four issues, postpaid; $26 for eight issues, postpaid. (Canadians must pay in money orders in U.S. funds only.) Orders should be sent to the address at the bottom of this introduction.

Before ending up and letting you get to this collection, we'd once again like to invite all of you with an urge to write to send in your contribution. As we indicated above, new writers are the lifeblood of *Trek*, and we're always delighted to receive material from them. To make things a little easier for us, however, please note the following instructions: Type the article, double-spaced; please don't send any articles less than 2,000 words long; include a return envelope with postage attached. Easy enough? Thanks, and we'll be looking for your submission very soon.

And if you don't feel like writing an article but would like to drop us a line anyway, please do so. We're always delighted to hear from our readers, and you might find your letter included in a future *Trek Roundtable*! Or if you have any idea for articles, features, or ways we can make *Trek* better or more entertaining, please let us know!

Without your feedback, we have no way of knowing if we're doing a good job or a bad one. After all, we consider this to be *your* magazine, and each and every one of you has a say-so. So say! You can reach us at:

TREK
1120 Omar
Houston, TX 77009

Thanks again for your support and advice and plain old *love* over these past years. We honestly could not have done it without you!

WALTER IRWIN
G.B. LOVE

DIVERSITY IN COMBINATION

by Alan Manning

We sometimes feel that the philosophy of IDIC is bandied about among Star Trek fandom a little more freely than the concept warrants. Some fans do, however, give it the thought it deserves and ofttimes manage to develop concepts and theories which transcend the original idea. Such examination can be found in the following article, which wonders if the diversity which all too often seems to be lacking in Star Trek's stories is alive and well at the core of Star Trek's characterization.

"Infinite diversity in infinite combinations," or IDIC, is a prevalent motto and ideal in Star Trek fandom. Any individual aficionado of Star Trek has strong personal opinions about its meaning and typically constructs his or her own version of the imaginary universe implied by the series. Their common philosophical acceptance of frequently incompatible views developed by other, equally dedicated fans seems to keep them all from coming to blows with each other. In fact, IDIC may be keeping the peace between this minority and the general population, which considers such devotion to a television program frivolous.

On a higher plane, IDIC encourages diversity for its own sake, implying that contrasting opinions, life-styles, appearances, and so forth are somehow beneficial rather than merely tolerable. It is generally agreed that this was a major message conveyed by the television series, "evidenced" by the racially integrated crew of the *Enterprise* and occasionally positive portrayals of alien creatures and cultures. However, there are visible limits to acceptable diversity; the *Enterprise*,

14

through Kirk, is dominated by recognizably Anglo-American values, and a number of alien customs are changed by Kirk precisely because they violated those values. (See "The Apple," "Patterns of Force," "The Omega Glory," and "A Taste of Armageddon" for examples.)

While infinity is a highly useful concept in a mathematical system or as a philosophical ideal, in actual practice only limited variety and finite combinations shape our experience. By itself, the principle of infinite diversity in infinite combinations has no informative content; that means it allows any state of affairs, forbidding nothing, and experience is as much a matter of finding out *what is not* as it is a matter of seeing what is. Some may recall Spock's advice in "The Gamesters of Triskelion"—if you can't know where someone is, you may at least determine where he isn't. We may choose limitations ourselves, by picking specific qualities from a potentially infinite diversity; examination of all possible combinations of these qualities alone does tell us something: the number of unique combinations, and consequently, the characteristics of each combination due to the possession of certain qualities and the lack of others.

For example, let E represent the quality of *emotion* and L represent the quality of *logic*, our chosen bits of diversity. Since these are qualities and not quantities, it's pointless to use E or L more than once in a combination, and their order of appearance is arbitrary. This disallows combinations like EE or LLL; and EL is equivalent to LE. In the process of combination a quality can either be included or excluded; as was said, it is also important to know what is not, so a zero would indicate that a quality has been excluded. Under these conditions there are exactly four unique combination-entities: EL, OL, EO, and OO. The first entity has both *logic* and *emotion* at its disposal; the second, however, is only disposed to *logic*, and the third only to *emotion*. The fourth entity is the decimal zero, indispensable in mathematics for its place-holding value; it has no overt qualities and so the other three may obscure its importance, but it exists by logical necessity, as background; it is the slate, one might say, on which the next three entities are written.

Readers who have not, by now, begun to detect a familiar pattern in all this should turn in their phasers and have their pointed ears clipped.

Entities EL, LO, and EO clearly designate the most fundamental characteristics of Kirk, Spock, and McCoy respectively—these characters have been referred to countless times as the Three, the Triad, the Friendship, the distinct aspects of a Whole Man. If the world of Star Trek goes around, it is because they turn the crank. However, it is rightly said, and not often enough, that the *Enterprise* is also a character, indeed a key character in Star Trek. It is the background without which there would have been no story. As a piece of machinery, the *Enterprise* is neutral with respect to *emotion* or *logic*, and she is bound to the other three, as an entity complementary with logical and emotional Kirk, in a relationship unemotional and illogical: "I give—she takes. . . . No hand to hold; no beach to walk on," laments Kirk ("The Naked Time"), and then, illogically, he declares, "The *Enterprise* is a beautiful lady and we love her!" ("I, Mudd"). The fourth combination entity *OO* quite appropriately designates the *Enterprise*.

So, while IDIC in its unlimited sense fails at the level of plot (what with Kirk blasting computers, pulverizing perverse cultures, and quoting the U.S. Constitution), it succeeds at the level of characterization, in finite terms—two elements of diversity, *logic* and *emotion*, have exactly four possible combinations: one, the other, both, and neither. The inherent, complementary pattern of these combinations reflects to a striking degree of specificity the basic characterization pattern of Star Trek.

This diversity in combination produces a special kind of pattern known as a *paradigm* (pronounced PEAR-a-dime), an ordered system generated by the combination of a finite number of principles. One paradigm readers are probably all too familiar with is the pattern of verb conjugation English teachers oblige us to learn: *I run, you run, he, she, it runs, we run, they run.* This paradigm has a logical gap where there is no special plural form for *you* as there is for *I* and *he* (*we* and *they*), but this lack tends to be repaired by the increasingly acceptable southernism *you all* or *y'all*. This demonstrates the natural tendency to fill all possible positions in a paradigm sooner or later. Once a paradigm is established, innovations which violate its boundaries are unpopular; things like *me runs* or *them run* are denounced as "ungrammatical."

Commenting on the early days of the series, the cast and creators of Star Trek seem to agree that the complex relationship between Kirk, Spock, and McCoy developed spontaneously, as if by magic, and once "the Big Three" were established it seemed impossible to produce an episode focusing on anyone else. It is as if the positions of a paradigm were spontaneously filled, and thereafter all real activity was limited to it. Structural oppositions in the pattern developed in the character; a bickering feud got started between Spock and McCoy, and Kirk began to manifest a troublesome pseudosexual attachment to the *Enterprise*. Events like these have been described and discussed in detail, but more often than not, no real *explanation* for them is ever offered. *Why* does Star Trek showcase three and only three of its regular cast? *Why* do Spock and McCoy oppose each other literally and symbolically? *Why* is Kirk romantically involved with 200,000 metric tons of metal and plastic? Why do we enjoy watching this so much, in rerun, year after year?

The hypothesis offered here would explain these and many other Star Trek phenomena as the inclination to match characters with a paradigm generated by specific qualities, in all possible combinations.

To continue, then, as the series developed there came to be four regular supporting cast members: Scotty, Uhura, Sulu, and finally Chekov. This would be the natural consequence of adding the quality of support to *logic* and *emotion*, making a total of three instances of diversity. The inclusion or exclusion of three qualities in combination yields 2^3, or eight unique entities: *OOO, EOO, OLO, ELO, ELS, OLS, EOS, OOS*. While this string of figures seems like some arcane religious chant, it is intended to represent the character types which naturally develop given those three themes. The first four designate the *Enterprise*, McCoy, Spock, and Kirk, as we have seen, with the added stipulation that they are non*support*, i.e., supported rather than supporting by nature. This does not mean the Three are incapable of lending a hand to those in need; Spock does show emotion now and then, and McCoy is not incapable of logical reasoning, so the Three occasionally help others out of a jam, too, but it is more typical for them to be helped by others to accomplish their own goals. Naturally, it is Edith Keeler who offers help to Kirk ("The City on the Edge of Forever"), and Kirk who steals the scene by explaining the poetic significance of that gesture to her.

For Scotty, Uhura, Sulu, and Chekov, all of life's meaning lies in supporting the *Enterprise* and the Three. It seems certain that *ELS* designates Scotty. Of all the supporting cast, this character is the most completely developed. His expertise in techno*logical* matters equals that of Spock, and yet Scotty is quite an emotional character, particularly where the *Enterprise* is concerned. This is expected because *ELS* and *OOO* are paradigmatic complements, each possessing features missing in the other. The old adage that opposites attract is exploited here, just as it is in the relation between Kirk (*ELO*) and the *Enterprise* (*OOO*) at a different, nonsupport level. Scotty's love for the *Enterprise* is supportive, while that of Kirk is not. That is why she is Kirk's "lover" and Scotty's "baby." Complementary difference between *EOO* and *OLO* (McCoy and Spock) is exploited another way; opposites attract but they also argue a lot.

While indications that Scotty matches up with *ELS* are strong, the correspondence between *EOS*, *OLS*, and *OOS* and Sulu, Uhura, and Chekov seems harder to establish. Throughout the series they are either being upstaged by the Three or they are so busy doing their jobs that their personalities never really develop. This problem solves itself because the jobs come to match those paradigmatic types instead; what these characters do to support the others becomes more important than who they are.

Like Scotty, the communications officer holds a technological position (stress *logical* again) and works with intricate codes and complex equipment. This post also demands the single-minded ability to send messages as they are given, without personal or emotional coloring. *OLS* is probably best matched by Uhura.

The position of helmsman surely requires a special "feel" for the ship in order to execute often delicate maneuvers successfully. Such sensitivity might qualify as an emotion, at least in an extended metaphor relating control of the ship's motion to e-*motion*. The helmsman should take no time to consider the logic of any action. His job is to carry out the captain's orders to move, quickly and accurately. *EOS* designates that position, usually held by Sulu.

This leaves Chekov with the role of just plain *support* (*OOS*), nature unspecified. In the episodes before Chekov was added, this paradigmatic position was probably held by Yeoman Rand, and in her absence it could be filled by assorted crewmen such as Lieutenant Riley. These are characters-at-large, with flexible duties: some days the navigator, some days the assistant science officer, some days part of a landing party, some days toting papers for Kirk to sign. *And* when the script calls for someone to be poisoned (Riley, "The Conscience of the King"), someone to be accosted by strangers (Rand, "The Man Trap," "Charlie X"), someone to be thrown into the agonizer booth (Chekov, "Mirror, Mirror") or shot ("Spectre of the Gun") or frightened ("The Deadly Years") or burned (*Star Trek: The Motion Picture*), this character type is the favorite victim. Chekov seems to fill the role best; as David Gerrold points out (*The World of Star Trek*), he has a great way of screaming.

Given the typology of their duties, Uhura (logic-support), Sulu (emotion-support), and Chekov (unqualified support) could be expected to manifest those traits in their personalities, should these ever be developed. Vonda McIntyre's "Hikaru" Sulu is surely a romantic character in her Star Trek novelizations. A bit of this also appears in Joyce Tullock's comments about *Star Trek III: The Search for Spock*: "There is Sulu, the dashing, sexy swashbuckler. . . . There is Uhura, with her warmth, beauty and elegant presence of mind. Here is a dignity which rivals even that of Mr. Spock. . . . Mr. Chekov . . . seems to be the most clearheaded of the crew, in fact, lacking both Scott's rebel cynicism and Sulu's passion for adventure . . . (*Best of Trek #8*).

Majel Barrett fans may perceive a flaw in the hypothesized paradigm because it fails to provide a position for or explain the character of Nurse Chapel, but in fact her lack of "fit" in the eight-member paradigm explains why she is not used in the later Star Trek films. If she matches any type it is *EOO*, as a feminized version of McCoy, complementary and therefore attracted to Spock. Significantly, it is she who temporarily carries Spock's *katra*, consciousness, soul, or whatever, in the episode "That Which Survives," foreshadowing McCoy's service in *The Search for Spock*. Figuratively, these *EOO* characters have room for Spock's *OLO* in their persona; together they briefly make a whole *ELO* being. But in the end, Chapel is not the real McCoy, as it were; when the true Spock/McCoy relationship is portrayed, her role is superfluous.

Because the three-quality paradigm generates exactly eight positions, the number of characters that can be included in the "family group" is eight, counting the *Enterprise*. Guest stars, as aliens, bad guys, love affairs, etc., are no problem, because they come and go, interacting but not intruding upon the *Enterprise* family. With the advent of Star Trek cinema, however, new characters appeared with evident intentions of joining the family. Even Gene Roddenberry must have thought this would work; David Gerrold notes that Decker and Ilia both were first created as regular characters for a new Star Trek television series, but as the script for the aborted series evolved into a feature film, Decker and Ilia were sacrificed to V'Ger and the nth dimension. Harve Bennett then took creative control of Star Trek, and marched out his new generation of characters, Saavik (apprentice-Vulcan) and David Marcus (son-of-Kirk). In *Star Trek II: The Wrath of Khan*, Saavik is acceptable, but David is clearly excess baggage. In *The Search for Spock*, Klingons get to kill David, while rookie actress Robin Curtis never lets her performance of Saavik live.

This all does not mean that characters cannot be added to Star Trek successfully; it does mean that new players cannot be stuck on the old paradigm with thumbtacks, glue, and good intentions. Arrangements must be made and prices must be paid.

Star Trek II: The Wrath of Khan pays a price for Saavik which makes her acceptable; Chekov is transferred to the *Reliant* crew, then Saavik, not he, holds the *OOS* position aboard the *Enterprise*. Complementary relations between *ELO* and *OOS* sustain the chemistry between Kirk and Saavik, evidenced by their verbal fencing, just short of being openly flirtatious. Saavik is here the support-character-at-large; she is the apprentice commander, the navigator, landing party member. She gets all the jobs Chekov had, except screaming.

Saavik can take a few liberties here with her ostensible Vulcan background—a little aggression here, a few tears there—because the paradigm only stipulates her *support* quality. Her Vulcan nature is as incidental as Chekov's Russian accent—both interesting, but flawed on several points. Perhaps if Spock had stayed properly dead she might have moved to *OLO* and might have been paid Leonard Nimoy's salary too, thereby inducing Kirstie Alley to keep the role. But in that case Saavik would have to clean up her Vulcan act.

Chekov suffers greatly in the trade to *Reliant*, but Walter Koenig benefits as an actor. As victim-of-Khan he garnered more on-screen time than Sulu and Uhura combined; sometimes it pays to escape the paradigm, but when it comes to long-term survival, there is safety in being numbered among the Eight. *The Search for Spock* returns Chekov to his original support role, and the price for that arrangement is Saavik. It could easily have been Chekov, as senior surviving officer of the *Reliant* (survey ship for the Genesis Project), assigned to explore the Genesis Planet with David Marcus, where they could have had a revealing discussion about the proper role of the military in scientific research. But Chekov was returned to the fold, and Saavik was thrown to the Klingons.

On Genesis, Harve Bennett gathered together all the problem-characters he created in *Wrath of Khan*: the planet itself, Spock's animate corpse, Saavik, and David Marcus. David was doomed from the start. Besides having no place on the *Enterprise*, the script forced him to be a distasteful boob. In fairness to his creators, it is conceivable that he could have evolved as Luke Skywalker did, from fool to hero, but *Star Wars* was structured *a priori* to accommodate such a character; Star Trek was only structured *ex post facto* to dispose of him. On Genesis there were two forces at work, *aging* and *death*. The planet itself ages rapidly and dies. The body of Spock ages rapidly from its regenerated youth along with the planet, but is rescued and lives. Saavik does not age and lives—*AD, AO, OD, OO*—creating another paradigm does make a place for these characters, but it is doomed from the start to dismantle itself.

In some respects, that is also the way the extra characters from *Star Trek: The Motion Picture* neatly remove themselves from the continuing adventure. Decker, Ilia, and V'Ger form a separate group corresponding with the same *EL, EO, OL, OO* pattern which formed Kirk, McCoy, and Spock, with the *Enterprise* as *OO* background for both groups. Decker, Ilia, and V'Ger fuse into a single superbeing; all identical qualities are the same quality, so *ELEOOL* equals *EOLO*, which suggests that both qualities are included and excluded at once. To resolve this paradox the superbeing vanishes into another dimension, leaving the *Enterprise* to its old crew.

Perversely, Saavik is left to the old crew at the end of *The Search for Spock* and the *Enterprise* perishes. This just barely seems a fair trade because a restored Spock is produced in the bargain. Incredibly, after all the action, explosions, deaths, and reshuffling of characters, the paradigm endures. Exactly eight continuing characters remain when the dust settles: Spock, Kirk, McCoy, Saavik, Scotty, Uhura, Sulu, and Chekov. After death, confinement in McCoy's persona, and refusion in his physical body, it is doubtful that Spock is still his former nonemotional, merely logical self. This leaves his former paradigmatic position, non-*emotion*, *logic*, non-*support*, available to someone else. A painfully obvious candidate is Saavik. If few fans liked Robin Curtis's cold portrayal of her, it is because she matched that paradigmatic type too well and *too soon*. Contrasted with Kirstie Alley's warmer, almost seductive *OOS* version of Saavik, Robin Curtis was so cold she made our teeth ache. This leads to a major blunder because her main role in *The Search for Spock* was *OO* in the Genesis paradigm. In contrast to the aging, dying world around her, Saavik should have been shown fighting actively, even passionately, to sustain her youthful attitude and her life; in this context, a textbook Vulcan, wisdom-of-the-ages approach was as wrong as it could be. Failure to match the right paradigm at the right time has cost this character its original popularity and maybe its future.

To fill the *OLO* position, Saavik might get another chance in the future film(s), but there is at least one attractive alternative. The character of Sarek, nicely recreated by Mark Lenard, could be taken up as a continuing character instead; in a vicarious sense, Sarek keeps Spock's old position filled all through *The Search for Spock* by pointing out to Kirk that Spock's soul is still lurking about. As Spock's father, Sarek is a well-established fixture in the Star Trek universe, and hence a more reliable choice than Saavik.

In any case, Saavik, or Sarek, or someone like them, is necessary for the immediate future because Spock has been promoted to *OOO*, the center or background position formerly held by the *Enterprise*. At the end of *The Search for Spock*, Sarek explicitly informs the audience that Kirk's ship was the price of Spock's return. A curious exchange of fates has taken place: Spock's battered remains fall like a meteor into the atmosphere of Genesis in *Wrath of Khan*, and in *The Search for Spock*, the burning wreck of the *Enterprise* streaks across the Genesis sky. Spock is rescued from his fate, but the *Enterprise* is left to hers.

By definition, there cannot be a star trek without some vehicle to travel between stars, so the erstwhile crew of the *Enterprise* must board another starship in order to continue the adventure. Even so, there may never be an *Enterprise II* or any other ship which is also a real character, Kirk's lover and Scotty's "baby." By willfully discarding the *Enterprise* in exchange for Spock, Kirk and Scotty abandoned that disproportionate affection for a material object; to restore it would be a step backward.

Instead, Spock assumes the paradigmatic position *OOO*, which is a convenient pattern for someone recently resurrected to match. There is now as much freedom to redefine Spock's character as there was to redesign the *Enterprise* sets for the Star Trek films. It will also be convenient for Leonard

Nimoy, as director of coming films, literally in the background of every scene shot, to play a role which is now figuratively the backdrop of all other main characters in Star Trek.

This outcome of *The Search for Spock* is so convenient for Mr. Nimoy that some might wonder if he planned it that way. We can imagine Nimoy and Bennett plotting together in some dark corner of a Paramont sound stage to assassinate the *Enterprise* and place Spock on the throne. . . . Besides bordering on paranoia, such a scenario ascribes to the conspirators more explicit knowledge of the internal workings of Star Trek than they probably have. In order to succeed, real plotting demands a working knowledge of cause-and-effect rules which operate in the situation being manipulated. These imagined conspirators are the same people who brought us David Marcus and derailed the character of Saavik. How much can they possibly know?

In reality, Star Trek is an art form, and all the people who bring it to the screen are artists, usually just doing the best they can. When a creative decision is made, it is because it "feels right," "looks good," or "sounds like it will work." A sequence of these subjective, noncalculated decisions has directed the evolution of the world of Star Trek to its present point. Paradoxically, the whole purpose of this essay has been to demonstrate a Star Trek paradigm, a tightly organized pattern which dictates the acceptable number of regular characters, the typical qualities each should have, and the complementary associations between them. It would be a good bet that your average writer/producer/director would not realize that such a paradigm even exists in Star Trek. How can such a pattern be used and how can it survive, without the conscious control of its creators?

This phenomenon, while puzzling, is not without precedent. Children learn to use all major components of their native language long before they can be taught any explicit rules of grammar in school, which are rarely learned anyway. People who hear an ungrammatical sentence are more likely to spot it because it "sounds bad," not because they recognize that any rule has been violated. Conversely, they recognize a grammatical sentence because it "sounds okay." Knowledge of language is so basic that we have access to it without being aware of it, and we can learn a language (at least when children) by simply being exposed to it, rather than by laboriously learning the explicit rules. The Star Trek paradigm can be seen as the explicit form of a *paralanguage*, a symbolic structure having qualities similar to a real language (just as a *paramedic* is something like a real doctor, but not quite the same). Like children exposed to a language, people who watch Star Trek episodes long enough begin to sense the typical paradigmatic roles of the characters without being consciously aware of what they are. Some people are more adept at learning new languages than others; so too, the degree to which some people are deeply moved by Star Trek and find meaning in it, while others find it bizarre and insignificant, may be in keeping with their natural ability to learn the paralanguage associated with it. A question: Do Trekkers score higher on language aptitude tests than the general population?

Those who do come to understand Star Trek can detect instances when the proposed paradigm is not being correctly matched in an episode or film because "it feels wrong" at certain points. On the production side, those with creative control over the series make decisions about what the characters will do and say based on what "feels right." Their subjective judgment is hopefully also guided by the same paralanguage, learned by watching previous episodes or reading the series guidelines. If there is anything a fan fears or hates, it is a television episode or film "mutilated by someone who doesn't understand Star Trek," i.e., someone who hasn't learned the paralanguage well enough to be guided by it. Of course, even the most literate among us occasionally make grammatical errors, slips really, with language, that we don't detect until we've said them, so even reasonably experienced people like Roddenberry, Nimoy, and Bennett may try something which isn't an obvious mistake until it's on the screen in the final cut, too late to be fixed. In learning to recognize and produce acceptable forms of a paralanguage, Star Trek filmmakers come to obey constraints of its paradigmic structure without explicit knowledge of it; if they make occasional errors, it is fortunately true that these can be recognized and corrected later, just as long as there is another Star Trek movie in the works.

It was explained at the outset that the Star Trek paradigm originates from a finite application of IDIC, which in itself may explain the popularity of that expression among Star Trek devotees. It happens that diversity in combination is a highly efficient method of generating character types. In television and film, efficiency is always a must, because of time limitations. While a novelist can take hundreds of pages to establish characters and plot, screenwriters have to tell their whole story, with believable characters, they hope, in an hour or two, with a handful of scenes and a limited budget. More characters means less time devoted to plot only, and less time to make each person real to the viewer. Not surprisingly, more programs fail in this balancing act than succeed. But if all characters are variation on the same qualities, then to develop each is to develop them all, directly, by similarity or indirectly, by complementarity.

Consider, for example, the original Spock, unemotional and logical. Time spent illustrating his logical behavior on-screen is also time spent illuminating the logical qualities of Kirk (*ELO*) and the logical duties of Scotty and Uhura (*ELS*, *OLS*). Spock's unemotional behavior establishes the emotional nature of Kirk, McCoy, etc., by contrast. In like manner, portrayal of any and all members of the paradigm reinforces the features they possess in all the others as well. Most of the character development thus takes place in our minds by association, and only a small fraction one-eighth to be exact, is physically manifest on camera. Because the developmental potential for each character is multiplied eightfold in this manner, it is small wonder that the Star Trek characters become very much alive to those who understand the paralanguage best, the ranks of Star Trek fandom.

A bare handful of syndicated television programs enjoy a level of economic success comparable to that of Star Trek. For some reason, people find these programs watchable even after years in rerun. It is enlightening to count the number of main characters in some of these:

Bewitched—Samantha, Darrin, Endora, Larry Tate . . . 4

I Dream of Jeannie—Tony, Roger, Jeannie, Colonel Bellows . . . 4

I Love Lucy—Lucy, Ricky, Fred, Ethel . . . 4

Gilligan's Island—Gilligan, Skipper, Mr. Howell, Mrs. Howell, Ginger, Professor, Mary Ann, the island . . . 8.

These are precisely the number of characters that would match two- and three-quality paradigms (2^2, 2^3). Each of these programs has identifiable theme qualities which will generate patterns that do match its characters quite well. Identification and elaboration of these will fill many more essays; readers wanting intellectual exercise may tackle these themselves.

Diversity in combinations is such an effective characterization strategy that those few programs which are lucky enough to chance upon it should have much greater chances of survival, in syndication if not on prime time. Evidently, characters which are so developed that they seem real are enjoyable to watch, even when the outcome of the episode is well known, as if a *historical event* were being experienced directly, and not the nth repetition of a mere story.

So long as the producers of those cultural artifacts we call entertainment are not consciously aware of IDIC and paradigms, the phenomena described here can work to their advantage only if it all develops spontaneously; but in theory, one could deliberately pick qualities, generate a paradigm, and match characters to it before shooting a foot of film. If this ever becomes standard practice, we may get better programs, and IDIC will have become a first principle of *cultural* engineering, just as Newton's $F = ma$ is a first principle of mechanical engineering. Should that happen, I hope people remember they heard it here first. Nowhere is IDIC and the paradigm principle of characterization more clearly revealed than by the *Enterprise* and her crew—one more discovery made on their epic journey.

THE BRILLIANT DOOR

by Joyce Tullock

Joyce Tullock was one of the few regular Trek *writers that we asked to comment on her personal feelings about Star Trek's twentieth anniversary. She was among the very few to agree—very reluctantly—to do so.*

Apparently, discussing one's innermost feelings about Star Trek was just too difficult a task for most. And as you read the following article, you'll realize that it was difficult for Joyce as well. Trouper that she is, however, she came through— dare we say? —brilliantly.

Back in the third grade, I had to write an essay on the first day of school. It was supposed to be about "what I did on my summer vacation." It was very hard for me to say anything. Not that a lot didn't happen during summer vacation, it's just that the stuff you remember, that really, really is important to you . . . well, it's personal, even to a third-grader.

That kind of thing never changes, so when, for the one and only time I sat down and tried to write a personal account of Star Trek's influence on me, I just got stuck. And kind of angry at a certain someone for even suggesting I do so. I got defensive. After all, it's nobody's damn business what Star Trek means to me. Don't I write about the series enough anyway? Can't people get the point of what I'm thinking?

Anger, as Dr. McCoy might point out, can be a useful tool. If you apply a Spockian logic to it, that is. And so it is that I have found a starting point for my little article.

First and foremost, it seems, Star Trek has always been a very personal experience for me. As personal as my social security number, bank balance, and shoe size. I don't care to

27

flaunt my feelings about it to just anyone. They might misinterpret them. Sometimes I think even *I* misinterpret them. And it seems pretty obvious that the anger I feel about having to talk about it means that Star Trek must have had a greater effect on my life than I'd like to admit. After all, I've spent a good deal of time these past years trying to express what it is that I see in Star Trek. One might ask: ''Why?''

I could get real defensive here. I could tell you about all the people I know who have revealed themselves to me, telling me how Spock has influenced, even changed, their lives. Yes, I could just tell on everybody else. It would be easy, and fun. But it would not be accurate. I would not have the whole story, only bits and pieces friends and acquaintances and casual readers have given me.

Not that Star Trek ever taught me honesty and journalistic integrity. There are too many episodes where Star Trek's scientific credibility, for example, does not want to be examined closely. And even moral judgment is left in question from time to time, for it seems as though Captain Kirk is all too ready to impose the WASPish Western ways of our society on alien planets. Not that I blame him particularly. I'm as blind as he is about some things. I would never presume to outguess or outjudge the noble Jim Kirk. He is a hero of grand stature. I always marvel at the way he handles so many impossible situations and questions and world-wrenching problems with such grace and adroitness. I've always wondered how he did that, and have never been able to imagine myself handling life so well.

Maybe I've always been a little jealous of Jim Kirk. And if that doesn't give you a hint about what Star Trek means to me, I feel very sorry for you indeed.

Spock, on the other hand, has always been a character I could grapple with. I've always liked his type. Even when his type was Michael Rennie in *The Day the Earth Stood Still*. Now I realize that the good Vulcan is many things to many people, and I don't want to step on toes. But to me, he is . . . oh, what do you call it? . . . *Future*. I've heard him referred to as an emotional idiot. But those remarks don't come from anyone who has studied the series. You have to take time to know Star Trek, after all, just like anything else. You have to learn to know Spock, for after twenty years, he is quite real. And in the context of Star Trek and the universe it contains—with a Vulcan race which decided on peace over passion and war thousands of years before Spock was born—Spock must be seen as an alien. He must be seen as one who does not follow the "rules" as we know them, and as we demand they be followed in our world. To many people, I suppose, Spock must seem offensive, hence the label "emotional idiot." All because he's an alien. You know, I think I like Spock because of that. Because of his being "alien," I mean. I have been an alien all my life.

Now are we getting personal?

It's all right, though. A lot of people I know are alien. Some are my friends and some are not, but at least we all have that much in common. I bet Mr. Spock would be pleased at something in that statement. After all, look at the fellow: In the series he's a lone alien aboard the *Enterprise*, trying to make do with the likes of Jim Kirk and Leonard McCoy for friends. Now we all know that Jim Kirk, while being a Terran, with many of our rutty Terran ways, somehow has become such a special man, such a diplomat, that, socially speaking, he pretty much passes the Vulcan test for good manners and propriety. Yes, Jim's been around, and maybe, just maybe, I'm a little jealous of that too.

But Spock's other friend, Dr. Leonard McCoy . . . well, he isn't the kind of guy you would expect to see at your average Vulcan social affair. I've said it before, in other articles, but this is my one and only time of being personal so I just have to say it again: I like McCoy because I can relate to him as a real, honest-to-goodness human being. Of the three, his character is the most complete, the most believable, the most "for real." The irony of it being that understanding McCoy takes more work. That statement sounds illogical, but it's true, and I'm sure McCoy would be more than happy to back me up on it.

McCoy is embarrassingly human. Overall, he's a nuisance, and generally annoying. He suffers from foot-in-mouth disease. He is humanitarian in principle, sometimes hypocritical in deed, and forever trying to reconcile the two. He likes people, but he wishes they'd leave him alone. In other words, he's the kind of man who'd love to be a hermit—if only he weren't so busy with humanity.

Leonard is mixed up, and like Spock, he is alien. He is Spock's psychological negative. That is, Spock seems to be an individual with direction, discipline, a sense of future. McCoy, on the other hand, is a tad chaotic. The universe is not all mapped out before him, described in the language of physics and mathematics. One would guess that McCoy had to work really hard to be satisfactorily good at math. To be honest, though, it's just something I like to imagine: that McCoy isn't good at math. It isn't necessarily so.

And if Spock gives me a sense of future, then McCoy gives me a sense of *Past*. But hold on, 'cause this is where the science fiction comes in and ties Spock and McCoy together in the kind of literary symbiosis I love—the past McCoy represents is our present. I like that, because it makes Star Trek more real to me. It's like the hub at the center, the quiet spot, the recognizable, where I can sit and watch through McCoy's eyes as the future happens all around me. I don't think it's going too far to say that I bet a lot of people view Star Trek the same way, whether they are consciously aware of it or not. I don't think you can really help it.

And the fact that McCoy is there too, in that beautiful future, with Spock and Kirk, makes me hope that something of the kind of person I am will make it to a better future, somehow. That's a very selfish feeling, and it is personal.

I remember how things were in the sixties when Star Trek made its first public appearance. Not to reminisce, but we'd been through one hell of a decade. We'd lost a young president who'd promised us a future, and we'd lost others, valuable people who had actually stood for ideals. All of us who were old enough were in a trauma in those days. No kidding, it really was a time when you would sit down to dinner with the TV on and watch young Americans and Vietnamese die. People talk about the young people of the sixties, with their flower songs and peace movements, as being unrealistic, escapists. I don't think anyone, young or old, was escaping in those days; we were all on a pilgrimage, looking for the Holy Grail. And we probably knew more about reality than any generation since Hiroshima.

We were definitely looking for something. and it's no accident that a lot of the things we were looking for popped up in a daring new series called *Star Trek*. For one thing, it was clear that in Star Trek, our own painful, complicated time was history. That is, we had made it through the nuclear age. But we'd been through some nasty times, as characters like Khan of "Space Seed" and Colonel Green of "Savage Curtain" reminded us. These fellows represented everything civilized man has always tried to rise above: racism, fascism, tyranny, cruelty. And in Star Trek, it seemed pretty evident that the men of planet Earth *had* risen above those things—for the most part, anyway. How refreshing it is to learn from Dr.

Marcus in *Wrath of Khan* that the Fleet had preserved the peace for one hundred years. Just think of it!

Some fans refuse to accept the movies as genuine Star Trek, by the way. They have all different kinds of reasons, too—from Kirk being too "imperfect" (huh?) to Spock's death and resurrection being too contrived, too "Hollywood," if you will. Well, I don't blame anyone for complaining from time to time, but I can't agree with this authenticity thing. Although sometimes I'd like to. Like everyone else, I sometimes forget that Star Trek is not my own personal property. That's why Paramount has a hard time with people like me.

That's also why Star Trek is still around.

From the time the series was canceled it has been a comedy of errors. Bjo Trimble spearheaded the movement to save it, but some people think we might almost be better off if we'd been left without that last season. I'm not one of them. There were some dogs in the last season, but there were some gems, too. It was worth the pain.

The people who gathered behind Star Trek. seeking to keep it alive in their own writing, if necessary, have become sort of legend to the Trekkers. In the early days of Star Trek fanzines, for example, there was some fantastic talent. Connie Faddis of *Interphase*, for one. She set the pace for the zines we see today.

Of course, that was then and this is now. Since the time of *Interphase* a whole new generation of fans has turned up— and this is not a generation that has to do with age, but with tastes, with talent, with what they see in Star Trek. Fans write more about inner feelings than did the early writers—although there were some fine, introspective writers in the early days as well. But now fan writers, always trying for something different, tend to examine the characters as people, not so much as heroes. It makes it much more difficult to write the relationships and keep them in character. Even Paramount is trying it, giving us a Kirk who makes personal and judgmental errors. A Kirk who is growing old, facing the pain of separation from the people and things he loves. The fallibility and maturity of the man in all three movies is refreshing and wise. Paramount is to be commended. It is to be even more commended for *finally* allowing the other characters to have some time with the audience. Paramount had to learn the hard way, but the last two movies have proved that Star Trek is more than Jim Kirk or any one of the characters.

Unlike Paramount, however, fan writers have known that

all along. They *know* Star Trek, and usually work hard at making the science in their material at least marginally credible. The serious writers really work hard, on both the amateur and professional levels. Maybe Star Trek isn't "growing up," but it is certainly growing. While the fan novels still beat out the pros in character development, character relationship, and true "Star Trek feel," we've seen some good professional novels in the last few years, like Howard Weinstein's *Covenant and the Crown* and Diane Duane's *Wounded Sky*. These stories are the genuine article, true Star Trek. No more perfect than the episodes or movies or fan stories, but filled with the warmth and the wonder, just the same.

But an indication of how much Star Trek is growing up is seen most clearly in the works of the fans themselves. Bev Zuk's novels, *Honorable Sacrifice* and *The Final Verdict*, absolutely shine. She treats her subjects with maturity, clarity, and professional prose style. And Laurie Huff of *Galactic Discourse* edits a zine that rivals *Interphase*. She has a gift of putting graphics, story, and artwork together in such a way as to make a zine that is, of itself, a work of art. These people care about Star Trek, and it shows in their work. It is not a living to them, but a nonprofit hobby. No, that's not right, either. To these people, the appreciation of Star Trek is an art. Maybe that makes them and their kind the truest writers of all.

But what makes us do it? That's the real question. Star Trek fans, the creative ones anyway, seem driven to go about a virtually thankless, profitless task. Why?

I think the answer takes us back to that personal stuff I mentioned earlier. You know—the topic of this article, which I so slitheringly avoided. Star Trek is personal. And for those who write and draw and edit it, it is frighteningly so. Because when you write, when you create with pen and ink, you have to call up things inside. When you're creating, it doesn't matter if you're professional or amateur, you're using personal things—some happy, some painful. On some level, you're discussing and defining things you never knew before about yourself and the world as you see it. And speaking about such personal matters so openly can prove quite dangerous. But that's the point, I suppose: Star Trek works particularly hard on creative people, and draws from them, challenging them to define what it is they see in this world of the future, how they apply it to the world of today. Even the most cynical creative fan knows—when you write, draw, paint, or edit Star Trek you are, on some level, in search of that Holy Grail.

For me, the Star Trek experience has been remarkably rewarding. It helped me come to terms with my own view of the universe. And yes, I'll admit it, with my own view of myself. I've learned, for example, that I've never, ever been able to see the universe around me in black and white. I've learned to live with that and appreciate it. That's gotten me in trouble a time or two, though. For example, I've had people complain that I am an atheist because of my remarks in the *Best of Trek* article "Bridging the Gap." To them I would say, "Read it again, and tell me who is the atheist and who is the believer." I enjoy writing articles like that one, because they allow me to express openly the way I see the world. In analyzing the series, I discovered a lot that surprised me about myself, about Star Trek and science fiction, and about our own society.

I have had to pick the episodes and characters apart sometimes, and in doing so, have found bits of my own personality. It's a very rewarding thing, very exciting, very frightening. So I guess you could say Star Trek has helped me to understand my own perspective. If I learned anything else in watching Star Trek, I learned to give as much attention and respect to my own view as I do to anyone else's. And more important, I've learned that the best way to expand my point of view is to listen to others.

The feelings evoked in and by Star Trek are deep, mysterious. No wonder some think of it as cultist, for there is no good bread-and-butter, black-and-white way to describe to an outsider what Star Trek means to those who number themselves among its fans. It has a lot to do with the mysterious, surrealistic magic of science fiction, of course. And with the powerful literary presence of such ideas as isolation, alienness, of hope for the future, of the imperativeness of human brotherhood. Then, of course, there are the deep, virtually endless meanings found in the triad friendship of the unified personality of Spock, Kirk, and McCoy.

It's the triad that stands out most in my mind. It's the triad, I would venture to guess, that is at the core of the very "personal" nature of Star Trek. Kirk, Spock, and McCoy are the point of center from which I can view a world of imagination. A world that is as alien or as twentieth-century as I care to see it. They are the key, or more correctly, the equation of

Kirk, Spock, and McCoy is the key. It is not so much the men, but the relationship they have to one another and their world. It wouldn't have to be a Kirk, or a Spock, or a McCoy—it just happens to be so. It is their part in the equation: the outgoing human spirit of Kirk, the sensible, controlled logic of Mr. Spock, the warm, positively irrational emotions of McCoy. They are us, bits of us, altogether.

Spock and McCoy, with their ongoing battle of emotion versus logic, past versus future, impulsiveness versus stoicism, and on and on and on . . . they are indeed bits of me. They present a challenge for the writer, for in writing them, in understanding them, one must dig deep. For myself, and for many others I know, these characters have opened a brilliant door.

And if I cannot tell you what it means to me, I will tell you what it means to you: Look in the mirror.

BOOTS AND STARSHIPS

by Walter Irwin

*There's seldom any problem getting Walter to the keyboard—
the problem's more often getting him away!—but in this
instance, for once, he proved reluctant. Like many others, he
was loathe to discuss his personal feelings about Star Trek,
feeling that his already published articles and features were
more than sufficient. But canny G.B. pointed out that maybe
not everyone on earth had had the privilege of being thrilled
by Walter's previous writings; more seriously, each volume
attracts new readers who've never seen any of the earlier
ones. So didn't Walter owe them something, too?*

By the time our readers see this volume, it will be 1986 and
close upon the twentieth anniversary of Star Trek. A twentieth anniversary is a good time to look back, to take stock, to
ask questions and seek answers. Several articles in this volume discuss "What Star Trek Means to Me"; this is supposed to be one of them.

Instead, I'm going to present to you a speech I made at
Deltacon in Baton Rouge, Louisiana, last September. The
speech is not about my feelings about Star Trek; it is, however, about the way in which I see Star Trek, a view which is
unique unto me, and a view which probably says more about
me than I could ever say otherwise. I'll also have a few things
to say afterward.

By his own admission, Gene Roddenberry's original concept of Star Trek was based, in part, on the Horatio Hornblower
series by C. S. Forester.

The image of the seafarer, the explorer, is a powerful one,

which has been used to good effect in the legends and fiction of many cultures. From Odysseus to Ahab, the stories of men who cannot resist the lure of the sea are part and parcel of humanity.

Forester, when creating Hornblower, used this tradition to the utmost. His captain is all of the things we expect our heroes to be: courageous, self-sufficient, loyal, handsome, compassionate, steadfast, and just the tiniest bit flawed. The Hornblower stories are also set in that most romantic of seafaring times, the era in which England was stretching her colonial arms around the world, building an empire upon which the sun would never set. It was a time when men set forth upon tiny wooden ships, braving the elements and enemies on every side, simply for God and country. And maybe just a smattering of Adventure.

The Hornblower books, well written and exciting, sold in the millions. By the time that Roddenberry was planning Star Trek, the Hornblower series was an institution, virtually a template from which any seafaring series dared not stray too far.

Roddenberry had no intention of doing so. He envisioned his captain as being firmly in the Hornblower mold. The parallels were nothing if not obvious: a captain in charge of a vessel, weeks, even months removed from contact with his government, required to act as diplomat, governor, general, despot as the occasion arose, an explorer who also served as ambassador of his culture and arbiter of others, and a natural leader of men, but humanized by a dollop of hubris, ambition, and the occasional doubt.

It was around this familiar and romantic theme that Roddenberry built his series. Star Trek wasn't to be "Wagon Train in Space"; it was to be "Hornblower Explores the Stars."

But somewhere along the way, something went wrong.

In each of the early Star Trek episodes, we see a little bit more of this concept lost. The introduction of faster-than-the-ship subspace radio, the establishment of an entire fleet of starships, all seemingly within the same area of space, and mostly the introduction of Starbases and the consequent command structure.

The focus of the "commander alone" concept was first watered down, then completely abandoned. The long tentacles of Starfleet Command reached farther and farther out into space, until it seemed that in many episodes, Captain Kirk and his crew went home every night for dinner.

Thus, the concept became quite something else in execution. Instead of the intrepid explorer, Captain Kirk became a soldier, a keeper of the peace, a patroller of borders and neutral zones.

In short, the *Enterprise* became part of the cavalry. The myth of the seafaring man was exchanged for the equally powerful, and, to American audiences, more familiar, myth of the horse soldier.

Portions of the United States Army, divided into groups of officers and men designated (and numbered) as cavalry, patrolled the American West from after the Civil War until during (and shortly after) the First World War. Their duties included aiding and protecting settlers, enforcing borders, tracking down and punishing marauders, limited exploration and mapping, diplomacy and treaty-making, and law enforcement in the absence of federal marshals. The cavalry operated out of a series of forts established along, and sometimes beyond, territorial borders. The ongoing settlement of western lands, the building of railroads, and the continual expansion of telegraph lines allowed officers to keep in touch with their superiors in Washington.

This era has become part of our folklore. The sound of "Charge" blown on a bugle is known by every schoolchild; the name Custer is synonymous with both incredible bravery and incredible stupidity; when one hears the word "fort" an image of upright log walls and attacking Indians immediately springs to mind.

Although there is enough truth in the annals of the cavalry to supply any television series with material for several seasons, most of our enduring images of the cavalry have come from fiction. Thanks to the stories of writers such as James Warner Bellah, who wrote, among many others, the stories on which the John Wayne movies *She Wore A Yellow Ribbon*, *Fort Apache*, and *Rio Grande* were based, and Ernest Haycox, to name only two, we get a glimpse of what life as a dollar-a-day man in the cavalry was really like. Many other writers, some equally fine, most just hacks, have contributed to the legends. Most persuasive, however, have been the innumerable movies and television shows featuring the cavalry. It is safe to say that a substantial number of stories which we think of as "westerns" are tales of the U.S. Cavalry.

So what, you may be asking, does a series set in space, on a starship, have to do with boots and saddles?

Just this: The Duties of Captain James T. Kirk, commander

of the *Enterprise*, over the course of the series, included aiding and protecting settlers, enforcing borders, tracking down and punishing marauders, limited exploration and mapping, diplomacy and treaty-making, and law enforcement in the absence of Starfleet authority. The *Enterprise* operated out of a series of Starbases established along, and sometimes beyond, territorial borders. The ongoing settlement of new planets, the building of faster and faster ships, and the continual expansion of subspace radio allowed officers to keep in touch with their superiors in Washington.

Sound familiar?

This transmogrification was not necessarily a bad thing. As a matter of fact, by grounding the Star Trek world in a legend/format more recognizable to American audiences, it probably accounted for the (eventual) success of the series.

Star Trek is nothing more than the logical extension of the lusty American creed: ''Elbow room!'' It is the twenty-third-century equivalent of Manifest Destiny, the promise of a United States from ocean to ocean which stirred colonists to keep moving west. Star Trek, in its devotion to the work ethic and down-home American values, reaffirms the rightness of exploration and colonization—without exploitation—by free men who remain free.

Little wonder, then, why the series very quickly became a reflection of our own past struggles to capture and colonize our West. In episode after episode, the battle aims were restated, the battle lines redefined, the battles refought. In ''Where No Man Has Gone Before,'' the second pilot (and the first Kirk episode), the aim of the *Enterprise* is to discover what is on the ''other side'' of the barrier surrounding the galaxy. ''Mudd's Women'' presents us with itinerant traders, fiercely independent miners, and ''mail-order brides,'' all staples of western fiction. These are but two very early examples, made before the introduction of the elaborate series of Starbases, outposts, survey ships, etc. that made the *Enterprise* ever less alone and ever more dependent upon the chain of command.

Roddenberry was also faced with what virtually amounted to a *fait accompli* in the area of characterization. So vivid were the portrayals of his leads that he was forced to adjust the concept of the series to accommodate them. William Shatner's Kirk was simply too active, too brash, too *American* to be the brooding, introspective captain. And the quick emergence of Nimoy's Spock and Kelley's McCoy required a readjustment of the series which showed them constantly interacting with Kirk as part of the regular chain of command. This resulted, of course, in the development of the classic Triad, or Friendship, which completely refocused the show and further affected the development of each character. This interdependence of character called for situations in which the three would be working as a team, thus further removing Star Trek from the original concept.

In short, Gene Roddenberry's dream of a "Hornblower in Space" was not successful. This is not to say, of course, that such a series could not be successful; nor were all of the "seafaring" elements dropped from Star Trek. (Most, however, survived as elements of nostalgia: naval rankings, Kirk's yearning for "the wind at his back," etc.) The lure of firmly grounding the *Enterprise* and its crew in a more audience-recognizable and appealing milieu, one which was also easier to write and act, was virtually irresistible. One might even say, given the time and the place and the people involved, that it was inevitable.

If you read between the lines (and I hope you could), perhaps you realize that, to me, Star Trek came to represent everything that is good about our country—today, in the past, and in the future. Most fans like to say that Star Trek represents hope for the future, a promise that we will overcome our difficulties and differences and build a world of freedom and tolerance. I see it a little differently: I believe that Star Trek represents the best in humanity, as evidenced in American principles and life-styles . . . *today*, not in some "maybe," Utopian future. Principles and life-styles not perfect by any means, but better than most and damn well preferable to the death of the mind enforced by totalitarianism and the death of spirit caused by socialism. Principles and life-styles which can accept, and have accepted, again and again, new and different cultures, and can take the best from them, tolerate the rest, and emerge ever stronger and enriched.

Star Trek says that all men are better off when free and left to their own devices. As a product of Twentieth-century America, it says this in American terms, to a largely American audience. But the message is nonetheless clear and demanding: Man must be free, he must continue to explore and grow, he must continue to ask, "Is this all that I am?"

THE NAMING GAME

by Nicky Jill Nicholson

Way back in an early issue of Trek, *we ran an article outlining how most of the beautiful women who appeared in Star Trek had names that ended in "a": Mea, Shahna, Marla, Odona, etc. Harmless fun. Nicky Nicholson, however, takes us one step farther: She examines the names of each character in relation to the kind of person they are, wondering if the name "fits." She also manages along the way to make a good case for establishing some characters' "real" names. (We fear, however, that that debate is far from over.)*

An individual's name does more than distinguish him/her/it from a host of similar individuals. The name, to a great extent, both defines and reflects the person it represents. A name also presents an instantaneous image, a "thumbnail sketch," so to speak, of the name's owner. This impression may not always be accurate: many people have taken an immediate dislike to a new acquaintance, merely because they have, in the past, known and disliked another individual with the same name. However, preconceived notions aside, it is your name, more than any other single facet of your personhood, that tells the world who and what you are.

This is even more true for a fictional character than it is for an actual person. In a very real sense, the name *is* the character. Many an otherwise excellent book has been ruined (at least for me) by the author's unenlightened choice of character names. On the other hand, I've also read a few books whose plots were decidedly shopworn, but whose alluring, mystical, otherworldly names held me enchanted from beginning to end. If the name isn't *right*, it destroys the character, and it can destroy the entire fictional work as well.

Say the following name aloud: James Tiberius Kirk.

Nice, isn't it?

Notice the crisp consonants (J,T,B,K) that dominate the vocal sound. These terse phonetics conjure a mental image of an alert, active individual, erect, confident, and capable. One might expect a starship commander to project just such a first impression.

The name is appropriate for its character in the sense of literal meaning as well. The name James is of Hebraic origin, and means "the supplanter." A supplanter is a person who takes over someone else's position and/or property. James T. Kirk was introduced in the second Star Trek pilot, "Where No Man Has Gone Before," as the replacement for the USS *Enterprise*'s original commander, Captain Christopher Pike. Thus, Pike was supplanted by Kirk.

Tiberius was the name of one of the most famous rulers of ancient Rome. The name originally referred to the "lord of the Tiber River," but the meaning which filters down to modern times is that of a leader, a man of great power.

The name Kirk is apparently of Norse origin, and means "dweller at the church." Now, although Captain Kirk has never been an overtly religious man, he certainly displays many qualities for which religion would have us strive: truthfulness, compassion, loyalty, self-discipline, and strength of spirit. The name perhaps exaggerates the fact, yet does not invalidate it.

An additional point is the fact that both James and Kirk are fairly common names in this country today. Since James T. Kirk is supposed to have an ancestral background connected with the American West (established in the television episode "Spectre of the Gun"), it seems reasonable for him to have an American-sounding name.

So, on several different levels, the name James Tiberius Kirk was an excellent choice for this particular character.

One might look at the name Leonard McCoy in the same light. I may be crazy, but the very phonetic sound of the name McCoy calls to my mind the medical officer's dry bark of "I'm a doctor, not a—!" This might be thought a Scottish name, but it is a very common name in America, quite proper for a man from Georgia. The prefix "Mac" (here shortened to "Mc") means "son of," and the man's name Coy is derived from an Irish Gaelic name meaning "battle follower." His first name, Leonard, is of Frankish origin and means "lion-brave." What courage it takes for a man of such compassionate nature to remain in Starfleet service, where he must see his dearest friends so often in deadly danger!

The same may be said for the names of most of the other Star Trek characters. Whether intentionally chosen or not, the names are suitable for their characters in terms of phonetic imagery, literal meaning, and national or regional origin. Thus: Montgomery Scott, Pavel Chekov, Christine Chapel. The names *are* the characters.

However, some controversy has arisen concerning the names of three of Star Trek's regular characters. Just to add to the confusion, I would like to offer my own views on these three people-puzzlers.

First of all, there's Spock, and by extension, Vulcan names in general. Spock, Sarek, T'Pau—are those their first names or their last names? Or, to phrase the questions more precisely, are those their given names or their family names?

In "This Side of Paradise," Spock told Leila Kalomi that she couldn't pronounce his first name. In "Journey to Babel," Spock's mother, Amanda, told Captain Kirk, "I doubt you could pronounce the Vulcan family name." One must bear in mind that *family name* and *last name* do not necessarily mean the same thing. Right here on our own little planet there are a few cultures wherein it is customary for the family name to precede the given name. Thus, when Spock told Leila she couldn't pronounce his first name, he still might have been referring to his *family* name. Vulcans are apparently known by their *given* names, regardless of that name's "position." An interesting side note is that in her Star Trek novel *The Vulcan Academy Murders*, Jean Lorrah suggests that in Vulcan society it is considered particularly courteous to address an individual by his given or "first" name.

The second name in question is that of Mr. Sulu. Some sources, reportedly including actor George Takei, insist that Sulu's first name is Walter. Other people, including the authors of several Star Trek novels, give Sulu's first name as Hikaru. I think this deserves some discussion.

In the first place, I feel that Walter is simply the wrong name for this character. Try saying it aloud: "Walter Sulu." It sounds (to my ear at least) a great deal like "Waterloo." Not the kind of image we'd like a Starfleet officer to convey. Also, Walter is more or less an American-sounding name, inappropriate for an Oriental character. My third objection to the name is its original Germanic meaning, "powerful warrior." Of course, Sulu is no slouch when it comes to fighting, but he has never struck me as really being warlike or violent in nature.

Besides, I think I know where the name Walter came from in this context. In his book *Chekov's Enterprise*, Walter Koenig humorously lamented the fact that some people around the studio seemed to have a hard time telling him and George Takei apart. Apparently Mr. Takei thought it was extremely funny to hear people call him Walter, and I've got a sneaking suspicion that *that* is where the idea came from to have Walter become Mr. Sulu's first name.

The alternative choice, Hikaru, is a very excellent alternative. It is an authentic Oriental name, its phonetic imagery balances between crisp alertness and relaxed humor, and it means "shining one." As the premier helm officer of the *Enterprise*, Sulu shines indeed.

For the above reasons, I find myself forced to the conclusion that the proper name for this character is Hikaru Sulu. If some of you want to pretend that his middle name is Walter, feel free.

My most vehement pronouncements concern Uhura's name. In her article "Star Trek Mysteries Solved . . . Again!" (*Best of Trek #8*), Leslie Thompson made the following flat statement: "Uhura's first name is inarguably Penda. No compromises there."

I'm sorry, folks, but I thoroughly disagree. I have examined every scrap of Star Trek material at my disposal, and I cannot find a single reference to the name Penda in connection with Uhura or any other Star Trek character. On the other hand, the authors of Star Trek novels (Diane Duane, Janet Kagen, and William Rotsler, to name a few) are unanimous in giving Uhara's first name as Nyota. This I'll buy. Nyota is a Swahili name which means "of or belonging to the stars." It's *right* for the characters. It sounds African, it sounds feminine, and it certainly has an appropriate meaning. Further, I firmly believe that the choice of professional writers should take precedence. Thus, Uhura's first name is indisputably Nyota. And I won't compromise, either.

The appropriateness of names operates on another, more subtle level as well. In order to preserve what J. R. R. Tolkein referred to as the "inner consistency of reality," there must be a kind of continuity between the name itself, the character's personality, and the culture from which the character supposedly springs. Accordingly, with relatively few exceptions, most Vulcan male names begin with the letter

S and end with the letter K, and are generally limited to one or two syllables. Vulcan female names, again with few exceptions, begin with a T, as in T'Pau and T'Pring. This gives the overall feeling that the names (and the characters they represent) do indeed spring from a common culture.

Even the names of Star Trek guest characters were often chosen with uncanny insight. My favorite example is the character of Lieutenant Mira Romaine, from the television episode "The Lights of Zetar." In that episode, Mira Romaine repeatedly had visions of future events. Generally, the name Mira is considered of Latin origin, and means "wondrous one." Interestingly enough, however, *mira* is also a legitimate word in the Spanish language. It is a form of the verb *mirar*, "to see," and can be translated "she sees."

Unfortunately, the same care was not always given to the selection of names for planets. Most Star Trek worlds were called by utilitarian names that reflected the planet's location in space, as in Ceti Alpha V and Gamma Hydra IV. Other planet names were largely derived from Earth's folklore and legends, chosen with some appropriateness but little imagination. Thus, we have planets with names like Charon and Gideon and Sarpeidon. However, there was some creativity even here: I remember with pleasure Star Trek world-names such as Triacus, Vendikar, and Thasus. Those names surely were derived from some truly alien culture and language.

One aspect of science fiction naming has always annoyed me. This is the tendency to lump every facet of an alien culture under one general name, and Star Trek is as guilty of it as any other SF production. The word "Vulcan" is a perfect example. Think how many things that term covers! The planet is Vulcan, the people are Vulcan, the language is Vulcan. This makes no sense to me. Our planet is Earth, our people are humans, and our language is English—and it seems logical to assume that other races would have separate words for all those things as well. The term "Romulan" particularly distresses me, being so obviously an Earth-human invention.

Some Star Trek writers evidently agree with me on this score. In her Star Trek novel *My Enemy, My Ally*, Diane Duane informs us that the Romulans' name for their own people is Rihannsu. They call their home star system (and by extension, their empire) Eisn, and their twin worlds are named ch'Rihan and ch'Havran. Now that's more like it!

John M. Ford performed the same service for the Klingons

in his Star Trek novel *The Final Reflection*. Mr. Ford accepts the term "Klingon" as the name of the people, and I can't dispute this matter, since the word is clearly not derived from any human language. However, the author also points out that the name of the Klingon homeworld is Klinzhai, and the language is called *klingonaase*. The core of all these terms is the prefix "kling," which refers to the basic principles of life and power. Ford also adds the interesting note that Klingon officers change the first letter of their name to the letter K when they attain command rank. That's why all Klingon commanders have names that begin with the letter K; it's an honorific. Nice touch.

I can't conclude an examination of Star Trek names without mentioning the one recent Star Trek novel in which names play a very important part. I'm referring to Janet Kagen's delightful novel *Uhura's Song*.

One of the first important points made in the story is that Uhura's friend Sunfall calls herself "of Ennien"—yet there is no place named Ennien on Sunfall's home planet. This information, along with other clues, eventually leads the *Enterprise* crew to the world from which Sunfall's people first came— the planet Sivoa. In Sivoan culture, it is a dire insult to call someone by anything other than his or her proper name. As a matter of fact, instead of saying "When I grow up," Sivoan children say "When I have my name." The Sivoan characters tend to have descriptive names, such as Fetchstorm for a youngster who likes to cause trouble, and Stiff Tail for a rigidly conservative individual. On making initial contact with the Sivoans, the universal translator renders Nyota Uhura's name literally as Starfreedom; and later, a Sivoan adolescent whom Uhura has particularly befriended chooses Another Starfreedom as her own adult name. And in the midst of all this, a mischievous impostor has taken the name of a Starfleet doctor and assigned herself to the medical section of the *Enterprise*!

Names.

Names can make magic—or prevent it. They can lure the imagination into their inventor's world, or create stumbling blocks that are impossible for a reader (or viewer) to overcome.

Star Trek writers have, for the most part, chosen the names they have used with great finesse. Let's hope they will continue to do so.

ONE MORE TIME: TIME TRAVEL IN STAR TREK

by Kay Kelly

Time travel is one of the most enduring themes of science fiction, and Star Trek is no exception. As much as the ability to travel through time fascinates us, so almost as much does the mechanics which allow such travels. How can time travel work? Is there more then one method? What are the dangers? And why has the issue always been so confused, even obscured, in Star Trek?

Kay Kelly, using examples from the Star Trek episodes involving time travel, as well as scientific "evidence" from the rest of the series, makes some attempts to answer the above questions. And, no, a modified DeLorean automobile doesn't figure in the answers.

As I write this, the last two Star Trek novels have involved time travel—proof that the subject holds as much fascination as ever. I don't plan to discuss the novels. But they set me to thinking about time travel in "official" Star Trek . . . and I realized no one, to my knowledge, has presented views like mine in *Trek*. Nor has anyone discussed time travel in a long (that word again).

So I'm going to give it a shot. And to further distinguish this article from all others, I'm going to take the perverse approach of stating my proposed "rules" first.

"Rules" for Time Travel

1. In the time of Star Trek, three basic methods of time travel have been discovered:

A starship can "create a time warp"—to be explained in

more detail later—either by imploding its engines (as in "The Naked Time"), or by approaching a star at many times the speed of light and breaking away at almost the last moment (as in "Tomorrow Is Yesterday").

Travelers can journey to the past and return through the Guardian of Forever.

Travelers can also journey to the past and return by using an Atavachron. The original Atavachron on Sarpeidon has been destroyed. But Starfleet might be able to construct another, based on Spock's tricorder readings.

All three methods have advantages and disadvantages.

2. There is no reason to believe "alternate timelines" are created when history is apparently changed, and left in existence when changes are apparently reversed. When a time traveler "changes history" he makes a real, meaningful change to his own universe. In "City on the Edge of Forever," when Kirk sacrifices the woman he loves, he saves millions of people who would have been slaughtered by the victorious Nazis.

3. When a time traveler makes a change that prevents his own birth, he winks out of existence. Admittedly, this creates a paradox. But if we accept the reality of some kind of reincarnation, we can at least answer the "immortal soul" question. The life force that animates every individual always has existed, and always will—in one identity or another.

4. A person or object can exist in two places at the same time. I would accept this on theoretical grounds alone. But in fact, we must accept it because we see it happen in Star Trek—even without citing the animated episode "Yesteryear."

When the *Enterprise* is hurled back three days in "The Naked Time," her officers see the chronometers running backward—not making a sudden jump. They are too distracted to notice this phenomenon at the beginning of "Tomorrow Is Yesterday"; but they do mention it later as a feature of backward time travel. Most important: While traveling "fast forward" they somehow manage to return Captain Christopher and the Air Force sergeant to Earth, using the transporter.

Clearly, while the ship is traveling backward and "fast forward," it is actually in the intervening times, however briefly. That means that while the crew is going back and forth in "Tomorrow Is Yesterday," they are aboard the *Enterprise* throughout the period of their own youth! But this does not interfere with their being born, growing up and attending Starfleet Academy, etc. If it did, no one in Starfleet would remember them upon their return.

5. "Two of" a person or object cannot exist in the exact same place at the same time. When a person or ship, using instrumentation, attempts to move into a space/time he or it already occupies, the universe makes an adjustment. The person or ship already there winks out of existence, and is replaced by the new arrival (usually, though not necessarily, a "later" version).

It follows that when time travelers using a starship want to "erase" a change they have made, the simplest method is to go back to the beginning of the experience, momentarily "overlay" the earlier version of their ship, and then take off in a different direction. The crew will be aged by the amount of time that has passed in their real lives, and will retain all their memories.

6. As previously stated, a person can exist in two places at the same time; but a person as he is at a specific point in his life—i.e., at a specific age, down to the second—can only exist in one place. This may cause a problem in fluke situations.

Time Travel via Starship

The mechanics of time travel via starship are never explained in Star Trek. Terms like "time warp," "whiplash," and "slingshot effect" are simply bandied about. We are expected to believe the universe "knows" whether the *Enterprise* officers want to go forward or backward in time; they appear to use the exact same method for each!

I think it is possible to make sense of this—and explain why we are not given a clear explanation in the most obvious episode, "Tomorrow Is Yesterday."

I read recently (in the August 1985 *Analog*) that scientists believe it "should"—theoretically—be possible for a type of light to exist that would travel backward in time. It is called "advanced" light. However, the phenomenon has never been observed in nature; nor has anyone been able to create it in the laboratory. It is generally believed that for reasons we do not yet understand, backward-traveling light actually cannot exist, but we do not *know* it cannot. The idea is, at least, scientifically respectable.

Supposedly, if backward-traveling light did exist, it could only be used to send "signals" back in time. Even that prospect is mind-boggling. But now, let us connect it with the transporter technology that is—like it or not—a "given" of the Star Trek universe.

As generally understood, the transporter breaks down people or objects into atoms. The atoms are transmitted over some kind of beam (as in "Beam me up"), and reassembled at their destination. For a person, there seems to be a momentary break in consciousness. But we cannot be sure. The "journey" is almost instantaneous; the "break in consciousness" may be only a moment of disorientation.

Let us suppose that when a starship either implodes its engines or approaches a star at many times the speed of light and breaks away at almost the last moment, its warp engines produce a massive burst of energy—*which is converted into "advanced" light*. Then something else happens. From the point of view of an external observer, the ship and crew are broken down into atoms or subatomic particles, and the particles are "beamed" into the past on waves of backward-traveling light. From the point of view of the crew, however, they and the ship remain solid throughout the journey—which is perceived as rapid, but not instantaneous.

With only light as a "propellant," we would expect a journey of 300 years into the past to take 300 years (and result in a spatial displacement of 300 light-years). In a sense, it does. When the *Enterprise* officers find themselves in Earth orbit in "Tomorrow Is Yesterday," they observe only that they had been headed in that general direction—not that they had been near Earth. But some time distortion connected with the "beaming" process (perhaps a great many "momentary" breaks in consciousness?) has caused them to experience the passage of only a few minutes. And they have not aged or grown younger.

Once the principle is understood, a scientist of Spock's caliber can work out the details—mass of the star, angle of approach, speed and breakaway point—that determine how far the ship will be flung into the past. The "advanced" light will be traveling in space at normal light speed. And the ship's apparent displacement in space will be further affected by the rotation of the galaxy.

Now, how does the ship return from the past? (Bear with me as I seem to contradict "Tomorrow Is Yesterday.") The most logical answer is that it returns by a method understood today. It goes "fast forward" in time by traveling at high sublight speeds.

We know that if a ship were to travel at nearly the speed of light, a very few years, months, or even weeks (depending on the speed) would pass aboard ship—both subjectively and in terms of the crew's aging—while many more years passed on Earth and other planets. If a ship could accelerate to something like 99.9999 percent of light speed, a few days on shipboard could probably be made to equal 300 years in the "real world."

Traveling at light speed or faster is, according to our physics, impossible. I cannot imagine how it would affect the passage of time. Would we still go "fast forward"? Would we begin going backward? In any case, Starfleet's warp drive prevents time distortion. When the *Enterprise* travels at warp speeds, elapsed time is the same aboard ship as on planetary surfaces.

But starships seldom travel at high sublight speeds. When warp drive is activated, there is usually a sudden jump to Warp One (light speed). Maximum speed under impulse power is not very high. In *Wrath of Khan*, it would not have enabled the *Enterprise* to escape the range of the Genesis Torpedo in four minutes. (And Genesis cannot have too great a range: One of its intended uses was to terraform a moon, presumably without damaging its primary.)

It is possible to accelerate gradually to light speed. In *Star Trek: The Motion Picture*, there is an acceleration buildup count of: "Warp point eight . . . point nine . . . Warp One." This may have been a safety precaution in a crowded solar system. And it may be a relatively new capability in the time period of the films. The warp engines are being pressed into service to do something for which they were not designed; and some device is being used to prevent the ship's going "fast forward" in time.

Now, consider the situation in "Tomorrow Is Yesterday." Since Kirk, Spock, and Scott have never faced this problem before, they are initially stumped. None of them has traveled at high sublight speed; and it has been years since they thought about the theoretical consequences of doing so.

They soon remember. But when we hear them talking about their plan for returning to their own time, Captain Christopher is always within earshot. They are not 100 percent sure they will be able to erase his memory.

The most damaging thing Christopher has learned is the possibility of faster-than-light travel and time travel. The progress of Earth might be greatly accelerated by definite, upfront knowledge that those "impossibilities" are possible.

As an example of what might happen, the history of the Federation could be so changed that Kirk's parents—or Spock's—would never meet!

Understandably, the *Enterprise* officers do everything in their power to mislead Christopher regarding the details of their plan. They know that if they talk doubletalk, and he remembers it and repeats it to scientists who recognize it as doubletalk, his story will be discredited. For his benefit, they even cause the chronometers to run backward when they should still be going forward—before the ship has broken away from the sun.

At this point, they are using the sun only to go back and correct the problem they have caused. It is not necessary for their return to their own time. And while they are at Warp Eight inside the orbit of Mercury they are, of course, spiraling toward the sun rather than plunging toward it.

Near the end of the episode, we do hear something strange when Christopher is not present. After the ship has jumped back in time and then started "fast forward" and back toward Earth, Scotty apparently reports on the acceleration: "Warp Eight . . . Nine . . . Ten . . . off the dial!"

I suggest he is actually holding the speed below Warp One, and Kirk and the others know it. But the warp speed dials are not yet equipped to show this, and they "go crazy." Scotty is only reporting on the meaningless dial readings—perhaps, initially, in the forlorn hope "Warp Eight" will correspond to Warp point eight, and so forth.

If necessary, Scotty has disabled the controls that keep shipboard time in sync with "real-world" time. But it is probably that at this point in Star Trek history, no controls exist for maintaining synchronization while speed is being held below Warp One.

To sum up: A starship travels back in time by creating a burst of "advanced" (backward-traveling) light, which "beams" it into the past. Backward-traveling light is a scientifically respectable idea; and the "beaming" concept is similar enough to the transporter to be consistent with the Star Trek universe. The ship returns to its own time by utilizing high sublight speeds. This is more tricky than it sounds, because neither impulse engines nor warp engines were designed for speeds in that range.

This method of time travel has obvious advantages. The ship's captain controls it, without being beholden to anyone.

And a fully crewed starship—if necessary, a fleet—can be sent into the past.

The disadvantages are just as obvious. The first that comes to mind is danger, but that exists with all techniques. The principal drawback of this method is that it *requires* sending a ship, whether or not it is really needed. The ship itself can be an embarrassment in many eras (as Kirk discovered), and increases the risk of changing history.

Travel via the Guardian of Forever

Travel via the Guardian is relatively straightforward, if only because the science involved is so far ahead of the Federation's that there is no hope of understanding or duplicating it. The Guardian exists; use it or not, as you will.

Its principal advantage is that it permits one or two people to go to the past without taking a ship.

On the other hand, using this method, they *cannot* take a ship. The remote Guardian Planet must be their starting point, and the waves of disturbance around it constitute an additional hazard.

Finally, the traveler is forced to abdicate control to the Guardian. In "City on the Edge of Forever," Kirk does not have the option of bringing Edith back to his time. It is clear the Guardian will only permit him to restore, as nearly as possible, the "original" history. (And Kirk is in a "Catch-22" situation. He cannot return to the 1930s with the *Enterprise* because, by then, only Edith's life and his happiness will be at stake. And the ship is valuable Starfleet property that cannot be used for his personal gratification.)

Travel via the Atavachron

The peculiarities of the planet Sarpeidon are too numerous to catalog here. But the Atavachron itself is a machine, pure and simple, with none of the mystical overtones of the Guardian. This suggests the time portal may also be an artifact . . . and Starfleet may be capable of reproducing it.

The greatest puzzle involving the Atavachron is the matter of "preparation." Of what does it consist? It has been pointed out that it cannot involve alteration of memories—because the Inquisitor, in the "Seventeenth century," still remembers the Library and the Atavachron. Nor can it involve immunization against past diseases: that would not prevent a person's surviving in his own time if he chose to return.

"Preparation" does not unfit a person for life in his own time if, after being "prepared," he does not go to the past. That apparently happens to Kirk after his return from the "seventeenth century," when Mr. Atoz knocks him out and tries to force him back through the portal. Atoz is no murderer; he has almost certainly "prepared" him. (The only alternative is that he means to dump Kirk a mere thirty years or so into the past, when he would already be alive. But it seems more likely Atoz has the portal set for his own destination.)

Consider this. When a person—a researcher, let's say—leaves the Library for another time, he sets the portal for his destination by gazing at a picture of it. But how does he return? The Library, once constructed, must have looked the same for centuries.

I suggest that when our hypothetical researcher goes through the portal, it traps and holds a portion of his "essence." (I can't help thinking of Peter Pan's detachable shadow.) He cannot survive long in the past without it; but, as a researcher, he has no desire to. When he returns, the portion of his essence held in the portal draws him to the correct era.

This is the original design. Later, someone decided to incorporate the option of permanent emigration to the past. "Preparation" assures that when an individual passes through the portal, no portion of his essence will be held. He can then survive in the past. But if he tries to return, he will be "left hanging" forever somewhere outside time.

The Atavachron/portal may be the most promising method of time travel. It may be possible to reproduce it anywhere, and create portals of varying sizes—so one or two people, or a fleet of spaceships, can be sent into the past.

But . . . there's always a drawback!

The explosion of the star Beta Niobe does not fit the pattern of either a nova (as Kirk calls it) or a supernova. A nova is a temporary brightening of a star that is a member of a close binary pair, caused by transfer of gaseous material between the two stars. The name Beta Niobe does presuppose the existence of an Alpha Niobe; but if they were that close, no planet could maintain a stable orbit. A supernova is a dying flare-up of a star of enormous mass; this type of star has a lifespan of only a few million years.

Intelligent life would not have evolved on a planet of a star destined for either fate; nor would any spacefaring race have planted a long-term colony there. The Sarpeidonites could be descendants of a team that staffed a forgotten scientific outpost. But the facts still do not fit. A nova is not like a time bomb! The idea of a planet having a shirtsleeve environment up to the moment its sun "goes nova" is ridiculous. If it ever was habitable, it should have been uninhabitable for generations.

We must conclude that the explosion of Beta Niobe is an anomalous cosmic disaster—colloquially called a nova, and common enough in Kirk's day that he is not shocked by it. That suggests two possibilities. The time portal may have been possible only because there was always something odd about the star. Or . . . an initially normal star may have been destroyed by excessive time travel in its vicinity!

"Alternate Timelines"

The theory of "Everett-Wheeler universes," in extreme form, holds that universes branch off in all conceivable directions whenever an apparent "choice" is made—and reintegrate whenever two or more "pasts" lead to "presents" with no discernible difference. Applied to "The City on the Edge of Forever," this would mean Dr. McCoy's "change of history" merely adds one more to the score of universes in which, for some reason, Nazi Germany won World War II. And Kirk's sacrifice does not undo the Nazi triumph: the timeline McCoy created still exists. Kirk simply creates another, so similar that it quickly reintegrates with the one he and his comrades had known as the "original."

Dramatically, we cannot accept that! We cannot tolerate this trivialization of Kirk's sacrifice. And there is no reason why we must.

Rejecting the Everett-Wheeler theory is not comparable to rejecting, say, evolution. As I understand it, the majority of physicists do not accept Everett-Wheeler. And many who do say this theory is meant to explain only the behavior of subatomic particles, not "universes."

The "other universes" we encounter in Star Trek—in "The Alternative Factor," "Mirror, Mirror," and "The Tholian Web"—can be explained without falling back on Everett-Wheeler. Many scientists believe a vast number of "bubble universes"—so called because they are pictured as separate bubbles in a boiling medium—came into existence immediately after the Big Bang. They are separated by a medium called "H-space" or "the false vacuum," which is even more hostile to life than normal space. Some of the universes may have wildly different laws of nature; yet they are so numerous there could also be near-duplicates.

Supposedly, it will never be possible to go from one to another. But we can surely find a science-fictional way around that! For example: the secret of faster-than-light travel is that part of the ship's mass is "draw off" into H-space, so that it never becomes infinite. But this contact with H-space weakens the fabric of the Mega-Universe, and creates "resonances" and physical conduits between universes.

"Tomorrow Is Yesterday"

The most puzzling time-travel mysteries in Star Trek occur in "Tomorrow Is Yesterday" and the animated episode "Yesteryear." What is going on?

In discussing time travel via starship, I have already addressed some of the questions raised by "Tomorrow Is Yesterday." The *Enterprise*, I suggested, does not return to the twenty-third century by the method her officers describe. They are deliberately misleading Captain Christopher for fear they will be unable to erase his memory. They actually return by the comprehensible method of traveling at high sublight speed.

But this invites another question. Why do they let Christopher hear their plans at all? Why not keep him under guard in his quarters—or, if necessary, in the brig?

The answer: Christopher is an intelligent, competent, self-confident young man—very like Kirk himself. Kirk likes him, and can't resist having a little fun with him. Also, on a very human level, Kirk and his friends want Christopher to like *them*—and to enjoy the greatest adventure of his life, whether or not he will remember it later.

Now, let's examine what the *Enterprise* officers do to resolve their problem in the Twentieth century.

They first run into trouble because the ship has sustained minor damage, and they cannot get their deflectors up quickly enough to prevent detection by U.S. radar. Air Force jets scramble. Captain Christopher gets a good look at the *Enterprise* and takes pictures. Kirk puts a tractor beam on Christopher's jet—and inadvertently causes it to break up. Christopher has to be beamed aboard the *Enterprise*. The Air Force recovers his film from the wreckage of the jet. And while Kirk and Sulu are stealing the film, an Air Force sergeant is also—accidentally—beamed aboard the *Enterprise*.

If Christopher and the sergeant are returned to Earth with memories intact, their knowledge may change history. This is especially true of Christopher. It has been argued that he does not know enough to do any damage. But in fact, he quickly learns two supposed scientific impossibilities—faster-than-light travel and time travel—are possible. Starfleet itself did not discover time travel until the Twenty-third century! And Christopher is a responsible officer whose word is likely to be taken seriously. Knowing at the outset that these goals are attainable may speed Earth's progress and change the history of the Federation. Our friends in Starfleet may never be born.

It has been suggested Spock could have used a Vulcan mind meld to erase the men's memories. Why does he not attempt it? There is only one possible reason: The mind meld can be used to erase someone's memory only if he wants it erased. (This hypothesis also answers any ethical questions about Spock's conduct in "Requiem for Methuselah.") Christopher might pretend to agree, but in reality would never yield.

An additional problem: Even without the film or the men's testimony, the *Enterprise* will be remembered as a hostile UFO that shot an Air Force jet out of the sky!

Clearly, the ship must go back in time—again—to change at least part of what has happened. Spock ponders the implications, and quickly arrives at my Time Travel Rule #5.

Let us call the ship that first appeared in the atmosphere *Enterprise A*. The "day-older" *Enterprise*, with Christopher and the sergeant aboard, is *Enterprise B*.

If *Enterprise B* jumps back in time and moves into the exact space/time occupied by *Enterprise A*, *Enterprise A* will wink out of existence. (*A* will not perceive the approaching *B* as a threat, because *B* will be traveling at high speed—and the crippled *A*, with a distracted crew, will not be anticipating or scanning for anything like that near Earth in the 1960s.) *Enterprise B*—with deflectors in working order—can then, quickly, take off on another course. History will be changed from that point on.

The ship could go back to the moment of its first appearance and prevent the initial radar detection. In that case the Air Force jets would never scramble. With such a drastic change, the "Christopher" and "sergeant" aboard the ship would wink out of existence. The two men—a day younger—would, of course, be alive and well on Earth.

But Kirk can't resist giving Christopher a few thrills—and

the Air Force, at least, a sportsmanlike hint. Remember, Kirk is of North American descent; and Starfleet Headquarters is in San Francisco. He can't help feeling a sense of camaraderie with these Americans.

So *Enterprise B* allows the jets to scramble—and moves in as Christopher (the one in the aircraft cockpit) is getting his first glance of the ship.

From here on it gets tricky.

The man in the cockpit is Christopher A. Aboard the *Enterprise*, the day-older Christopher B is hurrying to the transporter room. He has a fairly clear idea of what Kirk has just done with the ship.

It certainly seems that when Christopher B is beamed into the cockpit, he will "overlay" and replace Christopher A—and retain his memories. Doesn't it?

It seems that way to him, too! And Christopher has a good opinion of his own intelligence. And he's seen enough of Kirk's problems to know the *Enterprise* officers are not infallible. They're ordinary mortals. They can slip up. In this instance, he thinks they have.

But . . . they don't beam him into the cockpit! They never intended to. Instead, while he's on the transporter platform, they beam the day-younger Christopher A onto the platform and "overlay" *him*! They bring Christopher A to the verge of materialization—just for a fraction of a second, to be sure they have him. Then they beam him back into the cockpit. *Voilà!*

The disoriented Christopher feels something has happened, but has no idea what. By the time he gets his eyes focused, the ship he thought he had seen—traveling, now, at near light speed—is out of sight.

The *Enterprise* officers repeat the process with the sergeant. That may seem less necessary; he's been in shock most of the time he's been aboard. And if they simply don't beam him up at the moment they originally did, Sergeant B will disappear. But by now, he's snapped out of his shock and knows what's going on. He'll be alarmed if they do not appear to be preparing for his departure in the same way they did Christopher's. And he too has become a person they'd like to remember as a friend.

When it's all over, the Air Force is left trying to explain a "UFO flap" that caused its jets to scramble—and ended as suddenly as it had begun, with the disappearance of the offending radar blip. If Christopher and the sergeant are hypnotized—and Christopher may be—each of them will remember a split-second glimpse of a starship transporter room.

A "sportsmanlike hint."

I'm tempted to point out that Kirk himself was still a very young man at this time. But if we know Kirk, he'll have the same spirit of mischief when he's ninety.

"Yesteryear"

"Yesteryear" offers a different set of puzzles. Since even the most famous animated episode is not as familiar as the live-action shows (I myself have seen it only once), I'll take time to summarize the plot.

Kirk and Spock use the Guardian of Forever to go to "Orion"—presumably, a planet with a good view of the Orion Nebula—thirty years in the past, to observe an astronomical phenomenon. Several officers wait for them on the Guardian Planet, and pass the time by viewing the history of Vulcan.

When Kirk and Spock return, no one recognizes Spock! No one but Kirk remembers him, either on the planet or aboard the orbiting ship. And the *Enterprise* now has an Andorian first officer.

Checking computerized Federation records, they learn that Spock of Vulcan, son of Sarek and Amanda, died in an accident at age seven. The child's death led to the breakup of his parents' marriage; and the still-young Amanda was killed in a spacecraft accident en route home to Earth. Sarek never remarried, and has presumably led a lonely, unhappy life. So more is at stake than Spock's status in Starfleet.

As Spock recalls the childhood crisis, his life was saved by a visiting cousin named Selek—a man he had only recently met, and never saw again. Now, as he tries to picture Selek, he realizes for the first time that the "cousin" was his adult self! The implication seems to be that Spock has been edited out of existence because he was on Orion on the past date when he "should have been" on Vulcan, saving his own life.

Even the Andorian first officer agrees they should try to set things right. So Spock uses the Guardian to return to Vulcan, impersonates "Selek," helps Sarek see the error of some of his ways, and ultimately does save his own life. But he cannot restore history quite as he remembers it: In the final version, the child's pet dies.

We have here a minor and major puzzle. The minor one is

that even the officers on the planet's surface—within the Guardian's influence—have forgotten Spock. This seems inconsistent with the workings of the Guardian in "City on the Edge of Forever."

The major puzzle, of course, is the plot itself! How can we accept an "original" reality in which a person only lives to reach adulthood because his adult self goes back in time to save his child self?

I say we can't. *The "original," whatever it was, has been changed and forgotten before the episode begins.*

Try this one on for size:

In the original reality, either the child Spock was never in danger, or the crisis was resolved without the nonexistent "Selek."

The *Enterprise* arrives at the Guardian Planet, on a mission that is not considered dangerous or particularly important. It has not yet been decided whether Spock will accompany Kirk to Orion; it's a casual decision that could go either way. It's finally decided Spock will remain at the Guardian.

Because Kirk has gone thirty years into the past, Spock lets his mind drift back to that period in his life . . . a childhood he does not remember as happy.

He and the others have asked the Guardian to display the history of Vulcan. Spock is not of such historical importance that his childhood would actually be shown; but it is, like everything else, somehow "there" in the background. Partly because Vulcans are natural telepaths, and partly because he has been thinking about his childhood, something happens that could not have been foreseen. Spock feels an irresistible telepathic "pull" from his unhappy childhood self—and before anyone can stop him, he leaps through the portal!

Since he has not gone to Vulcan's past for any reason, he could probably return by willing himself back. Either that telepathic pull is so strong that he cannot, or he is accosted immediately and asked to identify himself. He invents the character of Selek, and becomes so embroiled in the lie that he cannot plausibly leave without accepting Sarek's hospitality.

Now events unfold as in the history Spock will later remember as the "original." "Selek" saves the life of the child Spock.

After leaving his family, he returns through the Guardian. Kirk is back by now, and everyone is anxiously waiting for Spock. He explains that he unintentionally "changed history" on Vulcan, but has already corrected any problem he caused. The landing party returns to the *Enterprise* and prepares to leave.

But now they run afoul of those "waves of time disturbance" around the planet (mentioned in "City on the Edge of Forever"). And the ship and crew are regressed a day in time! This is not the same as being "thrown back" a day, with memories intact. Rather, everyone aboard the ship *actually is a day younger*—and as they perceive it, they are just *arriving* at the Guardian Planet.

To complicate matters further, the ship and crew have regressed a day, but the Guardian has not.

At this point, the change Spock made to Vulcan's history still holds, but he does not remember making it. If he were to think about his childhood, he would remember the version in which "Selek" saved his life. But he would remember it only from the child's point of view.

Now we pick up where "Yesteryear" begins. This time, the casual decision as to whether Spock will accompany Kirk to Orion goes the other way.

But history is not changed because "Spock is on Orion the day he should be on Vulcan." Remember, a person *can* be in two places at the same time. The problem is that Spock is—let's say—thirty-seven years, six months, and two days old; and it's the Spock of *that specific age* who formerly went to Vulcan. If the time wave had erased the crew's memory of one day without actually regressing them, there would be no problem; the day-older Spock could go to Orion without affecting what the day-younger Spock had done on Vulcan.

It would be handy if, in the absence of "Selek," Vulcan history simply reverted to the original. But, apparently, whenever the past is changed, it's a new roll of the dice.

Why do the officers waiting at the Guardian not remember Spock when he returns from Orion? Because they have just viewed a "history of Vulcan" in which, somewhere in the unseen background, Spock died at age seven.

It's tempting to speculate on what might have happened if "Selek"—on either visit to the past—had failed to save the child Spock. He would have winked out of existence when the boy died. But the officers waiting at the Guardian would have remembered him; and if it happened while Kirk was on Orion, he also would have remembered. I think we can assume Kirk would have gone to Vulcan to straighten things out.

But . . . what if someone else had gone to Orion, and Kirk had been on the *ship*?

Apart from that horrible thought, the scariest thing here is the effect of the time wave. The *Enterprise* crew undoubtedly figured it out later when they discovered their clocks were running a day behind everyone else's. And in future, they'll steer clear of the Guardian unless their original mission is a lot more important than this one!

Time travel has always been a staple of science fiction, and as such was part of Star Trek almost from the beginning. Time travel stories and situations will continue to be used in new Star Trek tales, and we can only hope that future time travels in Star Trek will be as interesting, exciting, and endlessly fascinating as those before.

STAR TREK AND ME

by G. B. Love

Editor G. B. Love takes time out from his busy schedule to make a rare solo appearance in these pages. As usual, he was reluctant to write, but we convinced him that the coincidence of Star Trek's twentieth anniversary and the tenth Best of Trek volume was too important for him to be among the missing. He agreed—reluctantly, but we think we detected a little enthusiasm creeping in. Don't you?

Twenty years. I really can't believe it's been twenty years since I sat down to watch the first episode of Star Trek.

If memory serves, that first show was a "special preview" presented by NBC; Star Trek, along with the *Tarzan* TV series, debuted a week earlier than the rest of the schedule so that viewers could get a look at what NBC ostensibly considered its best." An attitude that changed rather quickly. Star Trek didn't—if you'll excuse the expression—take off like a rocket, so NBC quickly began to retrench. Fan legends aside, I strongly suspect that NBC didn't cancel and replace Star Trek for the simple reason that there was nothing "better" readily available.

But the fan efforts did get media attention. And whatever NBC's reasons for continuing the series into its third year, popular opinion would always have it that "the Trekkies saved the show." Such populism could not be tolerated—what if fans of other programs began to protest, speak out, write letters? With chilling efficiency, NBC set out to kill Star Trek in cold blood, and in a manner which would leave the network able to shrug and say, "We tried, but the ratings just weren't there." So Star Trek was moved to the 10:00 p.m. Friday time slot, a time when the show's young fans would be in bed and the older fans would be out on dates. As added insurance, the network preempted the show every few weeks.

I recall that Star Trek wasn't even allowed to expire gracefully—the final episode was preempted for a special on the death of President Eisenhower. A newsworthy item, to be sure. So newsworthy, in fact, that one must wonder why a program *earlier* in the evening was not replaced. The original showing of the final new Star Trek episode, "Turnabout Intruder," was ignominiously slotted between a pair of reruns.

Anyway, back to that first episode. I remember thinking that the spaceship didn't look right. It didn't follow the classic lines of the pointed-nosed, rake-finned spaceships of my youth, the spaceships of *Flash Gordon* and *Buck Rogers*. I was also surprised to see the interior of the ship looking like nothing so much as the corridors of a modern office building: executives, clerks, secretaries, service people all efficiently moving about appointed tasks, dressed casually, and of all races and sexes. Wasn't a spaceship supposed to be all iron and tubes and girders and pressurized submarine doors, with the dozen or so occupants dressed constantly in spacesuits and helmets? Apparently not.

No, I wasn't familiar with this new view of space, but I quickly became comfortable with it. It made sense, once you sat back and thought about it. This was, literally, what a capital ship would be in a hundred years or so; after all, sailors of today don't go around wearing life jackets and don't work only in boiler rooms.

I had no trouble with the pointy-eared Spock. Years of science fiction had prepared me for the friendly and intelligent alien, and I couldn't see green blood on my black-and-white TV anyway. Everybody else seemed likable enough, and I figured I would get to know them all soon enough. I had by then enough experience with series television to know that it took time to develop characters and background.

What really impressed me about that first episode was the story. Here were characters in a science fiction show talking about ethics, love, loneliness, and passion. And what was the reason for all of this bother? A monster. No, make that a *creature*. For the only monsters visible here were those within the minds of the humans (and Vulcan) onscreen.

I thought about "The Man Trap" after it was over. I think about it still, once in a while. And I promised myself that I would never miss an episode of Star Trek as long as it was on the air. (A promise I didn't keep, unfortunately, even during the original run.) So I continued to watch, enjoying the show, getting to know the characters, grooving (as we said back then) with the goodness of it all.

Then one day, Star Trek was gone. I missed it, but, heck, life goes on. There were three full seasons, enough for syndication. It would be back now and again; in a few years I could kick back and watch the show again.

Now this is the part of the narrative where I'm supposed to say a few insightful things about the Phenomenon. Sorry, I don't know a heck of a lot about it. All I know is that more and more Star Trek fans began showing up at comic book and science fiction conventions I attended (some of which I organized); before anyone knew it, Star Trek was a "fad" and the single biggest thing around. Star Trek conventions began popping up all over the country, memorabilia flooded the market, and literally thousands, maybe millions of fans, most too young to have watched the original run, began to demand that Star Trek return to the air.

Why all this happened at that particular time is, frankly, beyond me. It wasn't quite a long enough time for a nostalgia-type revival, nor was it a delayed reaction to the show's cancellation. (Personally, I feel that the fact the show *was* canceled had a lot to do with its appeal to these new fans.) All I can tell you is that suddenly Star Trek was the hottest thing in the country. In short order there were new novels, an animated series, and talk of a return of the show with the original cast.

That talk continued for quite a while.

It was about this time that we started *Trek*. Walter and I, along with Earl Blair, decided that there was a definite need for a fanzine which discussed *all* aspects of Star Trek and Star Trek fandom, good and bad, in a manner which was adult and serious, but still reflected the love and devotion the writers felt for the series. So we pooled our money and resources and produced the first issue. It was an immediate sellout. So was the second. And the third. And the fourth.

Before we knew it, we were publishing *Trek* on a regular schedule. In 1978, Signet/NAL published the first *Best of Trek* collection, allowing us to reach an even larger and more enthusiastic audience.

Since that time, we've seen three Star Trek films, all different in style and tone, all excellent and true to the spirit of the original series. We've also seen the resurgence of the space program, America's first women astronauts, amazing advances in satellite technology, and so much more. Most of all, however, we've seen the gestation of the *third* Star Trek generation—the children of the original Star Trek viewers, now old enough to appreciate and value the show.

I reckon it's time I said something about what Star Trek means to me. I'm not going to get too deep or personal here; I don't need to. Star Trek means to me exactly what it means to most of you. It is a vision of the future which is bright and hopeful and beautiful . . . and, most important of all, achievable. I see Star Trek as a sort of a role model of the future, something we can try to be, and can be if we only try hard enough. A simplistic view, right enough, but to me, the good things and the true things have always been simple.

Star Trek also has been a way for me to meet people— some of whom were nice, some of whom were silly, some of whom were interesting, some of whom were obnoxious, and some of whom became wonderful new friends. None of them, however, were boring. I cherish each and every one of them (while at the same time reserving the right to dislike some of them) and am looking forward to meeting many more.

To be honest, I'm more concerned with what real life means to me—and you—than what Star Trek means. After all, it's only a television show. I've never been one to hold the view that fandom is a way of life, and I hold that only something which transcends itself is of value to living in this world. That is, the fact that Mr. Spock is an alien means nothing, but the fact that he is accepted by his coworkers means quite a lot. See the difference? Another example: The fact that a ship called *Enterprise* flies through space on a TV series means nothing. The fact that it is possible to build such a ship in our future means everything.

That's how Star Trek is important. Not for what it gives us, but for what we take from it, and how we *use* what we take to improve our own lives. Examples of values such as friendship, sacrifice, love, honesty, compassion, etc. abound in Star Trek, but the examples are of worth only if we seek out and seize opportunities in the real world to apply those values. Star Trek isn't, after all, a *place* to live . . . it's a way—*one* way—to live.

I'm proud to say I've been a Star Trek fan for twenty years, and hope to be one for twenty, forty, sixty, a hundred years more. No other television show has captured my imagination in such a way, and I can't conceive of a world without it. I could definitely live in such a world, yes, but it wouldn't be nearly as nice a place as this one is.

Happy birthday, Star Trek. May you live long and prosper.

VULCAN AS A MERITOCRACY

by Carmen Carter

Here's another of those articles we love to receive and publish: one which rebuts, in depth and with passion, an earlier Best of Trek *article. Here Carmen Carter takes objection with Rebecca Hoffman's view of "Vulcan as a Patriarchy" (Best of Trek #4). We feel you'll find her views of the unusual and sometimes strange Vulcan life-style and societal hierarchy quite acceptable. So who's right? You decide. And if you decide neither of them is, then get working on your article!*

One of the greatest challenges in understanding another culture is that of identifying the bias present in our own view of reality. An amazing store of unacknowledged assumptions colors our every attempt to objectively interpret the actions of beings raised in another culture. A prime example of this unconscious ethnocentricity can be found in Rebecca Hoffman's analysis of Vulcan society as a patriarchy.

Hoffman has taken examples of objective Vulcan behavior and developed some rather subjective rationales for their occurrence. While her interpretations *may* indeed be correct, they are not *necessarily* correct. I would like to offer some equally plausible interpretation of the behavior she discussed.

The most blatant cultural assumption Hoffman made in her article is that Vulcan society has an either/or choice of a matriarchy or a patriarchy. Human cultures have often developed along these lines, but that is no proof that Vulcans are so simple-minded. To arbitrarily establish authority on the basis of one's biological sex is a rather illogical custom.

If one discards this limiting notion, a rather more intricate view of Vulcan life and society can be suggested.

Star Trek offers a firsthand view of Vulcan in "Amok Time," and it provides our first view of Vulcan authority in T'Pau. Here, Hoffman eloquently describes T'Pau's claim to power, and eventually attributes that rise to her individual abilities, abilities allowed to express themselves because of Vulcan's belief in equality of the sexes. To my mind, this belief in equality is in itself a denial of a patriarchal *or* matriarchal structure in Vulcan society. T'Pau is powerful because her talent and force of personality are undeniable. Her sex is immaterial.

Sarek, Spock's father, is possessed of a similar strength of character. Early in the series his son alludes to a resemblance between Sarek and the alien commander Balok ("The Corbomite Maneuver"). The resemblance is obviously not a physical one, but one of personality.

Sarek's demeanor in "Journey to Babel" fully corroborates Spock's view of his father as a forceful individual. Seen as just that, an individual rather than a male, Sarek's character has no relation to either a patriarchy or a matriarchy.

But there are many sources for authority, and personality is just one of them. Sarek is accorded military honors upon boarding the *Enterprise* (an action much regretted by the ship's surgeon, clad in dress uniform). These signs of respect had little to do with Sarek's personality (as yet unknown to the crew) or to his sex (women such as the Elaan were accorded respect as well). Sarek merited this reception because of his position as an ambassador from a powerful Federation planet.

In addition, Spock accorded his father respect (when they were talking) because Sarek is his parent. Again, this action can be seen as gender-neutral. Spock evidenced equal respect, if less formality, to Amanda as his mother. Any difference in their interaction is quite justified given that Amanda is a human and much less austere than her husband.

This Vulcan respect for family may also serve to explain the perceived power differential between Amanda and Sarek. In her own human way, Amanda is no less forceful than her Vulcan husband, but she does accord him with a noticeable public deference. She comes at his bidding ("My wife, attend") and bows to his wishes. The basis for this *public* acquiescence (in private she seems much more outspoken) may be due to his role as ambassador. However, it could also be due to an inequality of rank because of class or clan.

Sarek comes from a powerful Vulcan family, and a kinship with T'Pau might bestow a high rank on all members of her family (more on the nature of that status later). However, Amanda, as an outsider, has no such Vulcan connections. Therefore she would bring no status of her own into the marriage. On Vulcan, this difference in rank would probably be common knowledge and her deference properly interpreted. The human crew of the *Enterprise* (and the human viewers of Star Trek), true to their patriarchal origins, misinterpret this inequality of rank as a sign of sexual inequality.

Much has been made of the physical distance that separates a Vulcan husband and wife while walking. Again, taken at purely face value as shown in the televised episode, their action is easily attributed to Sarek's position as an ambassador.

However, if one considers the production scripts to be a part of the Star Trek canon (I don't), then we must believe that a Vulcan woman "habitually walks behind and to the side of any man, but especially her husband." Like a glass that is half empty or half full, a verbal description of this proximity in human language brings an emotional connotation to these words. Just as easily, it can be said that the Vulcan male walks ahead of his wife. *Why* he does this is never explained. To automatically interpret this distance as a sign of patriarchal prerogative is pure cultural bias. (For instance, early animal studies of primate troops, conducted by male anthropologists, often stated that males led the group and were thus dominant. Later observations by female scientists indicated that the males may have been at the front in the group's movement but that the females actually dictated the direction.)

Hoffman herself points out that the Vulcan custom may have its origins in pre-Reform times when a man would walk ahead to protect a woman from danger. Based on the few Vulcan individuals we have seen, there is some evidence for a slight sexual dimorphism in the Vulcan species. Sarek, Stonn, and the attendants at Spock's marriage ceremony are all tall and well muscled. Spock is more slender, perhaps because of his human inheritance, but all Vulcan males are undeniably strong. T'Pau and T'Pring are hardly frail by human standards, but they are certainly less muscular than their men. And while modern times may offer fewer dangers to a physically weaker woman (wild sehlats having become increasingly rare), the custom may yet persist. "Be prepared" is not an unlikely Vulcan adage.

In "Journey to Babel," Kirk observes that Sarek's "request" for Amanda to continue her tour sounded much more like a command. Amanda replies to the implied question "Why does it sound like a command?" with the words "He is a Vulcan. I am his wife." Her precise answer is in keeping with her long residence on her husband's planet. She correctly interpreted her husband's words as a request, but Sarek's statement *sounded* like a command because Vulcans do not say "My dear, don't mind me and my long estrangement from our son. Please continue with your tour while I pull myself together." Though Amanda is not a Vulcan by birth, she has married a Vulcan and accepts his culture. She does not expect human courtesy.

After Amanda reveals Spock's childhood fondness for a pet sehlat, Sarek reprimands her for embarrassing their son: "Not even a mother may do that." Hoffman sees this as "an unlikely restriction in a matriarchy." She misses the point. Sarek certainly doesn't mean that he, as a member of a patriarchal society, does have the right to embarrass his son. Rather, he means that *nobody* has that right, not *even* a mother. This implies that a mother has the greatest rights of all but that they do not extend this far. Actually, one could use this incident as evidence that Vulcan is, after all, a matriarchy.

But another explanation is available. Because of the telepathic powers of their race and their physical proximity during embryonic development, Vulcan mothers may develop especially strong ties with their children. This biologically based intimacy may result in a very strong maternal involvement, and a high status within the family circle, but does not necessarily have any bearing on the allocation of power in the society at large.

In "The Savage Curtain," the last episode of the series to depict Vulcans, the image of Surak serves to illuminate portions of Vulcan moral and ethical development. Violence and the emotions which engender violence were rejected. Given his role in instigating the Reform movement, Surak is rightly viewed as "the father of all we became." After all, it would be silly to call him "the mother of all we became." "Father" is used as a precise description of "male parent." There is no direct mention of how this pacifist philosophy affected the power structure within the society.

In typical sex-obsessed human fashion, Star Trek viewers accord the Vulcan *pon farr* with far-reaching significance. However, the occurrence of this mating fever has no necessary impact on the allocation of individual or institutional power and authority. On the contrary, the manner in which Vulcans deal with *pon farr* points to a respect for both sexes.

The bond which joins a Vulcan male and female serves the avowed purpose of bringing the couple into great communion. A bonded, yet unmarried, couple will "both be drawn to *koon-ut-kal-if-fee*." However, upon marriage this light bond will undoubtedly deepen, perhaps reaching the intensity to be found in a mind meld. Certainly one purpose of this bonding is to transform what might otherwise be rape into a telepathic sharing of uncontrollable passion. A patriarchy could take this sexual union as a right, but Vulcans have developed an intricate ritual which assures the male of a sexual partner yet protects the female from unwelcome intercourse by promoting a mutual arousal.

If a Vulcan woman chooses not to enter into this prearranged union, the male's sexual passion must be directed away from her. Unfortunately, the most likely way to channel a male away from his sexual lust is to arouse him into a bloodlust. The two states are physiologically similar, involving increased respiration, heartbeat, physical activity, and emotional upheaval. (Presumably, running a marathon just won't do.) Since Vulcans have a deep respect for pacifism, it is not surprising that a challenge is very rare.

Despite the *pon farr*, a regular and embarrassing lapse from Vulcan reserve, men have not been denied a place in the Vulcan hierarchy. After all, it could be logically argued that Vulcan men are too emotionally unstable to govern. However, with typical Vulcan pragmatism, there is an apparent acknowledgment of the infrequent occurrence of the *pon farr*. Presumably, as long as a male keeps track of his seven-year cycle, he can be trusted with positions of responsibility, such as ambassador.

How then to explain T'Pau's question to T'Pring? "Thee are prepared to become the property of the victor? Not merely his wife, but his chattel, with no other rights or status?" The origins of this phrasing might be found in pre-Reform ritual which has never been changed. Or, since the words were spoken in Vulcan, the ship's translators may simply have been unable to find human equivalents. More likely, however, is a return to the ideas of Vulcan status and rank.

The concept of status as seen through human eyes is concerned with wealth and privilege and as such is probably of no interest to Vulcans. Rank based simply on inheritance would also be seen as illogical. Under this system, undeserving individuals would inevitably be accorded respect above that of someone more ethical or responsible than they.

Vulcans are much more likely to see rank as an indication of the level of responsibility expected of an individual or family. High status brings a great burden of duty, not personal gratification. Thus, signs of respect are a constant reminder of this responsibility, not of privilege. T'Pau, by her very success, has committed her family members to a high standard of conduct. Sarek has upheld the family honor and expects Spock to do the same. Amanda had no family honor to uphold, but presumably has gained status over the years through her actions on Vulcan and her marriage to Sarek. Still, her rank will probably never approach that of T'Pau or Sarek, both of whom are many years older and have a good head start on her.

So what does this tell us about T'Pring? "Thee are prepared to become the property of the victor? Not merely his wife, but his chattel, with no other rights or status?" T'Pau does not pose this question until *after* T'Pring's challenge.

T'Pring, by reneging on her marital contract, has *lost* her status. A challenge, as discussed above, is not to be undertaken lightly and is a negation of the promise she made in the initial bonding ceremony. Presumably, if she had bothered to break the engagement earlier, a Vulcan equivalent of an annulment could have been arranged. But by waiting until Spock is well in *pon farr*, she has placed his life and the life of her champion in jeopardy. Surely that constitutes a sufficient reason for loss of respect. Like Amanda, she will enter her chosen marriage with no family-based honor and will defer to the greater honor of her husband. Unfortunately, ancient Vulcan rituals have no provision for Kirk's equal lack of status, unless his close relationship with Spock (the captain is "best man" at the marriage ceremony) bestows a modicum of rank.

Thus it can be shown that using the same incidents discussed by Rebecca Hoffman, one can nevertheless support a theory that Vulcan is not a patriarchy, or even a matriarchy. Rather an entirely different, and more subtle, view of Vulcan character and culture is possible.

Vulcans deal with authority in a decidedly logical manner.

Power is invested in an individual or clan that has proved its abilities by its actions. The signs of respect given to the members of this family are symbolic of the burden of responsibility which they have assumed. Thus rank and status are earned, rather than inherited on the basis of sex or "noble" bloodlines. They can just as easily be lost by dishonorable action.

Biological sex is irrelevant authority except when directly pertinent to a situation, such as in the close ties between mother and children. The physical distance between husband and wife when walking in public serves a protective function and carries no connotation of societal authority.

The mating cycles of Vulcans are primarily a matter of reproduction and continuance of the species. They do not determine delegation of authority. Very likely, when the cycle occurs, the Vulcan husband and wife are *both* permitted a temporary leave of absence from their ordinary duties so that they can deal with their shared passion in privacy.

All things considered, we humans could learn a thing or two from Vulcan culture.

THE SEARCH FOR SPOCK: FILM VS. NOVELIZATION

by Bill Abelson

What are the basic differences between a film and the novelization of that film? What will work in one and not the other? What must be sacrificed? What can be added, enriched? In the following article, Bill Abelson looks at both the film and novel versions of Star Trek III: The Search for Spock, *and comes to some surprising conclusions about each.*

As Diane Rosenfeld's article in *Best of Trek #4* detailed, Vonda McIntyre's novelization of *Star Trek II: The Wrath of Khan* expanded on a well-rounded film, adding depth in characterization, a couple of subplots, and, here and there, plot details, which made it much more unpredictable, intriguing, and entertaining to read than would've been a simple and straightforward retelling of the film.

For example, in the novelization of *Wrath of Khan*, we discovered that Kirk plotted a decaying orbit for Spock's coffin-torpedo, with the intent of its certain immolation, and that Saavik, showing the fierce, stubborn independence of a Spock—or a Kirk—redirected its flight so it would intersect the Genesis Wave, thus becoming part of the new world. And during the literary climax, McIntyre describes how Sulu is jolted by an electrical blast that shoots right through the helm consoles, and how his life is saved by the exhausting, untrained mouth-to-mouth efforts of David Marcus.

In her novelization of *Star Trek III: The Search for Spock*, McIntyre goes even further in her additions than last time— it's a 291-page book compared to *Wrath of Khan's* 216—and no event from the film occurs until page 78!

The *Search for Spock* novelization opens with a remarkably

disastrous onship wake set up by McCoy and Scotty in memory of Spock and Scott's nephew Peter Preston. Though not essential to the main events of the story, it reestablishes Carol Marcus's deep grief over the loss of her friends on Regula I, and states most firmly that Carol is *not* about to swing into any rekindled romance with Kirk. And the charming, difficult, but mutually rewarding Saavik-David romance—damnably trimmed from *Wrath of Khan's* final cut—is here maintained and consummated.

There is also immediate reinstatement of the strained feelings of the living spacelab scientists—Carol and David Marcus—toward Starfleet, and, as a result, a blindingly rapid re-deterioration of the Kirk-David relationship. Carol's absence from (she needs to escape the Genesis Project atmosphere and deal with the pain of her lover Vance Madison's death) and David's inclusion in the *Grissom* party are not only convincingly but dramatically accounted for, and poor Kirk must contend not only with Carol's and David's renewed hostility but McCoy's gradually manifesting "psychosis." Perhaps Kirk might have gladly opted for a continuing midlife crisis rather than all he's faced in these two adventures!

Most important to *The Search for Spock's* concerns, we also see a *gradual* building of evidence that Genesis doesn't work. Saavik and David's investigation of the project's Stage II on Regulus I turns up amok growth patterns and plants whose smell yields psychedelic consequences, rather than the caffeine effects intended!

A central question is whether the novel's extra plot elements and details are creations of McIntyre or Harve Bennett (the paperback advises the work is "based on a screenplay by Harve Bennett"). Whichever is responsible for the wake, the family politics around Peter's funeral in rural Scotland, Uhura's narrow escape to the sanctuary of the Vulcan Embassy in San Francisco, the Marcus/Marcus/Esteban/Kirk confrontation over Genesis's future, the Carol/Christine body identification on Spacelab, and so on, there's little doubt that the coloring of character and universe stem from Vonda McIntyre. Her imagination, daring and understanding of the Star Trek universe and ideals are rich. Her discursiveness enables her to explore with resounding and heartwarming success the concept of IDIC. We are introduced to and given intriguing and touching senses of the catlike Ferrendahl on the mercenary ship, and "Fred" of the crystalline Glaeziver race. She's even sensitive and imaginative (and prophetic?) enough to describe what it's like to be transported (one's environment seems to dissolve and re-form rather than one's self), and what it's like to be onboard a cloaked ship (objects appear slightly transparent and voices hollow, and madness is not uncommon).

Also explored in welcome depth are the Klingon qualities of loyalty and honor. The spy Valkris has undertaken her mission in order to restore her family's name to glory. This fact, and her presentation to Ferrendahl of a length of sparkling fringe—an heirloom of priceless personal value—is a further indication of Klingon blood love and honor, and an admirably clear strengthening of IDIC. Concurrently, McIntyre puts other aspects of Klingon mentality in their proper place—Kruge worries about every crewmember's potential as "a spy, a challenger, a traitor," much like the anti-Federation Empire of "Mirror, Mirror." To their credit, both the film and the novel vividly depict the mutual respect and honor Kruge and Valkris feel at the realization he must destroy her—as well as, of course, the ruthless Klingon willingness to kill crewmember and enemy alike without the faintest sense of remorse.

In the novelization, Kruge knows who Kirk is, and fails to board the *Enterprise* because having the admiral brought to him as a prisoner would represent a high personal prize. (By the way, isn't Kruge's "I wanted prisoners!" intriguing in light of Kirk's *Wrath of Khan* observation "Klingons don't take prisoners"?) On film, Commander Kruge—strongly played by Christopher Lloyd, who gives Kruge sufficient intelligence, guts, and pain that we can't *completely* despise him—is weakened slightly by his functioning as a comic foil, always being alerted by his officer Torg of a factor slightly beyond his scope of awareness.

The onscreen moment when Kruge and Torg hiss about "ultimate power" and "Success, my lord," while amusing, is worthy in tone of more pedestrian SF stuff, and seems an unnecessary shortcut to establishing (1) that the Klingons are super-baddies, and (2) Kruge's blinding obsession with Genesis.

The novelization revealed that Klingons use three levels of language. Assuming that this existed in Bennett's original screenplay, it may have been rejected as cinematically untranslatable. But was it really? Certainly the subtleties could not be explored in depth, and it was a great kick to hear spoken Klingon at all, but at least a passing reference could have been made. Again, this would deepen our sense of Klingon culture and society. The breadth of the Star Trek universe—and the base it provides for those all-important aspects of fandom, observation and speculation—should be joyously augmented, not shied away from. Why compromise for a perceived sake of simplicity? There are countless "in" references in *The Search for Spock*, so the "sake of the audience" rationale doesn't hold water. Remember, the television show relied on its audience's memory for detail before there *was* fandom!

In a mere five pages, Vonda McIntyre achieves the most satisfying and fully realized characterization of Mr. Sulu in the series' eighteen-year history. Here Sulu has progressed beyond the piratic mode of combat and ideas into a serious student of aikido, the martial art dedicated to "demonstrating to one's opponent the futility of violence." "The pattern of his motions was smooth and pure, the way he hoped and tried to form his life." The fellow has come a long way from the wiseacre with the silly grin of early episodes. *This* Sulu has vast potential, not only spiritually, but professionally; he is the only *Enterprise* crewmember to be truly growing and newly embarking. As the *Enterprise* returns to spacedock, he is on the brink of assuming captaincy of the *Excelsior*, a post surely requiring a being of highly developed wisdom, imagination, youth, *and* experience.

However, *Excelsior*'s chair—indeed, *any* chair—is withheld from him, perhaps permanently, because of the near-quarantine on Genesis-related personnel. Sulu's ensuing confrontation with Admiral Morrow approaches Kirk's most strong-willed moments. This ambitious Sulu, it is clear, would never have joined Kirk's search had not *Excelsior*'s helm been denied him—in which case *Sulu*, not Styles, would have been charged with the responsibility of stopping the *Enterprise*'s getaway!

McIntyre gives similar attention to the other members of Star Trek's regular cast. As a Chris Chapel fan, I was pleased to discover she is still part of the *Enterprise* crew (Vonda McIntyre's, at least!) (Janice Rand, queerly enough, is omitted from print for the first time, despite her cameo in the film.) As benefits Christine's nature, she plays a philanthropic and crucial role in aiding and comforting McCoy and Carol Marcus at potentially shattering points: as Bones is waking from his first and most upsetting Spockian behavioral outburst, and as Carol confronts the reality of her lover Vance's body and death. Even better, Christine has grown as well. She has accepted with the passage of time the impossibility of Spock's love, and achieved understanding of *why* loving her is physically impossible for him, all in her own uniquely compassionate and touchingly private way. Christine's prettiness and heart make her a thousand times sexier than space tarts like Elaan or Marta!

It is somewhat hard to believe, but the film version of *The Search for Spock* contains not even a passing reference to either Carol Marcus or Amanda Grayson. Amanda's neglected existence is particularly odd given that Spock's ceremony—his resurrection!—occurs on Vulcan. Such an omission is uncharacteristic of Star Trek. Though it was great that Mark Lenard filled his original role as Sarek, Jane Wyatt's absence—if that was the reason for the character's omission—should nevertheless not have left Spock's fascinating and lovely mother unaccounted for.

The detail given on Lieutenant Saavik in the two novelizations by McIntyre merits an article in itself. For instance, her act of relinquishing her phaser to David so he can investigate their pursuers—utterly inappropriate and without reason in the movie—is satisfyingly explained in the book. Saavik realizes that Spock should not be left alone, particularly at the onset of *pon farr*—he might *kill* David—and that David's guilt impels him to investigate. Her subsequent action while they are captives again rings truer in McIntyre's version. Onscreen, Saavik's fearful glance at the Klingon murder weapon is completely out of character. In the novel, she has typically formulated an escape plan that is foiled by David's impulsive (suicidal?) rush at the Klingon guard. Saavik's insolent snapping at that moment quite simply adds to her dimension as a character.

As readers, we get the treat of seeing that upon Spock's death, David quickly assumes the role of her teacher in the mysteries of human ways, particularly in elucidating all the human "little jokes" which Saavik, for all her brilliance, cannot fathom or even discern as jokes. And we share their delightful discovery—in bed—that Saavik actually *has* a great (and sexy!) sense of humor, and then David's painful uncertainty whether she still loves him after his actions on Regulus I and irresponsibility in establishing the Genesis formula. Additionally, David states his belief that there was only a *one in a million* chance that protomatter would gum up the formula—certainly making him more worthy of our respect. (Funny, all those million-to-one gambles the *Enterprise* crew took always worked out.)

Saavik seems more comfortable about Kirk in the films than in the novelizations—a consequence of the comparative absence from the screen of the Saavik/Kirk war of words and nerves. True, his evaluations of her *Kobayashi Maru*, and her constant quoting of regulations, are present in *Wrath of Khan*, but the former especially is quite scaled down and her highly quizzical impression of human behavior is almost totally slighted on celluloid.

The film also severely attenuates David's presence and personality, leaving Merritt Butrick very little inner tension to work with. No vicious, hotheaded responses to Starfleet military or its accomplice, Kirk, here, no sexual love story with the thus also lessened Saavik—just a nice guy, really, who shows flashes and hints of heroism and honesty and, in his damn-the-torpedoes approach to the Genesis formula, his father's reckless grandeur. In the end, though, the story of David Marcus is one of regrettably unfulfilled potential.

As part of an apparent effort to paint the good guys whiter and everyone else blacker than need be, the Nimoy/Bennett tandem ceaselessly sentimentalizes the screen images of the *Enterprise* crew. This practice ranges from the subtle (when Kirk tells Scott to be "tolerant" in the book he is *chiding*, but in the movie he is just kidding) to the blatant (the overuse of "I shall always be your friend" and "Good of the many," etc.).

The movie also sanitizes the Kirk-Sarek interaction to an annoying extent. After Sarek's initial entrance, which hits theaters like a thunderbolt, his anger softens quickly. (Would a Vulcan—especially one of Sarek's mettle—*ever* quizzically ask a human, "But how?") But in the novelization . . . ah! Spock's progenitor continuously laces into Kirk's perceived human failings through their investigation of the ship's flight recorder, and Kirk gives as good as he gets. (Sarek: "Even you might reach a moderate level of comprehension [of Vulcan philosophy]." Kirk: "I get the picture. It still comes down to 'None of your business.' ") The distance even remains—though appropriately colored with a great deal more respect—after the *fal tor pan* ceremony. This is as it should be; Vulcans and humans are still aliens to one another, and Spock ought to be the only one—or one of the very few—to have bridged the gap.

Scotty, as a film personality, retains his lovable mixture of equal charm and acerbity. (Surely his "Up your shaft" and Sulu's "Don't call me tiny" rank among Star Trek's most delightfully funny moments.) Vonda McIntyre's writing, however, displays a particularly unlikable interpretation of the man. In the *Wrath of Khan* novelization, he consistently and unnecessarily bitched to nephew Peter about the boy's precociousness (jealousy, perhaps?). In the *Search for Spock* novel, his relationship with his niece Dannan is chilly, almost nonexistent; he complains about her and her mother's life-styles at a time of mutual mourning for her brother. He is crabby and almost pitiable, sitting alone and silent in a corner of the darkening house while Dannan escapes to the lovely, autumnal Scottish sunset. In addition, this Mr. Scott is rude—beaming to Dannan's door just after dawn, knocking without forethought (''Even Montgomery Scott'' wouldn't beam directly into a private home), and entering in a sour mood.

These examples illustrate how important it is for a writer not to go too far in either direction when adapting a film. The Kirk/Sarek scenes are enhanced by expansion; the bitter exchanges are *natural*, because of the tension of the situation, their mutual love for Spock, Spock and Sarek's past problems, and the oft-illustrated Vulcan contempt for human ways. They fit. But the treatment of Scott merely makes him seem peevish—seemingly a strain in characterization of Scotty solely for the sake of some conflict.

I felt Spock's sudden wholeness came off as too easy, almost cheap after all the struggles up to that point. Perhaps Nimoy felt the struggle for Spock's parts had provided strife enough, and wanted simply to depict a gentle (if difficult) healing ceremony. McIntyre tries to bring this final scene to life with details of the procedures, the setting, and the crew's feelings, but it still lacks the clearly defined conflict necessary for real excitement. We would need to get into the intermingling minds of McCoy, Spock, and T'Lar—a challenging assignment indeed! As it is, we share Bones' experience for a moment, a moment which gives us a tantalizing glimpse of T'Lar's enormous psychic power, and McCoy's active agony in wrenching back independent consciousness.

McIntyre also most satisfyingly explains the film's most puzzling ''mysteries'' (this woman might do Leslie Thompson proud!): (1) The purpose of transwarp drive is intergalactic travel; (2) Uhura had to stay behind to scramble enough communications frequencies so that the *Enterprise* wouldn't be intercepted by every ship in the sector before reaching Genesis; (3) it is Saavik who broadcasts a cryptic alert message explaining the importance of the Bird of Prey's cruise through Federation space, and the fact that it was under control of (unspecified) Federation personnel.

The storyline of *Star Trek III: The Search for Spock* poses a curious and potentially perilous dichotomy for Star Trek's future: Will (or even *should*) the *Enterprise* crew remain in the Federation? The film gives the impression—a convincing one, unfortunately—that the crew really has nothing further to live for than the ship. Sulu's long-awaited captaincy is deferred, Chekov must await reassignment following *Reliant*'s destruction, and Scott is clinging to his old ways. (The engineer's disdain for the innovation of transwarp drive indicates that a curious crustiness has set in on the man since he eyeballed the Eymorg vessel of "Spock's Brain" and declared, "Isn't she a beauty. Ion propulsion—they could teach us a thing or two.")

The crew's lack of career development does make their eagerness to split with Starfleet easier to accept, but it seems somewhat wrong, somehow: Star Trek isn't really supposed to be the *Enterprise* vs. Starfleet. Sure, its officials are always stubborn, are sometimes alluded to sarcastically (Spock's remark in "Mark of Gideon"), and are sometimes even underhanded (Stone's offered "deal" to Kirk in "Court Martial"). But all of the crew's training and the whole opportunity to explore come from the organization! The *Search for Spock* film is steeped in a curious quality that might be termed "*Enterprise* provincialism."

In the television series other Starfleet personnel and administrators were consistently shown to be tough, seaworthy sorts (even if consistently lacking the *Enterprise* crew's vision and compassion). Commodores Mendez and Stone, Captains Wesley, Decker, Tracy . . . none of these guys lacked guts or brains. (Ambassador Fox and Nilz Baris lacked both, but they were politicians, not sailors.) Here in *The Search for Spock*, Starfleet Commander Harry Morrow and *Excelsior* Captain Styles fancy themselves sly and clever, but are pompous, arrogant prigs; and *Grissom*'s Captain J. T. Esteban, the Walter Mondale of Starfleet, is a nerd in captain's clothing, as square, predictable, and infuriating as your least favorite uncle. Add *Grissom*'s and *Excelsior*'s haughty helmswomen, and "Mr. Adventure," and the unlikable portrait is somewhat overwhelming. These figures, though effective as comic foils on a first viewing of *The Search for Spock*, don't fit in well with the Star Trek universe, especially since cumulatively they represent Starfleet in the film.

The lone exception in this morass is the security officer who detains McCoy in the bar: cool and strong, he also shows admirable independence and respect in giving McCoy every reasonable chance to simmer down before turning him in.

Starfleet didn't need to be silly, and almost pointlessly hostile to the *Enterprise* and crew, for this film to be amusing. Interesting question: Why would the fleet be so cutting, so denying, to the *Enterprise*? The *Enterprise* is the glory ship and crew of the fleet, depicted as publicly *revered* in the Roddenberry novelization of *Star Trek: The Motion Picture*. On the other hand, it is unbelievable because even brainless institutions—and I'd hate to think Starfleet is one—know how to play good politics with their PR. A more plausible explanation is that Starfleet got such cold feet about the Genesis uproar that it in cowardice took its fear out on the parties involved . . . the *Enterprise* and her crew, as usual!

McIntyre, thankfully, treats these characters as three-dimensional humans, not as easy setups for wrath or laughter. Morrow is older and more dignified, if stodgy; moreover, the sting of Kirk's situation is heightened, as we learn Morrow is a friend of thirty years' standing, was Kirk's first commanding officer, and has sponsored Jim's career throughout. J. T. Esteban is eminently sensible, and square, hardly the boob seen onscreen, and we learn this approach has enabled him to prevail over an "extraordinarily challenging" series of events in his career. Even "Mr. Adventure" actually has a name—Lieutenant Heisenberg—and is thought of far more respectfully by Uhura, who is actually glad he questions the irregular transporter procedures, since any other reaction would harm his future in Starfleet.

Why have Nimoy, Bennett, and company painted such an irritating portrait of the fleet? Perhaps they are testing our mettle and stretch as fans (always a good idea, at least in principle). After *Star Trek II: The Wrath of Khan*, the viewer was left with a whole ship, a near-whole crew, and clearly offered Hope. Here, everything—save the sheer physical survival of the familiar characters, now not even a "crew"—is in shambles. There is no ship, all the characters save Spock have conspired to commit treason, Federation relations with Vulcan may now be greatly strained, and the fleet as an entity appears less wise and foresightful than ever. Perhaps, then, it is time for our heroes, the one who always had vision anyway, to leave the base of Starfleet as a necessary part of their personal explorations and growth as life forms.

In any event, the *worst* resolution of the current situation would be Starfleet's issuing a general pardon, in the manner of "The Menagerie" (the situation is quite closely paralleled) or "Amok Time." How annoyingly anticlimactic that would be! Having the crew pardoned and the *Enterprise* rebuilt in the first five minutes of *Star Trek IV* is the last thing I, for one, want to see.

It's getting so one must read these novelizations to get the full story behind the films! More equitably and realistically, McIntyre's world might be seen as parallel-universe versions of the latest two adventures. Undeniably they have assumed a life of their own, one notably less sugar-coated than the latest cinematic offering. I hope fervently that Vonda M. continues to write the novelizations . . . and perhaps one day even gets a crack at a Star Trek screenplay of her own!

TREK ROUNDTABLE—LETTERS FROM OUR READERS

Star Trek fans like to write. Stories, poems, scripts . . . but mostly letters. Letters to each other, letters to Paramount, letters to the stars, letters to magazines, letters to us. And we're always grateful and happy to get them. Although we receive so many that it is impossible to print but a tiny fraction of them in these Trek Roundtables, *we do read each and every one. We do so because we're very, very interested in what you have to say. We want to know what you think of our collections, what you think about your fellow fans, what you think of the world in general. And if you have a story to tell or an unusual experience to share, then send it along to us. As you can see from this volume's sampling, you're not alone.*

Margaret Richey
Barnesboro, Pa.

I've just finished reading *Best of Trek #8.* I couldn't put it down. I read it straight through one evening. What can I say but that I love Star Trek? My husband can't understand me, nor my mother; she's insisting that one of these days I'm going to wake up with pointed ears from watching and reading too much Star Trek. Is there such a thing as too much Star Trek to a loyal fan? Certainly not.

I started watching Star Trek when I was around ten years old. I loved it then, and still do at age twenty-eight as the mother of four children. They love it as much as I do. We tune in every night at 7:30 for the reruns, and my husband is amazed at how we stay glued to the TV, not wanting to miss a word. My children and I love all the characters. My son says he likes Captain Kirk because he does daring things, Mr. Spock because he is so intellectual and extra-strong, but never fights unless he has to, because he loves peace and all life. They love McCoy because he always tells it like it is, and they love the spats between him and Spock. They love each crewmember for what he or she has to offer; put them all together and you get magic.

Parents who are looking for good programming for their children to watch should realize that Star Trek is great! Star Trek takes my son, age seven, into a world vastly different from the one he encounters every day. He sees we will make it, we won't destroy ourselves with atomic bombs, pollution, prejudice, and hatred. People are still people in the future and they do care about each other and helping the other. What better hope to give to our children? For it is in hope that we grasp the impossible and make it work. My son expects a future from Star Trek and is motivated to make it. He wants to learn about computers and have all the answers like Mr. Spock, to explore space and beyond.

Even if we find beings who may talk, look, and even behave different, he can accept them, because the crew of the *Enterprise* does it on every assignment, simply as a matter of fact. Children watching Star Trek learn and retain how true friends like Kirk, Spock, and McCoy stick together no matter what life throws at them. They are a team that lives, laughs, and loves together, perhaps as mankind and other, alien life forms will in the future. They see it on Star Trek and they believe it will happen. And so it shall; they will make our future along with us. These are a few observations from a mother I wished to share with you.

I've read the characters' ages are a problem to some. It's silly; bring in new actors to replace Shatner, Nimoy, Kelley, and the others, and I won't accept them or watch Star Trek. Adding new characters to enhance in their *own way* the theme of Star Trek *is* acceptable, but *never* can you replace those who made Star Trek what it is. They are the very essence of Star Trek. A friend is always a friend; you don't love him any less because he happens to pass fifty. I'm of the opinion they all look as good as they ever did, maybe better. You get the impression that Kirk, Spock, McCoy, and family will never grow old. They will be forever full of adventure and challenges, but that's Star Trek . . . it makes you feel young;

there's always something more to discover, explore, and, as Mr. Spock would say, find fascinating.

Irene Hanley
Edmonton, Alberta, Canada

I cannot hold out any longer! I am finally ready to admit that I am a *Trekkie*, have been since 1966, and always will be. This revelation will come as no surprise to my husband, children, or anyone else who has known me.

The first two years that Star Trek was on the air I was a young girl in Montreal. The reception on our set was extremely poor, as we were trying to pull the show in from New York. My father was hooked, however, and knowing me to be a budding SF addict (with a side interest in Beatlemania), he would keep me up past my bedtime until we could see our show through much snow and static. I fell head over heels in love with Mr. Spock's voice; I couldn't see him well enough to tell just what was alien about him. It was only from remarks from Dr. McCoy and Captain Kirk that I got the hint that there was something vitally different about his ears. Then, in the third year, I had been watching television in the Nurses' Residence, getting more and more upset that no one wanted to watch my program, suffering greatly from Star Trek withdrawal, when one night I found myself all alone in the lounge at that crucial time. There he was, and those ears, those gorgeous pointed ears! I could actually see Mr. Spock with no snow, no static! I fell in love all over again.

I remember being caught one too many times sketching pictures of his beautiful features or writing poetry about his melodious voice. I was almost kicked out of nursing school. But, tragedy of tragedies, I passed. This was probably due to the fact that the show was canceled shortly after I finally discovered his true features. And the program never came back to Montreal for many years, even when it went into syndication. I had no idea at this point in my life that there were such things as fan clubs for anyone but rock singers or movie stars. I had not heard they extended to TV stars. I missed all of that through the year. I had only my sketches and my memories to keep my fantasies alive. Eventually my nursing career, marriage, and two children kept me too busy for even these few escapes from reality. I had not even heard of the animated series.

Then it happened! I had a younger sister over to baby-sit.

She frantically tried to tell me about this new SF TV series they had developed from a cartoon series! I hadn't a clue what she was talking about and told her there hadn't been a good SF series since Star Trek went off the air. Well, she introduced me to the novels and reintroduced me to my favorite series, much to the distress of my husband and workmates.

After reading the article by the respiratory tech in *Best of Trek #7*, I decided I had to write. There is someone out there as insanely hooked as me, and in the same field! Let me tell you, after eighteen years of nursing and twenty years of being a Trekkie, I still get the two realities confused. I find myself continually transporting to the wrong universe at all the wrong times. An example: The first day the new University of Alberta Burn Unit opened I couldn't sleep all day. I had to work that night and was overcome with excitement. We had been drilling for weeks with the new equipment (monitors, computer outlets, respirators, IVACs, IMEDs, Hubbard Tank Lifts, etc., etc., etc.). I wanted to get at my new play pen like yesterday! I arrived at work, donned my scrubs and lab coat, and darted into the "glass alligator"—so our elevators with the Plexiglas wall (that nauseates a scared-of-heights grown woman like me) were named by a four-year-old burn victim that I had given the grand tour before we moved. I ran to the doors of the unit, pushed the intercom button, and shouted, "Beam me up, Scotty! If I don't get to Spock's cabin in the next five minutes, I'll have to wait another seven years!" There was no verbal response. The doors opened and I darted in to find all the nurses looking different shades of purple as at that moment our unit supervisor was showing some guests the use of the intercom. I had made my statement loud and clear to half the hospital administration, a few local politicians, and the local chapter of the Firefighters Association (whose valiant effort funded the unit). The unit supervisor, not to be outdone, introduced me as "Irene, one of our more subdued staff members."

Melanie Chronister
Pottstown, Pa.

"Oh, boy," I say to myself, "this is going to be fun!" Wait a minute. *Fun?* I hate writing letters, and I hate typing even more. Ah, but *this* is about Star Trek. It is only the second letter I've written about Star Trek, the first being to

Diane Duane about her book *The Wounded Sky*. (Which I, along with Hilary Ryan, heartily recommend. I must disagree with Barbara Devereaux that the ultimate Star Trek novel has yet to be written.)

I am within the inexplicable group of second-generation Star Trek fans; I was born the year the series went off the air (for all you doing quick calculations in your head, I'm almost sixteen). I was raised on Star Trek reruns.

I am writing to comment on *Best of Trek #8*, the second *BOT* I've read. There was a lot I enjoyed and a lot I disagreed with.

Peggy Greenstreet's letter was written clearly and with a lot of insight into what makes Star Trek tick. Especially her statement that the Friendship is *not* a triad, but a seven-sided group of people who know each other well enough to work as one. This was clearly demonstrated in *Star Trek III: The Search for Spock*. Not only did they work as one, but they displayed their own personal talents and abilities to reach a common end that all of them wanted as one. It should be carefully noted, as Walter Irwin and G. B. Love did in their discussion of *The Search for Spock*, that they did this not because they expected to have Spock return to life, but rather because they wanted to preserve what was left of him, at his father's request. It was an errand of mercy, perhaps to themselves as well.

Stan Rozenfield raised a question about aliens in Star Trek. In one aspect, I agree with him: I want to see more of them, particularly Catians and Edoans (I rather fell for Arex and M'Ress from the animated series). But while it is true that the Federation isn't Earth-based, Starfleet is. Jim Kirk speaks to Garth in "Whom the Gods Destroy" as if the Federation is something that happened within their lifetime. Most likely, Earth had the strongest military force, which the Federation contracted to act for it. So only now (during the series) are nonhumans joining. By the time of *Star Trek: The Motion Picture*, the ships' crews were probably much more varied. The *Enterprise* was simply an Earth ship.

Aliens *are* sometimes treated unfairly in Star Trek, but let us not judge too quickly.

All right, now that *that* is out of the way, we will get on with the business of the day—something that many people must have been thinking as they read the above: "But is she going to say something *important*, something about *The Search for Spock*?"

I should tell you I'm not, just for being so impatient, but that would be cutting off *my* nose to spite *your* faces; I can't help but talk about it.

To start off, I was a bit disappointed with *Star Trek: The Motion Picture*. Oh, the story was good, the effects were good. But Star Trek should be more than exciting special effects. That's not what drew its first fans. I think *STTMP*'s biggest problem was the transition to the movie screen; not only were the actors not comfortable, but the producers seemed afraid to make Star Trek the controversial, thought-provoking show it was in the sixties.

Star Trek: The Wrath of Khan was better; it was a step in the right direction; the actors were comfortable. But the producers were still afraid. If anything, *Wrath of Khan* was even more like *Star Wars*. And it lacked the . . . the Big Story, as Joyce Tullock calls it, man's struggle with his own humanity and what he will one day become.

And then, there was *The Search for Spock*. It was beautiful. It seems the film was searching for more than just Spock. It was searching for Star Trek's own eternal soul. And just as Spock is reunited with his, so we are reunited with Star Trek's. And we can look forward to dear memories to return to us, as they already have in this Star Trek, thanks to director Leonard Nimoy, who treated us to such delights as Tribbles, Klingons, Sarek, jailbreaks, and Jim Kirk going off against Starfleet orders to help his friend (although the friend this time will be McCoy).

Why did no one think of it before? Who better to bring us Star Trek than the one who has lived in the heart of it, one who *knows* Star Trek and cares about it? He made the film and the actors come alive as they haven't since, perhaps, the first year of Star Trek. Use of the shooting techniques of the sixties and a special showcase for each of the crewmembers were ways he achieved this end.

In this movie, two things happened that I wish had not. One was the demise of the *Enterprise*. I do understand why it happened; she sacrificed herself for the sake of the children she has carried within herself and protected. Hers was a sacrifice as surely as Spock's was. But I still wish it hadn't happened.

Another things was the misuse of Saavik, which was definitely a mistake. She had so much potential. The fault was not Robin Curtis's, or indeed anyone else's. The role was simply interpreted differently than we would have liked. It is possible that Saavik can still be redeemed and be made back into the Saavik of *Wrath of Khan*. Perhaps, even, Kirstie Alley could be coaxed into portraying her again. Many people will, no doubt, disagree with me, but I do not make this statement lightly. I just saw *Wrath of Khan* last night and carefully evaluated her performance. That cool, green-eyed, swearing young lady must be brought back.

All in all, *The Search for Spock* was a good movie and a *very* good year for Trekkies. It was certainly the best of the three movies. If I could eradicate the other two, I would not. They were good movies, if not terrific; and they were necessary steppingstones to *The Search for Spock*. But never, never let us return to their quality in the future.

Robert Willest
Holiday, Fla.

I am a forty-one-year-old male who has been interested in science fiction since I was six. As I grew older, the SF I read and saw on TV and movies became less and less believable until that unforgettable Thursday night in September 1966, at 8:30 p.m.

Before the show aired, I thought, "Here comes another silly space show." Thanks to the Great Bird of the Galaxy, I was very wrong. Each one of the seventy-nine episodes (even the "poor ones") has a special place in my heart and I have seen each one over twenty-five times, plus all the movies three times each.

I own over a hundred Star Trek books, including *Best of Trek #1-8*. I have just finished #8 and it is, without a doubt, the best yet, and I'm looking forward to many more.

Like most Trekkies, I have analyzed each episode and film, found mistakes, and have many opinions on plots, characters, etc., but instead of elaborating on them, I just want to say how thankful I am that they are even around to judge.

In my opinion, there has never been, and probably never will be (at least for a long time), a more enjoyable, educational, or believable SF series. NBC, you really blew it.

In closing, I would like to commend not only our beloved "favorites," who have done a superb job over the years, but the many fine actors and actresses who have appeared in "our galaxy." Also, a special thanks to the many fine authors, producers, directors, stage crew, and, especially, special effects personnel who have given all of us so many years of enjoyment, for without them, Star Trek would have been "just another silly space show."

Oh, just one final comment. Although I mourned the passing of our beloved Spock, I knew in my heart he would be returned to us and "things" would be as they should be, but I truly cried at the death of (I believe) our most cherished Star Trek memory—NCC–1701, the USS *Enterprise*, for she is gone forever. She will be missed and loved as much as anyone in Star Trek, because she was ours.

Patricia Frank
Los Angeles, Calif.

Did I see the same *The Search for Spock* that every other Trekkie did? Everyone keeps talking about Saavik and Spock's relationship since he underwent *pon farr* while on Genesis. What relationship?

Was not Spock's essence residing in McCoy far away on Earth? Did not Saavik state that the Vulcan child had no intelligence, the mind was a clean slate responding only to physical sensations? Spock's mind was not present! I'm sure Saavik's "meld" only offered solace and an easing of the pains suffered by the body from Genesis and the urges of *pon farr*. This physical young body of Spock's did not *know* who he was, or what was happening to it. And surrounded by Klingons and a planet that was breaking up did not seem to me a great time for actual intercourse.

Wake up, Star Trek fans; look at that movie again!

As to Saavik's seeming detatchment on Vulcan: Remember she had never been invited there. I'm sure Spock would not have inflicted on Saavik the censure of other Vulcans. He had suffered nonacceptance as a child; Saavik would have as well, being a child born of rape and mental violation. I believe her healthy emotional growth would have been impaired on Vulcan and that education in the rest of the Federation was necessary. Her detatchment was only a sign of her discomfort. If she seemed embarrassed in front of Spock at the end of the movie, couldn't it have been because there was no real recognition in his eyes? Also, he would have no recollection of the intimacy she had shared *mentally* with his body.

Heinz Werth
Sault Ste. Marie, Ontario, Canada

I have just completed reading the latest in your outstanding series of articles (*Best of Trek #8*). All I can say is this: superbly done.

Personally, I have been a Star Trek fan for several years now. I was twelve years old when it first appeared back in 1966, though I did not start watching it until later. My first connection with the world of space travel did not come about until December of 1968 when I happened to hear on the radio that three men had flown to the moon. The moon? Wow! That did it. Ever since the historic *Apollo 8* Mission, I have been following NASA's developments: *Apollo, Skylab, Apollo/Soyuz, Columbia, Challenger, Discovery*. (I still ask: Why is the *Enterprise* not spaceworthy?)

It was not until sometime about 1970 that I was finally introduced to Captain Kirk, Mr. Spock, and the rest of the crew of the Starship *Enterprise*. I can recall that first episode clearly. The *Enterprise* found a battered sister ship, the *Constellation*, and ended up facing "The Doomsday Machine." It is still my favorite episode. Needless to say, I have seen all seventy-eight original episodes, all twenty-two animated episodes, and all three movies. I just wish I could see the original pilot film "The Cage" in its entirely. Has anybody ever thought of suggesting to Paramount and/or Gene Roddenberry a release of "The Cage" on videotape to add to the collection Paramount is currently releasing?

Getting back to *Best of Trek #8*, my favorite article was "A Return to the Big Story" by Joyce Tullock. Her positive appraisal of *The Search for Spock* is outstanding; it expresses my own feelings of the film to a T. Sorry, Walter and G.B., your own discussion was good, too. I just liked Joyce's better.

Leslie Thompson's "Star Trek Mysteries Solved . . . Again" was again excellent. However, the discussion of Chekov . . . I'm sorry, Leslie, but I don't agree with you. I believe that Chekov may have just been transferred to the *Enterprise* at the time of "Space Seed." Further, I believe in the possibility that Khan may well have seen (even talked to) Chekov at some point, though offscreen. Eventually, Chekov worked his way through the ranks until finally we see him on the bridge as the navigator in the second season.

Concerning the Klingons, let me ask: How many different races are there on Earth? Do we all look alike? We've seen only two races of Klingons so far—those in the TV episodes and those in the movies. Just because we didn't see the "TV

Klingons'' in the movies doesn't mean they no longer exist, does it?

Editor's note: Rumor has it that Paramount does plan to release "The Cage" as videotape #1 in the series, Heinz. The problem is that the original color print no longer exists, and a new version will have to be pieced together from footage in "The Menagerie" and computer-colored footage from Roddenberry's black-and-white print. Perhaps, such a restored version will be available by the time you read this. Leslie says she's always held the view that there is more than one type of Klingon; two distinct types appeared on the original series, making a total of three we've seen so far.

Kelly Cowling
Ft. Worth, Tex.

Immediately after reading *Best of Trek #8*, I picked up the phone and shouted in my friend Melissa Tyson's ear, ''We're not crazy!'' My skeptical family members, however, still refuse to believe that I'm by any scale even close to normal.

I cannot describe my relief in finding others like me (I'm thirteen). My parents were beginning to get really worried. Once I was describing a Star Trek episode with such conviction that one of them leaned over to the other and whispered, ''She really believes it exists.'' This distressed me until I watched Star Trek later that night and I found that my strong devotion to the show was well founded.

People have ridiculed the efforts of myself and fellow Trekkies to find or explain the century in which Star Trek exists. Our only explanation was a parallel universe. Now that we know what it is, the question is, how do we get there? Is it enough to visit it for an hour every weeknight? That is what we live with, but as long as we bring part of that universe into our everyday lives, it will be all right. So, we'll continue to be a part of that odd species residing in the mysterious world of fandom. Yes, I'll continue painfully parting my fingers in the Vulcan salute and spending hours to train myself to raise my eyebrow—all the while delighted with the knowledge that I'm not alone and I'm *not crazy*!

Cam Walton
Waco, Tex.

I just finished reading my first *Best of Trek* book (#2), and now I can't wait to buy and read the others. Some questions I had about Star Trek were answered, and I'm formulating others. I never knew such enlightening books existed—but have long wished that they did!

I'd like to find out a few things that were mentioned but not defined in the book. First, what is the "philosophy of IDIC"? Being a relatively new Star Trek fan (I was an addict as a child but have forgotten most everything I saw) I obviously need more basic information to grow on. Second, how can I get a list of all the episodes in the order in which they were shown? And last, but not least, how can I find back copies of your magazine?

I want to thank you gentlemen and everyone else who writes about Star Trek for helping yet another foundering science fiction fan realize that Star Trek not only entertains and educates, but inspires.

I hope to continue my pursuit of ST's subtle messages to mankind, and would pursue even more if the television stations aired more shows, and if the bookstores thought it more important to the growth of young SF fans.

Editor's note: IDIC is both a Vulcan symbol and a philosophy: Infinite Diversity in Infinite Combinations. In short, it celebrates the Vulcan reverence for all life and the beauty which may be found in differences.

Gail Eppers
Racine, Wis.

On the door to my room is a sign that says "Starfleet Headquarters/Restricted Area." Inside is my haven. Whenever I feel down, I go in there, browse through a *Best of Trek* or some other Star Trek book, read through my Star Trek scrapbook, or try on my insignias. If I'm home alone, I might play one of the movies or one of the over forty episodes that I have on videotape. Before I know it, I don't feel down anymore.

I just finished *Best of Trek #8*, and though I've written letters many times, I vowed that this time it would get in the mail. The first thing I always read is Trek Roundtable. I wish you would give more complete addresses so I could write to some of them. I especially like the letters from people in faraway places. It's nice to know that Star Trek is everywhere.

Another thing I wanted to say is that I have *not* been a fan from the beginning. I was around but I was fresh out of diapers when it started, and no one in my family had the slightest interest in "those silly space shows." But I don't remember exactly when it all started for me. I do recall how, though: *Star Trek Log One*, by Alan Dean Foster. My brother (who regrets it to this day) gave it to me one day to feed my reading habit. In the first story, "One of Our Planets Is Missing," Kirk reaches a set of buttons by climbing on Spock's shoulders. McCoy rocks on his heels and muses, "Isn't science wonderful?" It was the first time I laughed out loud reading a joke. I was so intrigued, I started watching the episodes (I'd hardly grown out of cartoons yet), and the rest . . . well . . . obvious.

Something else that may seem strange: It was not Spock who kept me coming back. Sorry, Mr. Nimoy, but it was Captain Kirk. It was that he cared so much about people. I grew up hated and hating, and Captain Kirk showed me I didn't have to hate back. Through him, I learned to understand and accept people's faults and not condemn them. Even if we were enemies, I could value their life. I know this is a big part of IDIC, but it was Kirk who showed it to me in action, by not shooting the Horta and by joining forces with Kang.

Thank you, Captain Kirk.

And thank you, *Best of Trek* people. I love what you're doing and I am looking forward to *Best of Trek* #9 . . . and #10 . . . and #11 . . .

Editor's note: It's our policy not to publish full addresses for a number of reasons, not the least of which is to protect our correspondents' privacy. We regret that this sometimes prevents fans from getting in touch with each other, but we really can't do otherwise. By the way, this seems like a good time for our occasional reminder that when you write to Trek Roundtable, your letter becomes the property of Trek Publications, and you give us permission to publish your letter, edited in any way we see fit. But you already knew that, didn't you?

Sheila Chaffman
Pelahatchie, Mo.

I have just finished reading an article in *Best of Trek* #8 that has me very irritated. That article is "Beneath the Surface: The Surrealistic Star Trek,'' written by James H. Devon.

What exactly had this man been watching before he wrote that article, a triple-X-rated movie?

I am twenty-five years old and far from prudish, and I found *Star Trek: The Motion Picture* nowhere near the sexual fantasy that Mr. Devon seemed to imagine.

Spock and Kirk have always been very masculine to me, and I too have noticed all the sexual overtones of the television series and the movies, but never to the extreme that V'Ger had been sent from Earth as a reproductive vehicle for the future. Another example that Mr. Devon evidently didn't think of when he explained how the *Enterprise* was a symbol of male and female is that the dilithium crystal was the egg and the matter-antimatter must have been the sperm. A sickening thought, isn't it?

Star Trek is as stated at the beginning of each television episode:

"Space, the final frontier.
These are the voyages of the Starship *Enterprise*.
It's five-year mission
to seek out new life and new civilizations.
To boldly go where no man has gone before."

Not:

"Space, the final frontier.
These are the sexual fantasies of the sexy ship *Enterprise*.
It's five-year mission
to seek out new metaphors of new perversions.
To boldly write about what no man has ever seen before."

In closing I would like to say that the destruction of the *Enterprise* in *The Search for Spock* has started what many of us, the fans, feel will soon be the end of Star Trek, because eventually all the characters that we have learned to love over the many years will be gone and replacing those characters with other characters or actors will never be accepted.

Margaret Banks
Alexandria, Va.

This is my first fan letter of any type, so bear with me, folks! I've been a Star Trek fan since the first episode in 1966, so that dates me a little. I am a naval officer, stationed in Washington, D.C.

Best of Trek #8 was especially good; I particularly enjoyed

Trek Roundtable. I have a few comments to make, and maybe even an answer or two!

I'm referring to the article "Kirk and Duty," specifically Kirk's career pattern. Since Starfleet follows U.S. Navy rank structure, promotion patterns most probably do also.

Kirk would have spent two years as an ensign before his next promotion to lieutenant (junior grade). He was referred to as a lieutenant in the article, but most likely the writer(s) mean lieutenant (j.g.).

An officer spends about ten months to two years before promotion to the next grade, lieutenant, depending on performance and date of rank.

My next comment also is that later on in the article, Kirk is promoted "several grades" from lieutenant to first officer. That actually isn't completely correct. First officer is a position, not a rank. On a smaller ship than the *Enterprise*, the first officer (or executive officer) could be a lieutenant commander, the next step up from lieutenant.

In present-day Navy career patterns, the step between lieutenant and lieutenant commander is about four years. Those accelerated to lieutenant commander could conceivably do it in two to three years. Kirk's promotion from lieutenant to first officer was probably an accelerated promotion to lieutenant commander. That means Kirk could be three years ahead of his Academy contemporaries. Since his sterling performance continued at its rapid pace, he also was promoted early to commander, and eventually to captain, making him a captain at thirty-four. That would indeed be an accomplishment, even today!

Also, in "Mysteries Solved . . . Again!" I didn't quite agree with the answer given to the question about the dilithium-cracking station on the Tantalus V penal colony. There wasn't a dilithium-cracking station on Tantalus V, but there *was* one on Delta Vega ("Where No Man Has Gone Before"). Am I right?

Editor's note: Thanks for the inside information about naval promotion procedure, Margaret. The question of a cracking station on Tantalus arose because of the use of the same matte shot (slightly altered) in both episodes; in other words, if it's a cracking station in one episode, it's gotta be a cracking station in another. Why not just say they were both automated, and the one on Tantalus had a penal colony next door? See, Leslie, it's simple.

Daniel Maunder
Los Angeles, Calif.

"She is a beautiful lady! And we love her!"

That is why NCC 1701 can "go out in a blaze of glory," but the *Enterprise* can never die. To those who were assigned to her—thought they may *say* that they *served on* her—there will always be the memory of *serving with* her . . . and being in love with her.

This concept was brought even closer to me two months ago when my mother died. After cremation (. . . blaze of glory . . .), I realized that she isn't dead, only her body is. She (my mother) is a beautiful lady! And I love her!

Such a truth may not be the best way to start a fan letter, but I believe that it is a truth that needs to be known by every one of us.

Having been a Star Trek fan ever since I saw Gary Mitchell's silvery eyes (and Spock's elegant ears), you may think it a bit odd that I write this letter after so many years of remaining silent. Well, so be it. I can no longer avoid writing how a fifteen-year-old punk grew up to become a thirty-five-year-old man—with Star Trek as an "ersatz family."

In 1965, I was still numb from my sister's death (1963) and my parents' divorce (1965). Star Trek provided me with the family I desperately craved. Kirk, Spock, McCoy, and Scotty were the father and brothers I needed (I am the oldest son and was living with my mother). As the series progressed, I could see that the *Enterprise* wasn't just a ship—it was a family unit.

If I were to make a "family tree," it would be like this: "Grampa" McCoy, "Uncle" Scotty, "Papa" Kirk, "Mama" *Enterprise* (or Chapel), "Uncle" (or eldest son) Spock, Sulu and Chekov (sons), and Uhura is *definitely* the eldest daughter.

During the years between 1965 and 1970, I nearly died twice. Once from falling off the roof (nearly breaking my back) while adjusting the TV aerial (wonder which show was coming up?), and the second time from a brain tumor that was diagnosed "malignant, inoperable, terminal." No operation—no tumor—I am *not* writing this letter from the grave.

While the tumor left me amnesiac (totally, at first), I have been recovering memories—and friends—ever since. That last sounds a bit like Spock in *The Search for Spock*, but the point of this autobiography is to let you know *why* Star Trek has meant so very much to me—and how much I appreciate every person (and the characters they built) who *is* (not was) part of Star Trek.

To (briefly) continue my "autobiography"—since 1970, I have been born again, have loved and been loved, have gotten married, have become an armed security guard, watched my mother as she was released from a burdensome body. Through every moment of this time, I have lived—and loved—the Star Trek family.

I am totally shocked that this "quick note" has erupted into four pages without my having said what I had intended. When I sat down to write to you, I had two basic ideas I wanted to share (and ended up sharing my life!). So I'll share them now.

The first is that I have long seen Kirk and Spock as brothers (twins—like Desus/Spock in *Black Fire*), with McCoy as their father and Scott as McCoy's brother. The second is to name my three favorite episodes—"The Empath," "The City on the Edge of Forever," and *Star Trek III: The Search for Spock* (the novelization). Each of these are special to me because they show the love/devotion/sacrifice for one another in the Kirk/Spock/McCoy trio.

The three scenes that will always be in my heart are: "Forget . . ." ("Requiem for Methuselah"); "He knows, Doctor" ("City"); and "I have been, and always shall be your friend" (*The Search for Spock*).

It is my sincerest wish that this "quick note" gives you—and every fan in the universe—as much joy from reading it as it gave me from writing it. It's doubtful that you can find a library computer with enough memory cells to hold all that I now wish to say about Star Trek—so I will conclude with a reminder: "She is a beautiful lady! And I love her!"

Michelle Edwards
Brooklyn Center, Minn.

When Star Trek first aired in September 1966, I was three weeks short of my third birthday—a bit young to appreciate it. I never saw any of the animated episodes either, but Star Trek was always around and I was always watching it. I remember in junior high my friends and I would spend hours talking about our favorite episodes. I remember, too, huddling in the corner of our basement with an old black-and-white, flipping channels back and forth in an agony of frustration, unable to choose between watching Star Trek or the exciting Montreal Olympics.

Sometime after that, Star Trek went off the air in my area, and although I missed it, I didn't think too much about it. Then it happened. *Star Trek: The Motion Picture* was released. Suddenly I found myself almost choking with excitement at the thought of seeing new Star Trek. Sitting in the theater, I could hardly keep still. The whole audience burst into applause and cheers at the sight of each of those beloved faces, and more than a few eyes were wet at the sight of that beautiful starship. I confess that I left that theater with only the barest impressions of plot, so filled was I with delight at what felt like a reunion with old friends.

But: Being the sensitive, observant person I am, I noticed my enthusiasm was definitely not matched. My friends had done a terrible thing—they'd "outgrown" Star Trek. They thought of it as just a TV show they used to watch and a mediocre movie that couldn't hold a candle to *Star Wars*. I figured I was out of step and tried to reshape my thinking.

Not long afterward, I was prowling the bookstore for something new and different to read. I'd always been dimly aware that Star Trek fiction existed, but I'd avoided it because I thought it wouldn't be able to compare with the visual medium. But I saw the novelization of *Star Trek: The Motion Picture* and decided to risk it. How blind I had been! I went back to that bookstore and began haunting several others as well. I bought and voraciously read all the Star Trek I could get my hands on. I found new novels, old ones, TV episodes, animated episodes, books about the Star Trek Phenomenon, magazines, blueprints, and so much more. Unbeknownst to me, Star Trek lived and breathed. And I was enthralled.

All of a sudden it hit me: I'd become a Trekkie. Really. Me, a twenty-one-year-old English major at the University of Minnesota, I'm a Trekkie. And proud of it!

I am, however, a rather quiet Trekkie by nature. Let me assure you that I've never, *ever* written a fan letter before, or written to any club, organization, institution, or magazine for any reason whatever. So why am I writing to you? Because I feel a need to give something back. Star Trek has given me so much, I can keep quiet no longer. I just finished reading *Best of Trek #8* and decided to accept your invitation to write. Perhaps you people can stand in for all those who have been a part of Star Trek from its creation through today and accept my resounding "Thank you!"

Star Trek has left its indelible mark on me. I have laughed, cried, cheered, ached, and reflected. I can't even read my Star Trek books in public anymore because I forget that I only travel to Star Trek's universe in my mind; my body stays behind to embarrass me with belly laughs, cries of dismay and exultation, or, at the very best, an idiotic smile of sheer delight. Believe me, I've gotten some strange looks from passersby.

But I'll never give it up. Curled up in the privacy of my room, I revel in the valiant compassion James T. Kirk brings to his crew and to others, the wise and noble spirit of Spock, Bones' sharp tongue and gentle hands, Scotty's stoic, unfailing, invaluable service, the dashingly skilled Sulu, enthusiastically idealistic Chekov, the elegant competence of Christine Chapel, and the gifted efficiency and beauty that Uhura radiates. How could anybody not respect, admire, even love people like that?

Wonderful as I have found Star Trek fiction to be, I still await each new movie with bated breath. In my humble opinion, each one has been more wonderful than the last. It's like a shot in the arm to sit back and watch the further adventures of "the finest crew in Starfleet."

Well, I've had my say and maybe now I'll go back to being quiet. Somehow I doubt it, though. Star Trek has a way of not only reaching me but demanding a response. Who knows, I might even write my own Star Trek someday! But for now, I definitely want to keep reading yours.

Todd Bennett
Provo, Utah

I just finished *Best of Trek #8*, and, as with the previous seven volumes, I was entertained, amused, amazed, infuriated, etc., etc. Why, you may ask, have I been driven to a letter of comment at last? Two things, actually.

One: I honestly can't understand how *anyone* could prefer *The Search for Spock* to *Wrath of Khan!* The second film not only was a great action-adventure film, but dealt with *real* emotions and themes such as growing old, responsibility, self-sacrifice, love of comrades, and others. The cast *looked* great, the *Enterprise* has never looked better, and the style of the film was snappy, visual, and exciting to watch.

None of these things can be said for the trite, boring mess that was *The Search for Spock*. Many of those who praised the third film in articles seem to see the mere *pretension* of an important theme as valid reason for praise, despite the fact that the film failed utterly to do anything with its high-flown pretensions. The emotion was plastic, the actors without exception looked old and fat. (James Doohan seemed barely able to wheeze out his lines as Scotty.)

This is the fault of a mediocre director and an average writer. Nicholas Meyer made the best Star Trek that is, and ever likely will be; a movie that was not just a sop for the Trekkies and Trekkers, but a film of universal theme and appeal. (It was interesting to watch the "expanded" version shown on ABC a few nights ago; with a single exception, the added scenes *detracted* from the film. The sole positive addition was the reinsertion of the line in which Scotty identifies Peter Preston as his nephew, a line important to the understanding of later events. The other stuff that was added served merely to slow down the action.)

If Paramount continues to make Star Trek films only for the fans, the series will die after one or two more. If they, instead, bring in some new blood, not *just* in the cast, but in the writers, directors, and cinematographers as well, the series could last as long as the James Bond series.

Pat Todd
Mulgrave, Victoria, Australia

As you can see from my address, you are getting a following far and wide—if I may be so bold as to call myself a following. If not, then after reading only half of your book I make myself your number-one fan.

As I have already said I am only halfway through your book and could go no further until I had tried to put my feelings down on paper. The book I refer to is *Best of Trek*, and I must assume from your constant acknowledgment of the number of Star Trek fans that this must have been reprinted several times and you must have also had follow-up books, so the only way I can define which book it is is to tell you that the introduction is dated 1977.

I hope the pause in this letter is enough for you to get over the shock that someone is writing to you about a book you wrote over eight years ago. Please take into account where I live and also the fact that any Star Trek literature is almost impossible to obtain. Believe it or not, the only way I became aware of the fact that any Star Trek books were being written was through a secondhand-book shop; since then I have begged or borrowed (not quite stolen) any books that I can get my hands on. I have also found a science book shop that has a limited amount of novels. This is where I obtained your book.

I hope you don't mind, but there is another reason for my writing this letter: I have at last obtained proof (your book) that there are other people like me in this world, and I don't intend to let you get away too easily.

You would find a statement like that hard to believe, I suppose, but here I have still found no one who would openly admit to the fact that they either watched, liked, or followed Star Trek. I do now, and when I do, I stand ready for the funny looks and the laughter. People have afterwards admitted to me, when we are on our own, that they love it but would dare not admit this in front of other adults.

How I envy the fans in America being able to openly admit their "love" and "admiration" for this phenomenon, regardless of age, color, or race. I was particularly touched by the letter written in this book by Fern Lynch, a sixty-five-year-old grandmother. I can picture a woman who was once afraid to admit she had become attached to a science fiction series, yet in the end it changed her life and her relationship with her grandchildren. Also, she stated in her letter that she had sent a tape to a young girl in Australia, which I think was the final word to make me put pen to paper and see if there are any more like me over here.

I am married and I am thirty-six years old. I have three sons, eighteen, seventeen, and fifteen; my eighteen-year-old likes science fiction, but doesn't think Star Trek is anything special. (He is born of the *Star Wars* era.) The other two regard Mum as an object of pity and retardation every time she has a Star Trek book within her grasp or a Star Trek film to go and see. My husband regards me as childish and someone who should be humored if the subject comes up, but I suppose you have gathered by now that is not often, as no one shares this interest with me. I don't even have the luxury of viewing the reruns of Star Trek, as over here they reran them once and stopped doing that halfway through. When I read that Star Trek went into three years on TV, I'm sure that they didn't even bother to show them all, so there might be some I have never seen at all. We have had the films over here, and each time I have seen them I allow myself the luxury of letting open the floodgates of emotion, full of respect for this "enigma" and what it stands for.

Well, I have rambled on enough, but I don't know whether or not you can begin to know what it is like for me to be able to put these feelings down on paper after twenty years . . . in the beginning denying I watched the show and then growing enough in myself to admit that I love it and follow it each week and not worrying what the reaction is.

I suppose you have gathered by now that I could go on writing forever; if I wasn't afraid of frightening you off, I would tell you in what way Star Trek has affected me (even if it has been mostly in silence), but another time.

Kathy Heinis
Kingsford Heights, Ind.

I have heard a lot of negative comments on Robin Curtis's portrayal of Saavik—that she's cold even for a Vulcan. I have another view of her performance: It shows that she is just as confused as is Spock about accepting the fact that she's a half-breed.

Most people's opinion of her in *Wrath of Khan* was right, in that she was almost totally Romulan. She showed such great anger almost every time she had something to say. At Spock's funeral she was crying, which must have been embarrassing to her. Imagine the array of emotions she must have been feeling, losing him so violently. It might have been at that point that she decided to discard all emotion, for when we see her again in *The Search for Spock*, she is almost subdued.

When she and David discover Spock's tube, she becomes confused, probably wondering where his body is. She even shows an annoyance with Captain Esteban. When she talks to the Klingon commander, you can almost see the hatred in her eyes (and even fear of her impending death). When David dies and she tells the admiral, I read it as if she will not give the Klingons the satisfaction of showing that it bothered her at all. She feels she has handled it all the best way she could. Remember, not much time has passed since she lost her mentor. I see compassion and tenderness when she deals with Spock on the planet, and she shows astonishment when she sees him growing in front of her eyes.

She has become overly Vulcan, now. To everybody else it look like she's a passive, but I see her suffering to hide her emotions too much, for at the end, when Spock sees her in line, she hides her eyes.

Perhaps she has just discovered she cannot hide all emotion. Perhaps she just discovered that she shouldn't be ashamed she has emotions and that she doesn't have to suppress or show them. Just control them. Perhaps she has grown, too. So she doesn't raise an eyebrow. She doesn't have to.

Spock found his way through V'Ger. Saavik found hers through Spock's death and rebirth. Whether or not we see her again, we know she has grown through the experience.

WHY KIRK WILL REMAIN
AN ADMIRAL

by Joseph A. Rochford

One of the smaller, but enduring, mysteries of Star Trek is the question of Jim Kirk's rank: It almost seems as if he's an admiral one day, a captain the next, an admiral again the third. Why so much confusion? Some of the answers can be found in the following article.

BONES: "This is not about age and you know it."

KIRK: "Spare me your notions of poetry. We all have our assigned duties."

BONES: "Jim, get back your command. Get it back before you turn into part of this collection; before you really do grow old."

SPOCK: "Jim . . . If I may be so bold: It was a mistake for you to accept promotion. Commanding a starship is your first, best destiny. In any case . . . logic clearly dictates that the needs of the many outweigh the needs of the few."

KIRK: "Or the one."

—Star Trek II: The Wrath of Khan

With all due reverence to Spock's shade and McCoy's psychiatry, James T. Kirk will remain an admiral. Most probably, he will never again, except in times of emergency, actively command a starship.

This may not be what Spock would have wished, what McCoy wants, or what Jim Kirk himself likes, but James T. Kirk is stuck. From now on, he will be *Admiral* Kirk.

This may seem to be a pretty strong statement, but it is supported by ample evidence. In that "interim" period between *Star Trek: The Motion Picture* and *Wrath of Khan*, few of us were sure just how Kirk would return. Consider the closing lines of Gene Roddenberry's novelization of *STTMP*:

[Uhura:] ". . . and Starfleet also requests that you and your department heads beam down immediately for debriefing."

[Kirk:] "Answer . . . request denied."

"Sir?"

"Simply answer request denied. Isn't that clear enough, Commander?"

Uhura understood, and she smiled. "Aye, sir. It should be clear to one and all."

But it wasn't. There was only one major piece of Star Trek literature during the period between the two movies to deal with Kirk and Company after the V'Ger incident. That was Marshak and Culbreath's *The Prometheus Design*.

In that novel, Kirk again commands the *Enterprise*. The old crew is back together. Though Kirk receives a "nonpunitive" reduction to first officer as the plot progresses, he is still cleary both an admiral and captain of the *Enterprise*. As Spock says, "Admiral, Acting Captain Kirk in command."

Scarce months later, *Wrath of Khan* came out and there was Kirk still an admiral. He was not in command of the *Enterprise*. He was teaching school. If he still retained the title of Chief of Staff, no reference was made.

In fact, it is never really quite clear in *Wrath of Khan* just who the captain of the *Enterprise* is. Spock is called captain, but is he is also teaching school, and just commanding during training missions? The old crew is split up. Chekov is exec aboard the *Reliant*. Sulu, we learn in Vonda McIntyre's novelization, is now a captain and will soon take command of a new Galaxy Class starship.

Though Scotty appears to be in his old niche, we aren't even sure exactly what he or Bones and Uhura are doing these days. All we know is that *Wrath of Khan* was tantamount to a high school reunion, and not all the classmates showed up, at that.

In trying to determine just what took place, we need to backtrack to the V'Ger incident. What follows is, of course, supposition. It may, however, go a long way toward explaining what happened.

We must recall that Jim Kirk was a hero upon return from the *Enterprise*'s historic five-year mission. He was the kind of hero that Starfleet (in light of the "New Human" movement) was more than ready to use. Kirk himself admitted this is Roddenberry's novelization of *Star Trek: The Motion Picture*, as well as that he didn't blame Admiral Nogura for doing so, he would have done the same thing himself.

The appearance of V'Ger gave Kirk the chance to "slip the leash," so to speak. So eager was Jim to get back command of a starship that Bones considers him a man obsessed.

We all know that Kirk and company prevail, but what we are not told is what was happening back on Earth and in Starfleet.

About one hundred years ago, the information explosion began. What had previously taken days, weeks, or even months to report took less and less time as new inventions arose: the telegraph, the transatlantic cable, telephone, radio, television. By 1969, not only was most of the world aware of the moon landing, a goodly percentage of the world's population watched it live!

By the twenty-third century, this information net will be expanded to a point which almost defies imagining. It is an era of subspace communication—an era in which Kirk asks, "Radio?" We may surmise that not only did people on Earth know about V'Ger, they were able to follow everything as it took place. So when V'Ger knocked out Earth's defenses, it is likely that the scientifically well-trained and quite literate society of Earth immediately knew about it.

Consider yourself to be a citizen of that Earth. You are familiar with complex scientific readouts, and you know what V'Ger's threat means. The *Enterprise*, Starfleet, the whole Earth defense network, in fact, is helpless before this seemingly all-powerful entity. You are about to lose your life, and you know it. And there is literally *nothing* you can do about it.

Then, at the last moment, someone called James T. Kirk ends the threat. Are you happy? Try ecstatic. Is Kirk a hero? Try a minor (if not major) deity. Is he important? Try a savior. Does Starfleet know it? Nothing is clearer to them than the fact that if James T. Kirk could be used before, he can now buy them practically anything they want.

At this point, we need to look back at Kirk's previous fame in order to determine why things are suddenly different.

After all, Kirk has saved entire planets, billions of lives, before; he has been eliminating various threats to life throughout the galaxy for years. His actions against Gary Mitchell ("Where No Man Has Gone Before"), Nomad ("The Changeling"), and the Berserker ("The Doomsday Machine") saved uncounted billions. He has more than once repaired the fabric of time ("City on the Edge of Forever," "Tomorrow Is Yesterday," and "Assignment: Earth") to ensure that history itself not be altered. He has even taken a part in ensuring that the very nature of the universe itself not be altered ("The Alternative Factor"). Kirk has ended a 500-year-old war ("A Taste of Armageddon"), and was heavily involved in the events which led to the creation of the Organian Peace Treaty ("Errand of Mercy"). He may even have been instrumental in the toppling of a corrupt galactic dictatorship in an alternate universe ("Mirror, Mirror"). In short, Kirk should have statues erected in his honor on the many planets whose well-being, even very existence, is owed to him.

So a case could be made for calling the V'Ger incident just another day's work for Jim Kirk. Except for one difference. Even though many of the events mentioned above had galaxy-wide, even universe-wide, implications, they did not immediately affect the population of Earth. Subspace radio often has a serious time lag, depending on where in the galaxy the *Enterprise* is located, and in many instances, news did not reach Earth for weeks. If, for instance, we were told that the world had been close to destruction last month (as we were after the Cuban missile crisis), but that everything is now okay, we wouldn't lose much sleep over it. But if we know that the end is near, if we live it, we will feel it forever. Such was the case with V'Ger. V'Ger threatened Earth, and the Big Dollars, the Big Influence, and the Big Press of the Federation are on Earth.

Kirk was hooked. If the "Kirk image" was important to Starfleet before, it was now beyond price.

Society is loath to put its heroes' lives back on the line unless absolutely necessary. During World War II, America's Ace of Aces, Richard Bong, was pulled from active combat. Like Kirk, he was relegated to training others. Heads rolled when it was discovered that someone had actually permitted Bong to fly a combat mission again. We can imagine a similar restraint upon Kirk.

Starfleet wanted to keep Kirk safe, and benefit from his experience as well. That is probably why *Star Trek II: The Wrath of Khan* opened with a training mission. That is also why Kirk (luck of the Irish!) found himself back on the *Enterprise* at just the right moment to take action against Khan.

Bear in mind that the *Enterprise* was the only ship in the quadrant (more luck), and that the potential destructivenes of

Genesis was just what was needed to force Starfleet to risk Kirk again.

Spock, however, sees the threat to Regula as an opportunity for his friend to counter the deep psychological pain caused by Kirk's inner conflict between duty and desire—desire to command a starship again. Kirk is a living legend, he's indispensable, and he knows it. He also knows that Starfleet needs him not as Captain Kirk but as *Admiral* Kirk. Sure he feels old. It's Kirk the legend that is needed, not Kirk himself or his command abilities.

Is this why he gives no real answer to McCoy, who pleads with him to get his command back? Is it why, when Spock tells him that the needs of the many outweigh the needs of the few, he answers, "Or the one"?

Other moments from *Wrath of Khan* give similar impressions. Saavik insisting upon an armed guard, even making up regulations (Kirk gave her the opening) to ram one down his throat. Spock telling Kirk, "Jim, be careful," as though he too realizes his friend's importance. McCoy answering, "We will," as though to minimize, to bring the moment back into perspective. Kirk must not be too cautious, think too much about what he means to Starfleet. That would dull his combat edge.

There are other questions upon which we can speculate. Did Starfleet cash in on the V'Ger incident and the Kirk image to build the new Galaxy Class cruisers? Does the Kirk legend act as a living hedge—is he himself worth ten cruisers vis-à-vis the Romulans and Klingons where Starfleet is concerned? What part does the new "more militaristic" image of Starfleet play in all this? The list could go on indefinitely.

Kirk will remain Admiral Kirk. If Star Trek is to remain faithful to its own sense of honesty to itself and its fans, it would be "illogical" to have Kirk return to the active captaincy of a starship. We all know how upsetting minor inconsistencies in our Star Trek universe can be to us—here we are dealing with a major one.

As did Horatio Hornblower, Kirk must rise in rank and importance. That does not necessarily mean that he will not be in command situations again. Genesis worked nicely to get him in the center seat; other crises will occur. Perhaps that event, foretold by the Organians, which will bring the Federation and the Klingons together will happen. . . .

THE AMERICAN IDEAL IN STAR TREK

by Lisa Kenas

Ofttimes we forget that Star Trek was produced, written, directed, and acted by people living in, and believing in, twentieth-century American society. Even those Star Trek writers, etc., who were not convinced that the United States was perfect—and there were a number of them—believed in our constitutional ideals and guarantees. In this article, Lisa Kenas examines how those beliefs and ideals affected the Star Trek universe and characters.

Star Trek is a television series that premiered in 1966 and was in production through 1969. For the sixteen years since its cancellation, Star Trek has been visible almost everywhere through syndicated reruns; it is perhaps the most successful syndication of any television series. Yet, what is truly amazing is that Star Trek's popularity is still growing; with three major motion pictures released and a fourth currently under production, Star Trek today has more followers than ever. One reason for Star Trek's popularity is that viewers are able to relate easily to the characters and situations because the Star Trek universe is a dramatization of American ideals; truth, justice, and the American way are the cornerstones of the Star Trek universe and an integral part of every episode. American ideals are perhaps best summed up by the words written in the Preamble of the United States Constitution: ". . . to . . . establish justice, insure domestic Tranquillity, provide for the common defense, promote the general Welfare, and secure the Blessings of Liberty . . ."

The characters of Star Trek often function as judges, galactic peacekeepers and defenders, humanitarians, and freedom advocates as they carry out their five-year mission of exploration.

The characters in Star Trek live on a large starship called *Enterprise*, which carries a crew of about 430 men, women, and assorted extraterrestrials. The *Enterprise* is one of many ships in Starfleet, the armed forces division of the United Federation of Planets, an alliance of many planetary worlds. Captain James T. Kirk is the bold commander of this vessel. Kirk's second in command is a pointy-eared half-human called Spock, who acts as both Kirk's friend and his adviser. Dr. Leonard McCoy is the chief medical officer aboard the ship and is also a close friend to both Kirk and Spock. Because the *Enterprise* patrols areas very distant from Federation head-quarters, communication between the ship and Starfleet Command is often impossible. In these instances, the captain of the *Enterprise* gives the final decision on any action to be taken. Thus, the captain must be able to function not only as a soldier, but also as a diplomat.

Throughout the Star Trek episodes and movies, many parallels are drawn between American society and the Star Trek universe. Just as the pioneers felt they had to move westward, the crew of the *Enterprise* is engaged in a five-year mission "to explore strange new worlds, seek out new life and new civilizations, to boldly go where no man has gone before." In fact, Gene Roddenberry, creator of Star Trek, originally described the show as a sort of "wagon train to the stars." In Star Trek, the characters are not representative of twenty-third century man, but, instead, of twentieth-century American man. Likewise, the heroes of Star Trek bear a close resemblance to the heroes of the typical American western: brave men fighting for their freedom and striving to uphold ideals of truth and justice.

Although Star Trek's characters are typical American heroes, the show itself is in no way typical of television during the 1960s. In this time period, network television censors tended to be particularly sensitive to any politically based comments; subjects such as racism and the Vietnam War were generally considered to be off limits. Star Trek's science fiction format provided a way to get around such censorship, as writers were free to create alien cultures (perhaps very similar to American culture) and make comments about them with much smaller chance of having their work rejected by the network censors. Many of Star Trek's writers took advantage of this opportunity and wrote episodes that made a specific point about society. This usually meant that in each episode, a situation is created in which Kirk or the crew can make such a point. One way writers often accomplished this was by having the *Enterprise* crew confront an alien culture where some evil exists and then having Kirk intervene in the culture and correct its wrongs. Looking at the cumulative effects of this practice over three years of the series, one sees that Kirk often acts as a judge for the Federation rather than as an ambassador; he examines and evaluates each culture and intervenes when he finds wrongdoing. Of course, these cultures are judged by Federation standards and ideals, which are determined by American writers and directors. Since American writers and directors naturally tend to respect American standards and ideals, it is on this basis that each culture is judged.

Many times, the decision whether or not to intervene in a culture is the easiest decision Kirk faces; the real challenge is actually changing the ways of a world. There are many instances in Star Trek in which Kirk must use his diplomatic skills and function as a galactic peacemaker. In one episode, "A Taste of Armageddon," the *Enterprise* orbits one of two planets that have been involved in a century-long war. Computers on each planet determine where the next bomb will hit, and inhabitants of this area must then report to death chambers, where they are quickly and painlessly killed. Kirk and especially McCoy are appalled by the way in which this war is being fought; Kirk tries to explain these feelings to the leaders of both planets: "Death. Destruction. Disease. Horror. That's what war is all about. That's what makes it a thing to be avoided." Ultimately, Kirk and his crew manage to destroy the computers and once again establish diplomatic relations between the two neighboring worlds. In this episode, Kirk and the *Enterprise* crew function not only as peacemakers, but also as humanitarians, teaching the peoples of both worlds the senselessness of war.

Sometimes the situation Kirk faces calls for more than just diplomatic skills. In the classic American western film, the brave heroes always come up with the right solution just in time to save everyone involved. Since Star Trek was originally billed as an action-adventure series, there are many times when Kirk and his crew must come to the rescue of a civilization, a world, or even an entire galaxy. Providing a common defense for all is an integral part of the *Enterprise*'s purpose. In "Operation: Annihilate," Kirk, Spock, and McCoy must work quickly to find a cure for the mass insanity that is spreading throughout the colony. In "The Doomsday Machine," Kirk must confront a giant planet-eating machine that is threatening the entire galaxy. As one might expect, Kirk is usually successful in finding solutions to these life-and-death situations. However, just as there are situations in American society for which no solutions exist, there are similar situations in the Star Trek universe.

"A Private Little War" is an episode in which the *Enterprise* visits the planet Neural. Klingons are attempting to take control of the entire planet by supplying arms to one segment of the population and encouraging them to fight for control of the planet. Thus the Klingons are spared the work of fighting and are able to remain unknown to the rest of the planet population, known as the Hill People. Kirk is quick to realize that there is no real solution to the problem; his only option is to offer the Hill People a means by which to defend themselves, and thereby create a balance of power. The *Enterprise* crew leaves Neural saddened by the knowledge that they have not solved anything and may have even complicated the problem. Yet, as Kirk is quick to point out, "War isn't a good life, but it's life."

"A Private Little War" was filmed at the height of the Vietnam crisis, and the episode draws many parallels to it. The question of whether or not the Federation has a right to interfere in matters on Neural is the point on which the episode is based. Like Americans, the Federation tries to hold to a policy of noninterference as much as possible. Just as the communists were arming one side in the Vietnam war, the Klingons were arming the Apella on Neural. Even more specifically, the Hill People of Neural are dressed in Mongolian clothing, and in the original script, the Apella are described as being of the "Ho Chi Minh type." This episode goes beyond simply dramatizing American ideals and actually examines the reasoning behind a very controversial American action. It contrasts contemporary military and political actions of American government with established historical ideals.

As history demonstrates, nothing is more important to Americans than freedom. One of the biggest points that Star Trek tries to make is that man is a free and self-determining entity. Many Star Trek episodes protest any restriction on man's freedom. In several episodes, the *Enterprise* encounters societies that seem to be natural paradises. Although the people of these socieites live in peace and tranquillity, Kirk and the crew find that something is very much wrong: These societies are stagnant and unchanging. In "This Side of Paradise," Kirk voices his thoughts on this matter:

"No wants—no needs? We weren't meant for that. None of us. Man stagnates if he has no ambition, no desire to be more than he is. Maybe we weren't meant for paradise. Maybe we were meant to fight our way through."

Kirk and the crew find that paradise can exist only at the expense of man's freedom and creative growth, a price just not worth paying. Acting as freedom advocates, the *Enterprise* crew takes the steps necessary to free the people of these parasitic societies.

Another point Star Trek emphasizes is man's hatred of captivity. In many episodes, Kirk or members of the crew find themselves held captive by an alien race of some sort. Kirk is always quick to point out that it is man's nature to be free, and without freedom and obstacles to overcome, man will wither and die. It always amazes alien cultures that humans would much rather die than have their freedom restricted in any way. For example, consider the reactions of the Keepers in "The Menagerie." The Keepers had hoped to breed a race of humans to repopulate their planet but found that humans were not suited for such captivity:

"The customs and history of your race show a unique hatred of captivity. Even when it's pleasant and benevolent, you prefer death. This makes you too violent and dangerous a species for our needs."

In all situations where a party's freedom is in question, the end result is always the same. No matter whose freedom is being threatened, the *Enterprise* crew takes all possible steps to restore freedom to all involved. Just as Americans hold freedom above all, so does the Federation.

Although Star Trek's audience is never told the exact rules under which the Federation functions, it is quite apparent that the Federation is governed by many of the same beliefs as are Americans today. The Federation represents the ideal society; it is a criticism of what America is today. More important, it is an optimistic vision of what America can become—a place where peace, liberty, and justice are more than just words. On a more universal level, Star Trek represents man's incredible potential to grow and change. In terms of physical boundaries, space may represent the final frontier. For mankind, however, the final frontier is not space, but the human soul, and in this frontier, exploration is just beginning.

A LEXICON OF VULCAN

by Katherine D. Wolterink

Kathy Wolterink's "A Linguistic Analysis of Vulcan" (Best of Trek #7) gave us the first look at spoken Vulcan as examined under the rules of phonetics. Now she follows up with this lexicon, once again ultilizing only spoken Vulcan as it was heard in the series and films. We don't often like to suggest that Best of Trek *articles be taken as gospel, but in this case we'd like to advise any authors planning to feature spoken Vulcan in future Star Trek novels or stories to at least give Kathy's articles a careful look.*

If you were given a phrase book which contained all the spoken Vulcan from the original Star Trek episodes, the animated episodes, and the three movies, then were dropped off somewhere on Vulcan, could you cope? If you were suddenly abandoned in the middle of ShiKahr, would you be able to introduce yourself, order a meal at an inn, find a bathroom?

This article is a lexicon of spoken Vulcan which contains all the information you would find in such a phrase book, along with a little you probably wouldn't see there. It lists 103 words and includes articles, nouns, pronouns, verbs, adjectives, adverbs, prepositions, conjunctions, and even a couple of interjections (something which must be rather rare in Vulcan). The entries in the lexicon are much like the entries in any standard dictionary. I've made a translation of each term—that is, a spelling of the word in standard English—which I hope will be pretty easy to read, especially since many of the terms will be familiar to Star Trek fans.

The spelling of some of the words differs slightly from the spelling used by other authors, such as James Blish or Alan

Dean Foster. Where there is a difference, I've given the variant spelling, following the translation of the word. Each term is followed by a pronunciation guide in the International Phonetic Alphabet, as in many dictionaries. This is followed by the translation. I included the context or phrase the word appears in, when I thought this might help identify it, in both Vulcan and English. I've also provided variant pronunciations where they exist. Finally, I took the liberty of organizing the lexicon by listing the terms alphabetically according to their grammatical function (part of speech), because that seemed more useful than the strict alphabetical list you find in dictionaries.

Articles

a (/ə/) a; one

el (/ɛ/) the, as in *el kro-eel* (/ɛl krɔɔll/) the way

ti (/ti/) the, as in *ti porta porsen* (/ti portə porsɛn/) the last emotion

tō (/to/) the, as in *tō Kolinár* (/to Kolinár/) the Kolinár

Nouns

Reasonably enough, Vulcan uses both proper and common nouns.

ahn-woon (/an-wun/) a ritual weapon rather like our bolo; a long leather strap with a round weight at each end

atayven (/ətevɛn/) achievement

cárterite (/kártɛraɪt/) answer

cose (/kɔs/) minds

dis-hofne-yeas (/dishɔfni3s/) consciousness

Ee-chiya (/itʃiyə/) Spock's pet sehlot; also "I-Chaya"

fal tor (/fal tor/) refusal; an abbreviated form of the phrase *fal tor pan* (/fal tor pan/) the refusal

fal tor pan (/fal tor pan/) the refusal; referring to an ancient rite which attempts to rejoin the living spirit and the body of one recently deceased

formaji (/formaɛi/) sands

hauformala (/hauformala/) animal passions

Kalifí (/kælifí/) challenge, as in *Koon-et-Kalifí* (/kun-ət-kælifí/), the Vulcan ritual of "marriage or challenge" which traditionally occurs at the time of the male's first *pon-farr*; also "Koon-ut-Kal-if-fee"

Kahs-wan (/kas-wan/) traditional Vulcan rite of passage, a survival test for young males *kátra* (/kátrə/) living spirit, essence, soul

kitópila (/kitópilə/) goal

Kolinár (/kolinár/) Vulcan ascetic discipline designed to purge one of all emotion; also "Kolinahr"

kro-eel (/krɔɔll/) the way

kroks (/kroks/) thoughts

Koon (/kun/) marriage, as in *Koon-et-Kalifí* (/kun-ə-kælifí/), the Vulcan ritual of "marriage or challenge" which traditionally occurs at the time of the male's first *pon-farr*

L'langon (/ləlangən/) a mountain range on Vulcan, near the city of ShiKahr

lirpa (/lirpa/) a ritual weapon; a wooden staff with a fan-shaped blade at one end and a blunt, cone-shaped prod at the other

lematya (/ləmatʃə/) a carnivorous, leopardlike reptile which inhabits the deserts of Vulcan and whose claws inflict a deadly poison

ojica (/odɛikə/) logic

plak-tau (/plæk-tau/) blood fever; also "plak-tow"

pon-farr (/pɔn-far/) time of mating, occurring once every seven years in sexually mature Vulcan males. Also "pon farr"; "pon far"

porsen (/porsɛn/) emotion

rubicoff (/rubiIkɔf/) human blood (red as opposed to green?)

Saávik (/saæ'vɛk/) Lieutenant Saavik, half-Vulcan, half-Romulan officer of the Starship *Enterprise*, United Federation of Planets; a protégé of Spock's

Sarek (/sɔæk/) Vulcan scientist and ambassador; father of Spock

Sasak (/sæsɛk/) father of Selek

sehlot (/selɔt/) domesticated, bearlike animal native to Vulcan, often kept as a pet; also "sehlat"

Selek (/sɛlɛk/) a distant cousin of Spock's

Seleya (/səleiə/) Mt. Selaya, a religious retreat on Vulcan

sertific (/sətlfIk/) symbol

sha (/ʃa/) our race

ShiKahr (/ʃikar/) a border city of Vulcan; Spock's childhood home

Skon (/skon/) Sarek's father

Solkar (/solkar/) Sarek's grandfather

Spock (/spɔk/; Spok/) first officer of the Starship *Enterprise*, United Federation of Planets; son of Sarek of Vulcan and Amanda Grayson, an earthwoman

Stonn (/stɔn/; /ston/) the Vulcan for whom T'Pring dared to challenge Spock during the *Koon-et-Kalifí* ritual

Surak (/səæk/) Father of Vulcan; philosopher who introduced the principles of IDIC and nonviolence which revolutionized primitive Vulcan society; prime moving force of the "Great Awakening"

Tazmeen (/tæzmin/) a month of the Vulcan calendar

tel-shya (/tɛlʃaɪə/) a ritual form of execution used in ancient times on Vulcan; the victim's neck is broken by a single, swift blow; death is instantaneous; also "tal-shaya"

T'Lar (/t'lar/) the high priestess at Mt. Seleya; performs *fal tor pan* at Sarek's request

T'Pau (/t'pau/) Elder Statesman of Vulcan; officiated at Spock's *Koon-et-Kalifi* ritual; is the only person ever to turn down a seat on the Council of the United Federation of Planets

T'Pel (/t'pɛl/) mother of Selek; also "T'Pal"

T'Pring (/t'priŋ/) Spock's intended wife

Vucan (/vəlkæn/) Epsilon Eridani 3; the only inhabited planet of the Epsilon Eridani system; one of the founding members of the United Federation of Planets

zau (/zau/) ancestors

Prounouns

Like English, Vulcan seems to employ nominative, possessive, and relative pronouns. While objective pronouns don't occur in this sample, the existence of transitive verbs, which require an object, suggests that Vulcan does use them.

ben (/bɛn/) it
du (/du/; /tu/) you; nominative
kau (/kau/) our
te(/tɛ/) which
tu (/tu/) your

Although this sample contains only second person singular ("you" and "your") and third person singular and plural("it" and "our") pronouns, I think it's probably safe to assume that pronouns in first, second, and third person—singular and plural—all occur in Vulcan.

Verbs

There is evidence in the sample that Vulcan employs many of the verb tenses we use in English. Verbs occur in past tense, present (including present progressive and imperative), present perfect, and future. Vulcan also uses both transitive and intransitive verbs. It may use other tenses too, but no verbs in other tenses occur in this sample. A few examples might be useful:

past	was *orsi* (/orsi/)
simple present	is *duval* (/d'val/)
present progressive	calling *quisoreet* (/kwisorit/)
imperative	Halt! *kroyka* (/krɔɪkə/)
present perfect	[it] has come *kisár* (/kisár/)
future	will not achieve *krachi* (/kratʃi/)
transitive verb	give [me] *kípi* (/kípi/)
intransitive verb	prosper *brosper* (/brospə/)

ajeed (/aẓid/) achieved

brosper (/brospə/) prosper

came (/kɛm/) cast out

dongitu (/dongitu/) will you

duval (/d'val/) is

ehkserka (/ɛksɛrkə/) [is] shed

estirs (/ɛstəs/) touches

falikál (/falikál/) begin, as in *fal tor falikál* (/fal tor falikál/) Let the refusion begin

for (/for/) auxiliary verb, as in *sha orsi for sayven* (/ʃa orsi for sevɛn/) Our race was saved

ka-ri-farr (/karifar/) Let it begin!; also "kah-if-farr"

kimish (/kimʃ/) I am

kípi (/kípi/) give [me]

kisár (/kisár/) [it] has come

kitór (/kitór/) live [long]

koopstarive (/kúpstarive/) can you speak

krachi (/kratʃi/) will not achieve

kroyka (/krɔɪkə/) Halt!

navoon (/navún/) done

orsi (/orsi/) was, as in *orsi for sayven* (/orsi for sevɛn/) was saved

orti (/orti/) were, as in *orti came* (/orti kɛm/) were cast out

pokar (/pokar/) receive

prahgnáhst (/pragnást/) have not, as in *du prahgnahst ajeed Kolinar* (/du pragnást aẓ kolinár/) you have not achieved Kolinár

quisóreet (/kwisórit/) calling [to you]

sayven (/sevɛn/) saved

tarafél (/tarafél/) trust [me]

zoopzavo (/zúpzəvo/) have labored

Adjectives

aye (/aI/) these, as in *se aye formaji* (/sɛ al formaʐi/) on these
   sands

blomig (/blomIg/) a kind of soup; also "plomik"

porta (/portə/) the last; all, as in *ti porta porsen* (/ti portə porsɛn/)
   all emotion; the last emotion

retter (/rɛtə/) together

rutter (/r⌃tə/) one, as in *rutter eter retter* (/r⌃tə ɛtə rɛtə/) one and
   together

sosil (/sosI1/) total

Adverbs

ee (/il/) now

culchise (/kultʃis/) long, [a] long time

tehko (/tɛko/) here, as in *tehko krachi kitópila* (/tɛko kratʃi kitópil
   ə/) He will not achieve his goal here

tehquen (/tɛkwɛn/) elsewhere

tora (/torə/) here, as in *tora orti came* (/torə orti kɛm/) here were
   cast out

Prepositions

by (/baI/) by

cry (/kraI/) through

krasé (/krasé/) from [us], as in *pokar Krasé* (/pokar krasé/)
   receive from us

se (/sɛ/) on

Conjunctions

eh (/ɛ/) and, as in *kitór eh brosper* (/kitór ɛ brospə/) live long and
   prosper

et (/ɛt/; /ət/) or, as in *Koon-et-Kalifi* (/kun-ɛt-kælifí/) marriage or
   challenge

éter (/ɛtə/) and, as in *rutter éter retter* (/r⌃tə ɛtə rɛtə/) one and together

Interjections

dom (/dom/) so

op (/ɔp/) an expression suggesting that one has discovered
   something which one has not expected

I have a confession to make about this second interjection.
The definition I have provided, unlike those for the other

terms in the lexicon, is based almost entirely on speculations. The remark itself is practically unintelligible. This explanation makes sense in the context in which the word is used. It's about halfway through the Kolinar ritual. There has just been a dramatic pause, filled with a lot of loud background music suggesting the presence of V'Ger. The priestess has been staring off into space. She turns to Spock (with an expression that communicates about as much surprise as a Vulcan who has achieved Kolinar is probably capable of) and says, "Op. Kípi tu kroaks." (/ɔp kípi tu kroks/) "?! Give me your thoughts." Maybe she's simply saying, "Spock." That would make sense, but if you watch her mouth closely when she says it, it sure doesn't look like that's what she's saying. In this case I'd have to say your guess is as good as mine.

As you can see, if you're wandering through downtown ShiKahr, armed only with your little phrase book, you're in for a difficult time. Unless your conversations consist exclusively of discussions about Vulcan marriage customs, challenges, executions, rites of passage, and aesthetic disciplines, you're out of luck. Star Trek has not given the average tourist much help. In fact, nouns and pronouns make up slightly more than half of the terms in the lexicon (51.5 percent); together with verbs, they constitute 76.7 percent of the total. It's difficult to communicate intelligently using only nouns and verbs. However, it's easy to see how this sorry state of affairs came about.

Almost all of the spoken Vulcan that exists is in the form of isolated words, usually nouns, or ritual formulas, as in the Koon-et-Kalifi in "Amok Time," the Kolinar ritual in *Star Trek: The Motion Picture*, or fal tor pan in *Star Trek III: The Search for Spock*. For the most part, it is Old Vulcan associated with ancient social customs. Spoken Vulcan almost never occurs except at moments of crisis or dramatic climax. Consequently, the Vulcan we are familiar with is neither appropriate nor very useful for everyday conversation. While Vulcan society is characteristically formal, all social intercourse requires language which can convey the mundane and the trivial as accurately as the sublime and the crucial. Standing on a street corner in ShiKahr, you would probably find yourself wishing devoutly for a Berlitz handbook of Vulcan.

MEMORIES OF STAR TREK

by Colleen Arima

Colleen Arima answered our call for personal reminiscences with a pair of articles, both of which we present here. The first is a nostalgic look back at her first exposure to Star Trek and the later birth of a full-fledged fan; the second is a more intimate look at what Star Trek meant to her during the turbulent years in which she—and most of us—grew up. We think you'll not only enjoy Colleen's story, you'll find that you've shared a good bit of it.

My intitial reminiscence of Star Trek dates back to 1966, when I first read that a space opera was to invade network television. At the time it was quite a jump from the genre of the popularly viewed westerns to "a place where no man has gone before." *Bonanza* was my favorite program, so what in heaven's name would I need with a galaxy saga? In addition to my lack of interest, I had just entered the working world and didn't have all that much time for television. To make matters worse I have five younger siblings out of a total of eight, and growing up in a large family inevitably brews a fight over who gets to watch what and when. It was a daily struggle where we all learned valuable tactics no doubt useful in the years to come. Although the fights raged each evening, my brothers and sisters would invariably settle down for one hour a week to watch the show called *Star Trek*. I didn't care what was on the tube which totally engrossed them, only that it was quiet.

There was many an evening when I remembered other programs on the tube only because their theme songs were so irritating I couldn't for the life of me wipe them from my mind. My longtime suspicions were confirmed when I realized the monsters would watch anything on the screen. My siblings definitely had no taste. All I demanded was an hour on the weekends to ride with Ben, Adam, Hoss, and Little Joe as they defeated every bad guy that crossed their path. The five ogres could have their space crusaders and flying saucers.

In 1967 I decided to get married, but more important, I refused to relinquish my TV rights until I permanently departed the old homestead. My mother smiled approvingly but the monsters just growled. I didn't have to be intuitive to know the war wasn't over yet.

I was married in December, and since the weather at home leaves a lot to be desired, our honeymoon was in the land of Mickey Mouse and where Paramount Studios was churning out, among others, that Star Trek show. We never even got close to that studio, a television set, or Gene Who? Three weeks later we returned home all tanned and healthy-looking, but were immediately confronted by a perplexing problem. No one was left to fight over the TV with. My husband was agreeable to anything I wanted to watch, which was extremely irritating, since I was accustomed to a good nightly brawl. In spite of my extended viewing time, I had yet to develop an interest in a space opera and what I considered must be a total lack of credibility. I thought *Lost in Space* was a comedy. I was above children's shows and in this sense deemed myself an intellectual, and intellectuals watched shows like *Mission: Impossible*.

As 1968 slid in we were blessed with a new television set, with remote-control channel selector, which helped me avoid the undesirable fare which permeated prime time. By now Star Trek had been canceled, and after the summer season I failed to even notice its disappearance from the viewer's guide.

One holiday season five years later we attended a New Year's Eve party my mother was giving. Upon arrival I immediately noticed something amiss. The monsters, a bit older but monsters nonetheless, were gathered in front of the tube, unwilling to budge, fight, or converse. All through the night they sat glued to the television. It was soon thereafter I learned that the local independent station was running syndicated Star Trek episodes continuously for ten hours. I was now convinced beyond a doubt that they had no class and were hopeless causes.

Later that year I was socked in by the weather, the kid was

asleep and husband off on a business trip. To make matters worse, there wasn't anything on network TV worth occupying my rapidly expanding time. Abruptly, just like being in the twilight zone, my eyes were directed to the independent station's listings, and there it was. Star Trek. Why not? I rationalized. No one will ever know I watched it, and, besides, someone should censor the monsters' viewing habits. As the series was of course syndicated, I was extremely fortunate that the first episode I watched, "The Man Trap," was the also the first shown in 1966.

The freaks wrapped in tinfoil and draped in rawhide I expected to see never materialized. Instead, I was treated to a story where the officers and crew actually cared for one another and exuded a respect for all life forms. When Nancy Crater transformed into the salt monster, I had to applaud the makeup artist and whoever else was responsible for the realistic creature. The entire bridge crew seemed to possess a unique chemistry and rapport with one another.

My Star Trek viewing continued the following evening with "Charlie X," then on to "Where No Man Has Gone Before." It didn't take long before total addiction ate away at my very soul. I watched episodes every night of every week, even though it meant my husband and daughter were to exist on a diet of TV dinners. They soon grew tired of the frozen delicacies and joined me on the *Enterprise*.

As much as I enjoyed Star Trek, my impressions were not firm until halfway through the third-season episodes, which to me was about two months. My initial opinion of Kirk was that he was a bit young to command such a large ship and crew, but as I watched each show I became convinced he was in complete control, with a few exceptions such as "The Enemy Within." I appreciated the way Star Trek's creator, Gene Roddenberry, avoided the Captain Invincible image. Kirk was human and had his weakness as well as the power to command. He needed his senior officers as much as they needed him. And of course William Shatner's smile could melt the North Pole.

Spock was the most inventive alien I had ever seen. His pointed ears and upswept eyebrows were as significantly proper as his green blood. At last I had found a fictionary alien who didn't resemble Earthman, but differed drastically in areas of philosophy and physical features. Other splendid aliens were showcased in "Journey to Babel." Spock's internal struggle rounded him out as a viable character. My hat was off to Leonard Nimoy for his excellent portrayal and development of Spock.

Deforest Kelley (Dr. McCoy) was a character actor for years; I had seen him in villainous roles in many westerns. Now he finally got to play a good guy. As I listened to him, he reminded me of my own doctor and friend, who, praised be, isn't as cynical as McCoy. The good doctor advised his captain even if Kirk got annoyed. That's his responsibility, and he fulfilled it well. Again, I was relieved the "Great Bird of the Galaxy" didn't have the ship's surgeon fall madly in love with his nurse. Having the indispensable nurse in love with the stoic alien was much more intriguing, as revealed in "Amok Time."

Another source of fascination was the secondary characters of Scott, Sulu, Uhura, and Chekov. Although I would have preferred to see each featured exclusively in an episode, their storylines would probably detract from the Big Three of Kirk, Spock, and McCoy.

Mr. Scott (James Doohan) was like the trusted employee who has been around forever and was always available to keep those engines running. He acted as a liaison between officers and crew, as he very easily related to both. Mr. Doohan's knowledge of engineering was obvious, but fortunately was void of too many technicalities. Aside from his accent, and references to Scotland, his past was indistinct. Too bad he wasn't cast as an Irishman. Who would make a better Mick than the real thing? As it was, I had to wait for Lieutenant Kevin Riley, who first appeared in "The Naked Time."

As for Uhura, my impression was immediate. It was about time we saw a woman on the bridge, and a black one at that. Although Nichelle Nichols got to sing a few times, most of her dialogue was restricted to "Hailing frequencies open, Captain." Those ridiculous miniskirts should have stayed in the 1960s and tended to date the series. Uhura finally got to show her stuff in "The Tholian Web," where the fear of going mad is enough to drive anyone crazy.

How nice to see a crewman of Asian ancestry at the helm. Nice move, Gene. I couldn't agree more, as the silent minority, except for Charlie Chan, has always been typecast as evil. Lieutenant Sulu (George Takei) remained somewhat mysterious and seemed to have no background until I gave him one in "Sulu's Profile" in *Best of Trek #3*. My only complaint with Sulu was that as soon as he would report to the captain that the helm wasn't responding, Kirk, Spock, or Scotty would scurry to Sulu's console and frantically press buttons themselves as if Sulu were incompetent. If Sulu was supposed to be the best helmsman in the fleet, why didn't anyone take him seriously at the first sign of trouble? That got to be old rather quickly.

Chekov was brought onto the show in the second season because the Soviets made such a stink about the absence of a Russian aboard the *Enterprise* when the Soviet Union had contributed so much to the space race. The wig Chekov wore when he first joined the crew made him look like a Beatle clone and more than just a bit silly. His teenage appearance made it difficult to believe he was twenty-two. I thought the Federation was robbing the cradle. Walter Koenig should be commended for making Chekov work. He had the impetuousness of youth, yet the discipline of training. In the end, the last laugh was on the Soviets, as Chekov often bored others with his endless and vehemently exaggerated tales of questionable Russian achievements.

Aside from the miniskirts, Sulu's "ineptitude," and Chekov's wig, the series had other minor flaws. In the second season, "The Omega Glory" and "Bread and Circuses" were enough to cause me concern. I felt the attempted parallels to Earth's history failed miserably. Then again there were the Zeons and Nazis in "Patterns of Force." Another rip-off.

When the third season began with "Spock's Brain," I could see the quality of scripts was slipping. I was totally convinced when "Spectre of the Gun" aired, and we were asked to believe in the Clantons, Earps, and the OK Corral again.

My family has been watching Star Trek since 1973, and have enjoyed the characters, accomplished actors, and profound storylines. When I think back to 1966, I wonder how I could possibly have missed the original voyages. Since then I have attended several conventions and lectures by Gene Roddenberry, hoping to learn more about the creator of a show with a concept well ahead of its time. Star Trek is expanding again, but I can always go back to 1966, when the monsters Karen, Kelley, Tim, Bud, and Patti ignored my westerns and forged ahead with the *Enterprise* and her cast of characters. Without those five ogres, I'd probably still be considering myself too intellectual for space sagas.

HOW STAR TREK AFFECTED ME

by Colleen Arima

I never thought a television show could have such an impact on my life, or anyone else's for that matter. I was wrong, as the number of people affected by Star Trek is enormous.

When my formal education began, we children were threatened by the fact that the Russians stood ready to destroy us simply by pressing a button. They warned of expansion and their intent to bury us. They said our system was decadent and doomed to extinction. The great Bear across the ocean certainly posed a menace to all of mankind. This black omen, never far from our minds, destroyed any hopes I harbored of getting to know "thy neighbor." My childhood was consumed with the fear of instant annihilation, a fright that affected us all, only to manifest itself later during a tumultuous era.

While still in school one November in 1963, we learned that President John F. Kennedy had been assassinated. I was stunned, shocked, and saddened as the sketchy details reached us. No American President since William McKinley had died by a gunman's bullet. I went home in a daze; I remember people openly weeping on the bus and streets. This tragic incident had rocked America to the core. I recall sitting on a footstool in front of our television set watching dignitaries from around the world pay their final respects as the President's flag-draped coffin lay in the Capitol Rotunda. Two days later I saw his assassin gunned down on national TV.

The great American image was tarnished by the increasing problem of racial tensions and inevitable race riots. Militant blacks perceived all whites as the enemy, while redneck caucasians continued their fight against black rights. Sometimes bigotry was practiced in subtle ways, while other incidents ended in violence. As a result we were all victims.

Vietnam, a small divided country halfway around the world, was fighting a war against Communist aggression. At first we sent advisers, then soldiers to help train the South Vietnamese. It wasn't long before we were involved in the battle. Soon more and more American troops were dispatched to help as the civil strife escalated. Friends and neighbors began to return home in body bags. Others came home maimed or with wounds that didn't show. I vividly remember a family friend who had a distant look in his eyes as he described how his buddy was killed right next to him. The drafting of young men into the military services increased as more were sent overseas. They called it "America's first teenage war," as the average age of the GI was nineteen. It was common knowledge that Congress had not formally declared war against North Vietnam, and therefore many considered it an illegal war.

I began to wonder just what it was that we were fighting for. There seemed to be no way to win. College students and others took to the campuses around the country staging marches and sit-ins to express their disapproval of the conflict. They next went to the streets, where riot police often attempted to disperse the rowdy crowds with tear gas; the marchers retaliated. And violence at home continued.

Tensions in the Middle East also grabbed headlines as Israel went to war against the Arabs. Though the fighting lasted but six days, peace was shaky at best, and terrorism grew. The cost of human suffering was high and the value of life seemed low.

The drug culture in the United States burgeoned as numbers of young people died from potent and dangerous dope. Whether they were victimized by pushers or their own errant desires is uncertain. We were painfully aware that drugs had become a part of our lives. A classmate under the influence of LSD believed himself to be a bird and leaped from the roof of a ten-story building. Drugs were an evil permeated by disenchantment, greed, crime, and the futile desire to escape.

On April 4, 1968, the foremost civil rights leader of our time, the Reverend Martin Luther King, Jr., was fatally shot as he stood on a balcony. His sole purpose, as I understood it, was to peacefully attain racial equality. It wasn't but a few months later that Presidential candidate Robert F. Kennedy was gunned down. I had to believe that hate, assassination, violence, and indiscriminate killing had become a way of life, the accepted norm as it were. I often thought we were definitely on the eve of destruction and things couldn't get much worse. However, I was quite naive about politics and world affairs. Accusations were charged against the Presidential Administration for covert bombing raids into Cambodia, a neighbor of Vietnam, but were vehemently denied. I, along with many of my peers, became totally disillusioned with our country's government on all levels—not to mention mankind in general.

For a diversion one evening I absently turned on a syndicated show called Star Trek. It depicted man two hundred years in the future. I saw blacks, Asians, and whites all working as a team. It looked good, but I was still a skeptic. It revealed how man had gone beyond his own confines and reached out to other beings with peace and friendship. Aliens from distant worlds labored side by side with our own future generations. My cynicism was slipping. I saw hope amid the present despair, and a new vision for mankind. People in the future had learned from our mistakes and our lofty ideals were not so unrealistic after all. Our years of turmoil must serve as a lesson, a dark period to overcome and prosper as rational, sensitive beings. Star Trek gave me confidence and foresight. It expressed a positive standard worthy of incorporating into my life, as well as the philosophy that we can prevail through the direst of adversities.

THE NEGLECTED WHOLE—OR, "NEVER HEARD OF YOU," PART I

by Elizabeth Rigel

Loyal fans of Star Trek's supporting characters often chide us for not featuring enough articles about their favorites. But when we do run an article about, say, Sulu, we hear complaints from all the fans of Chekov and Scotty and Uhura and Chapel and Kyle and DeSalle and Saavik and Balok and . . . well, you get the picture. They get mighty upset. Although we reckon that our readers will never run out of new and fresh things to say about any of the Star Trek characters, we have to give Elizabeth Rigel credit. In this article (and a sequel to follow) she takes on the herculean task of discussing all *of the supporting cast of the original series. We think you'll be as impressed by her insights into them as we were.*

Star Trek lives in part by the Vulcan philosophy of Infinite Diversity in Infinite Combinations (IDIC). Therefore it is particularly discouraging that no one told the original scriptwriters about it. If you are a Kirk or Spock fan, life is good. The other regulars (remember them? They run the ship when the stars are captured) have faded into the background. Their supporters are drowned out, and articles are few. A casual viewer would be hard pressed to distinguish them from the extras in less than a month. So, after twenty years of frustration, let us introduce the "neglected whole." First, meet the ladies.

(Penda) Uhura
First Appearance: "The Man Trap"
Rank and Post: lieutenant, chief of communications
Rank and post by *The Search for Spock*: commander, first officer, communications

When Uhura (ably portrayed by Nichelle Nichols) first graced the bridge of the *Enterprise* in 1966, her future looked bright. As introduced, Uhura was a classy, witty, bright young officer who tackled her enemies and her career with a prowess rarely allotted blacks and/or women on television.

Her skills on the bridge are her most neglected characteristic. More than anything, the regularity with which Kirk takes her for granted confirms her status as "one of the gang." The captain will never understand what a pain in the nether region he is when he rants because the galaxy dares to have static in it. Nevertheless, Uhura shrugs off his outbursts, sends the message, pulls it in, coordinates the damage-control teams, and calls the medics. She leaps at the meager opportunities to man the helm in "The Naked Time," "The Corbomite Maneuver," "Balance of Terror," and "Courtmartial." In "Who Mourns for Adonais," she repairs equipment that Spock cannot. Indeed, her efforts made it possible for Spock to contact and rescue the landing party. And of course her brilliant work in disrupting the military's communication system was crucial to the successful *Search for Spock.*

A complaint of her bridgework (no pun intended) is that Uhura is rarely left in command ("given the conn"). In "The Trouble with Tribbles," Chekov was left in charge twice, although his rank and experience were not comparable to hers. In "Catspaw," Assistant Engineer DeSalle was left in command. (Apparently Scotty offers more attractive career opportunities than does Kirk. One season before in "Squire of Gothos," DeSalle was just another navigator.) Even as Spock was dying in *Wrath of Khan*, Kirk left the inexperienced Saavik in charge, although there were three officers of command rank on the bridge. Could it be caused by Kirk's muddled state of mind? If so, it has been muddled for some time. Uhura reminds one of the Vice-President, except that she doesn't even have the diplomatic duty.

Physically, she can more than hold her own. In "Gamesters of Triskelion," she was matched to train with Lars (whom she later fended off when he tried to rape her), though he was a foot taller. When the landing party was originally captured, both Shahna and Tamoon (who struck from behind) were required to subdue her. Both women carried six-foot pikes. Uhura was unarmed. (Lars and Shahna were also among the planet's finest warriors, as both were chosen to battle Kirk to the death.) In "Mirror, Mirror," both Sulu-2 and the phaser-wielding Marlena were finished so easily that the whole thing looked like a game. Uhura is not a person one would expect to see regularly in a fistfight, but she does not tolerate troublemakers.

Unfortunately, the sight of this lady in motion usually brings different images to mind. The men who chase her do not strike one as being interested in her good health.

Lars and Sulu-2 made their intentions clear enough. With sufficient provocation, they might have killed her instead.

In "Plato's Stepchildren," Kirk bestows an unwanted smooch on her, but the Platonians find this tame for a Saturday night's entertainment. They are more entertained by seeing Kirk crack a bullwhip at her head. (It is sad to note that the outcry over the Kiss exceeds that over the Whip.) It is easy to say that Kirk was not responsible, but the memory must still hurt.

Only in "The Man Trap" is it even hinted that Uhura was ever in love. The salt vampire, having scanned her thoughts, adopted the face of a handsome Bantu man for the purpose of luring her into a private conversation, then hypnotizing and killing her. Perhaps this is the face of the boy she left behind. Maybe he died, or he found another when she never told him that she cared for him. Only she knows why this image is so appealing. But the salt vampire's assault on her loneliness and homesickness is very effective. Only Janice Rand's noisy passage breaks the spell and saves her life.

The only "decent man" who ever made a pass at her proved to be a conceited little snob who soon dropped her for a blonde. However, he also gallantly kissed her hand, raved about her beauty in his highbrow way, and taught her to play the harpsichord, which delighted her musical soul. He did not attack her virtue or even threaten her life. So there you have it—in twenty years she has been Officially Kissed but twice (drooling doesn't count), and the nicest man she ever met was Trelane, a six-year-old boy!

The menfolk are not the only ones interested in the lady's appearance. Uhura must know, for example, that Vulcans do not make small talk, but she asks Spock, "Why don't you tell me I'm an attractive young lady, or ask me if I've ever been in love? Tell me how your planet Vulcan looks on a lazy evening when the moon is full." As to her previous lovelife, it is known only that she is not a virgin ("The Naked Time"). Probably the salt creature's disguise. And her romantic adventures in the series are anything but. But is Uhura vain?

Actually, yes. That scamp Harry Mudd figures that out right away. Just as he was the one to describe Kirk as being "married to his ship," he notices that Uhura is nervous of losing nature's best as time takes its toll. In a scene that was ultimately dropped, Harry almost convinced her to sample his Venus drug. (This illegal hormone/cosmetic would transform any plain model into a raving beauty in seconds.) This is enough that Uhura has a bad self-esteem problem, maybe even a screw loose. Male fans have informed this writer that you can't get any better than she is. Uhura is also intensely curious about the artificial bodies used by Mudd's androids— lifelike doubles that would last 800,000 years. "I want to be young and beautiful!" she says, and the androids believe her. The crew escapes, but the temptation was there. Why should Uhura care for such props?

In "The Children Shall Lead," Gorgan employs the "beast within her" (her greatest fear embodied) to paralyze her at her post. If she cannot work, no warning or plea for help can be sent. The "beast" in Uhura is the aged, weak, ugly reflection that appears in her mirror. That subconscious fear of ugliness and helplessness is Gorgan's most effective tool against her. But when Gorgan is undone, the "beast" is overcome, apparently for good.

In fact it seems that both Uhura and Nichelle Nichols have heard enough on the subject. At Kirk's whining that only the "young" (which excludes anyone from the series) belong in space, Uhura whips back, "Now what is *that* supposed to mean?" And Heisenberg the Wag's crack about her encroaching retirement earns him an armed escort to a locked coat closet. For her part, Uhura never could stand a smart mouth. And Nichelle Nichols is no doubt sick to death of hearing about: (1) the command debate (whether Uhura is really good enough to be captain, or if Starfleet is run by male chauvinists); (2) the thoughtless comments of critics, paid and unpaid, who don't care to see the "old guard" anymore and want to meet the "new blood." (As if something is wrong with a mature mind, a distinguished record, and a wise heart.) This is cruelly unfair to all the actors/actresses, but it is particularly senseless for Uhura. Of all the Star Trek performers, past or present, Nichelle Nichols looks the best. *She has not aged a day.* And she probably never will. Maybe Gene Roddenberry and friends found their Vulcanita after all.

Starfleet must have provided some interesting memories,

though. Fans and crewmembers will always cherish her talents with vocal and instrumental music. She will be remembered as the one who brought chaos to the Klingon Empire by buying the first tribble puppy or kitten (depending on your allergies). She learns that Nomad does *not* like her singing, but Nomad had a few wires crossed anyhow. She is generous to the faults of others, as when she permits the royal brat Elaan to occupy and destroy her quarters. Uhura even complimented T'Pring as "lovely," which is surely the kindest name any woman has ever had for *that* one. Less appealing, but more common, is her fear of strange places, which prompts the usual "Captain, I'm frightened." At least she has enough confidence to express herself. But she will not hesitate to admit her lack of confidence in Kirk when he leads his valuable officers into yet another fool trap. It is not merely her way, but the only way, to criticize his unsafe work habits. Kirk just yells at anyone else.

There are no other clues to her personal life. How does she feel about her family? What does she look for in a man? (Assuming she ever gets one.) And if she could live life over again, what would she change, if she could? These things remain unknown.

However, there is one last area of concern, and that is her career. Uhura bores easily, and that boredom makes her impatient. It's more than opening hailing frequencies ten times in "Corbomite Maneuver." It's more than angrily informing her boss the-Denevans-won't-answer-my-calls-so-get-off-my-back-sir in "Operation: Annihilate." No, she described the problem on Day One.

In the second pilot, "Where No Man Has Gone Before," the communications officer is a man. Uhura was either a backup or berthed on another ship. But in "Man Trap," the first episode, she complains to Spock, "I'm an illogical woman who's beginning to feel too much a part of that communications console." In less than a year (at most), her new job as department head had become boring and stifling. With some upward mobility, she believes, she would not be bored. (Obviously she chose not to get it through Engineering; Scotty would have gladly made room for her, perhaps as his main assistant.) She is a commander in *The Search for Spock*, so she has followed a fifteen-to-twenty-year command pattern, which is extremely good. True, it isn't comparable to Kirk's less-than-ten-year climb, but few could match his fanaticism. Many recruits spend twenty-five to forty years trying to attain a lowly captaincy, and some never achieve it. But to Uhura, Starfleet never moves quickly enough. Perhaps her goal is much higher than one starship, so that might explain her fidgets. Yes, it is irritating to fans that she has a small part. But that does not affect her promotion path. Career-wise, Uhura is not terribly put upon, folks. She's impatient (and so are we, but that's life).

The complication in the promotion scheme is the Genesis Experiment. In *The Search for Spock*, the conversation with Heisenberg indicates that Uhura has been a commander for a long time—perhaps too long. After all, no career can be said to be "winding down" when a promotion looms on the horizon. If Uhura is not being penalized for merely *knowing* about Genesis, then why is a ground post at a *deserted* transporter station the best job she can find? Why isn't Chekov joining Scotty on Sulu's ship, the *Excelsior*? No, there must have been a penalty. It is extremely unlikely that Uhura would share duty with Heisenberg (even if she chose to do so), because she is too important. Wouldn't Chekov have been suspicious if he had been the guard or transporter operator when Spock was caught tampering with the equipment in "The Menagerie"? Heroes simply do not sit idle with the diaper set. True, Heisenberg wasn't the brightest lad who ever lived, but his crack about Uhura's dead career makes more sense if he knows that she has been busted. He wouldn't know *why*, but he would know that she was.

It appears that Starfleet prefers quick-wits like Heisenberg and slow-wits like Saavik to run the show. The "yuppies" hit the big time! Ah well, those two cannot be the best represen-tatives of the next generation. But where does this leave our old crew, the "puppies" of the show? ("Puppie," for the reader's info, is the acronym coined by Jim and Jan W. of Michigan, for "Poor, Underpaid Professionals Praying for Increase in Earnings.") Obviously, they're out in the cold. But it's doubtful that Uhura will miss it much. She will shrug it off, repair (and clean) the Klingon ship, and sing for her friends as they sail off into the starlight . . .

(Janice) Rand
First appearance: "The Man Trap"
Rank and post: yeoman, captain's yeoman
Rank and post by *The Search for Spock*: unknown; in *STTMP*, lieutenant, transporter chief
Grace Lee Whitney, who plays Janice Rand, is often left

out of the permanent Star Trek family. Although she was billed as a regular character for that magical first season, young Rand saw only half of it. The captain's yeoman, although not crucial to the plot of an adventure series, did have potential for a dramatic series. Her fresh and somewhat civilian viewpoint of her stubborn boss and the military in general could have been quite interesting. The killing blow was the fact that Janice had to get a crush on Kirk to demonstrate more fully the loneliness of high command. In her ten or so episodes, Janice emerges as a surprisingly well-rounded young person and a darn fine worker. But one unrequited love (Chapel's feeling for Spock) was apparently quite enough, and when Janice was written the same way, it was time for her to go.

Her actual duties make her a combination of secretary, time manager, and nursemaid. If the paperwork is cluttered, she organizes it. When Kirk has unwanted visitors, she shoos them off (or warns them they must be accepted). If he is frustrated, she is his whipping post. And when he is overwhelmed, she is a comforter.

She probably did not meet many people during her short stay on the *Enterprise*. Uhura is one good friend whose songs are a fine way to pass the evening. Sulu is her best friend, though. They both have a writing hobby, and both named the plants. Janice probably takes care of them when he is particularly busy or on leave. It is easy to visualize them playing tennis or go; they probably jog, too. He is probably one of the few *Enterprise* crewmembers who have heard her sing, but he could not encourage her to sing in public. (Grace Lee is a fine songstress, but she did not have a chance to sing on the series before she was dropped.) When she appeared in Spacedock in *The Search for Spock*, it was most likely that she was waiting to board as a member of Sulu's new ship, the *Excelsior*. (The alternatives are that she works either in Spacedock, at the Academy nearby, or on some tugboat-style craft in port at the time.)

Janice also enjoys her work. In this new feminist age, the "traditional" yeoman's job is sometimes considered undignified or worthless. But Janice chose to endure four stressful years at the Academy to get that job. No one could make her endure that environment against her will; no one could make her drop out if she chose to stay. And after the books were set aside, Janice evaluated the opportunities—command, science, medicine, engineering, law, administration—and chose to be a yeoman. Obviously she is one of the best. She was assigned to the finest ship and the strictest commander within weeks of graduation. That's something to be proud of, provided she doesn't rest on her laurels.

At only twenty-two, Janice is mighty young to have such a difficult job. Her youth influences most of her behavior. She has a few faults, like all humans, but many of these can simply be chalked up to inexperience.

It is said that Janice scares too easily. Actually, death is never pleasant (to witness or experience), and it takes time to settle into a job where death is commonplace. There are also many things that are nonfatal but just as intimidating. Even Kirk is occasionally afraid. As he tells Janice in "Miri," "Only a fool has no fear when there's something to be afraid of." Maturity simply means an ability to restrain fears and other sensitivities so that one can better function. Yes, Janice has seen others die, as everyone has—perhaps through an accident, or maybe by a deliberate act or horrible disease. It's just that death is something that happens to someone else, and Janice wasn't personally fond of it.

Janice isn't easily frightened by the dead crewman she and Sulu found in "Man Trap." She is sickened, and even a little fascinated, but not a screaming wreck. The salt vampire has no effect on her. When it takes the salt from Sulu's lunch, she smacks it. When it follows her, she tells it to bug off. Certainly she knows that "Green" is unusually strange today, but she has handled strange men before. (Such is the curse of the beautiful.) She doesn't gasp and faint when she finds out why "Green" was after her, either.

While helmsman Bailey is falling apart in "The Corbomite Maneuver," Janice is making lunch. This might seem an odd thing to do when Balok is telling them to prepare for death. When Kirk is giving up in "Balance of Terror" because they will soon die, Janice wants to know if she should continue making log entries for him. As long as she is preoccupied, she does not panic or quit.

Probably the best example of her excitability is her screaming fit in "Miri." The sight of her pretty, youthful figure being wasted by oozing sores, to be followed by madness and death, overwhelmed her. Death is taking a long time, and there is little she can do for distraction, so she crumbles. Yes, Janice is fearful, but no more so than most young people. She would have outgrown it.

Another way in which her age influences her behavior is in

her mannerisms. She is new to the military world and has not had time to blend her individuality into the often faceless mass of the service. Some unity is essential for a smoothly running ship. But Janice hasn't yet lost that bright-eyed ideal that life is fun, even fanciful. She is still very much the teenage cheerleader, the belle of the prom, the one who yaks on the phone (?) continuously; but she has been transplanted to the difficult and sometimes painful life of galactic security.

As Charlie X discovered, Janice is *very* feminine. She loves perfume, and her favorite brand is only available planetside. Her favorite color is pink: her robe is pink and her quarters are flooded with pink lighting. She loves flowers (pink roses, of course) and those useless, harmless ceramic knicknacks all over the dresser. Her hairstyle is of the typical junior miss persuasion—soft, fluffy, and almost too pretty for work. (If she lost a hairpin she'd be blind for ten minutes. It is flattering, though.)

Her feminine ways also slip over into her job. Psychologists know that in a traumatic and ever-changing life, few sensations are more satisfying than a hot meal and the security of Mother's undying devotion. Janice is almost always feeding someone. The snacks and drinks are always welcome after and during a long, boring (or stressful) day on the bridge.

Janice always seems to know when to have the captain's coffee handy. This is more than her mother-hen personality, because she couldn't make him quit if he needed to. Kirk, like many workaholics, depends on his caffeine more than he should, but he is more nervous and disagreeable without it. If he gets intolerable, that's the doctor's area of influence. So she brings the cup faithfully and will go to unusual extremes to get it.

When the power was off in the galley in "Corbomite Maneuver," she went so far as to make the coffee with a hand phaser. After Balok's countdown to destruction, a hot meal and drink would be very soothing and welcome. But it must have been a real nuisance to make. Kirk had not issued phasers to the crew, but Janice was able to obtain one anyhow. Having got one, could she heat the equipment? Oh yes, and Scotty would chase her to the Klingon Empire with the ax of Lizzie Borden—unless he had absolute confidence in her ability. The alternative is that she dismantled the weapon and drained its fuel or power source into the machinery as Scotty did in "The Galileo Seven." Either way, Janice demonstrated a neglected knack for technology. (The only time she was seen to *operate* complex equipment was during her shift on the transporter in *Star Trek: The Motion Picture*.) The coffee incidents underscore her devotion to her boss. How many secretaries on Earth would go to that much trouble for such a whiner?

One thing to keep in mind, though: Starfleet did not train Janice Rand in weaponry to improve her cooking. Kirk usually brings her (or any yeoman) along when he must leave the ship on business, although he may not need her (fat chance). The reasoning behind this is not fondness for his rookies. Kirk is a hero, and heroes have enemies. As the fleet's best, Kirk requires additional protection. If something dangerous gets past his security escort, that innocent little yeoman with the phaser in her garter is the last line of defense. She must be prepared to attack or even die to defend him (even if the chivalric hero, employing a military lack of sense, tries to protect her instead). So much for equal rights.

This aspect of the job is probably distressing to her. Janice is by nature a peaceful and loving person, so it is just as well that she was never thrust into that situation. She loves people, even the misguided ones.

The memory of Charlie Evans will surely be with her for a long time. When Janice took him under her wing, she was unaware of his great powers and destructive temper. When she did realize, it did not intimidate her. To Charlie, her praise is eagerly lapped up, her scolding is like a rain of stones. When the weeping Charlie is taken away, she cries too. By giving him the affection he never had and could never return to, she probably made his lonely life worse. In a way, it's like losing her little brother.

Janice is also concerned for children in "Miri," including Miri herself. They are able to trap her only because she cares for them. (Never mind that after 300 years, only the self-sufficient are left. Children need attention, she decides.) When she tells Kirk, "Miri really loved you, you know," his flip answer brings a sad smile to her face. Amusing as it may be to outsiders, a crush is intensely sincere (and painful). When the adoration is spurned or made light of, the victim feels a thorough fool and never wants to be seen in public again. Janice knows that Kirk does not take Miri's (or Charlie's, or *her*) crush seriously.

How the tune must have changed when Kirk realized that

Janice could live without him. In "The Enemy Within," the evil Kirk was shaken to discover that "his" woman did *not* want him, or even *like* him. Finding himself rejected by the crew as well, he "explained" himself to her, asking her forgiveness, understanding, and company. He passed himself off as the "good" Kirk, but Janice was not fooled. "The impostor told me what happened and who he was," she said. With unusual strength and insight, she recognized that even this beast needed to feel loved and accepted. She could have betrayed him when she found him roaming loose, but she didn't. Instead, the Kirks were forced by their freedom to work it out themselves.

However, the near-rape would not have been quickly forgotten. As Grace Lee Whitney indicated in *Best of Trek #1*, the episode "Dagger of the Mind" was originally written for Kirk and Rand. Would Janice actually have planted a "love" suggestion in his mind? Perhaps. But since Kirk already has suppressed feelings for her, the suggestion might prove *too* effective. Recalling her experience with the evil Kirk, she might have panicked at the last moment and said, "Sir, there's a rock in your boot the size of your fist, and it hurts like fill-in-the-blank." When no rock was discovered, the true nature of the "threapy" exposed, but no one would be harmed. She's only affectionate, not stupid.

Kirk does have real feelings for her. But he has set himself up for failure in love. In "The Naked Time," he longs for a "flesh woman" (Janice) to love, but he is "not permitted," he insists. Yes, he knows that his addiction to command turns a woman into a hobby, not a companion. Janice is clearly not interested in that. Maybe he refers to a regulation prohibiting relationships with his personal employees—not an unwise rule. Should an affair begin and his yeoman's career take off, idle talk will mention her "inside influence." If she stagnates there, a lover's spat or harassment is suggested. The fling would not be worth the shading of their professional reputations. Kirk can afford to be sweet to her when they face certain death, but when they survive, he clams up again.

For her part, Janice only asked Kirk to flirt and look at her legs, as puppy love demands. When she had had enough of his peculiar baiting game, she decided to see some proof that he was (or wasn't) worth a commitment. Janice originally transferred elsewhere to observe his reaction, and also because she was embarrassed by the gossip and teasing. If, now that she was available, he failed to follow up on it, she was well rid of him. Obviously he didn't, so she is.

Janice does not seem to be the type who would join Starfleet to find a husband, as critics would contend. It could happen, of course, in which case she has nothing but our best wishes. Marriage is rather a good goal with the right person, because nothing is more important than love. And nothing is more difficult (but vital) than transforming squalling, selfish toddlers into moral, caring, good human beings. (Or good something-or-other beings.) Any boob can handle them when they've grown. However, a military marriage can be much more difficult that a civilian one. And Star Trek had enough trouble fitting in all the regulars and guests each week. If Janice did marry (particularly if she had children as well), we might never see her again. Even Spock's mother showed up only once and was never mentioned when he died.

Even if Jim and Janice had loved each other enough to marry while in service, it would not have lasted. He sulks, fights, constantly demands his own way. She would hate his tendency to be first in danger. His idea of shore leave would not exactly thrill her soul; hers would bore him. Occasionally he must be given orders to eat or sleep. He would soon cease to be charmed by her crying. She would eventually want a permanent planetside home; to him, home is in space. If they had children, it's a whole 'nother can of worms. To stay with her husband, Janice would have to dump the kids off on the grandparents. But since Janice definitely loves kids and only likes Kirk, she might stay with the little ones instead. (Then, being lonely or restless, his roving eye would grow back.) Taking the kids to Little League or a fourth-grade piano recital would bore him to tears. (He might even say that they needed more practice.) Janice would be the first to leave. He would be the last to care.

It does not seem that any intelligent woman, least of all Janice, would consider the military a good place to attract a husband. There are many more eligible males on the hundreds of (civilian) Federation planets. It doesn't take four years of slaving to reach them, either. True, the armed forces would provide room and board while the gold-digger was looking, but it still isn't worth the trouble. Most people who work in isolated starships must be loners by nature, so that's a waste of time. The comments that Janice is lovesick and feather-brained are unwarranted. After all, Kirk started it, and she was smart enough to end it with her career and self-esteem intact.

So, it was unnecessary to remove Janice Rand so quickly from the Star Trek family. A crush on one's boss, though embarrassing, is curable. Kirk's amorous adventures also tend to be brief and soon forgotten. They would have returned to a professional relationship. Then she could find a more compatible man if she wanted to, while still being Kirk's right arm. Because of the security nature of the job, it would not seem that the captain's yeoman was intended to be a high-turnover position. Clearly Janice was the best help he ever had. He uses up a flood of yeomen in a very short time, and none of them is seen more than twice. And he thinks that Kirk and NBC let Rand go!

What is she doing these days? One could hardly imagine her wasting away at the transporter for eight years. She could, of course, have joined the traditional paths to command—helm/navigation, science, or engineering. With her technical know-how, she might be into equipment design, with maintenance or repair being the bread-and-butter job. Or, employing her clerical and "people" skills, she could be Sulu's personnel officer. If she is not a member of Sulu's crew, she could hold a teaching or management position in the Academy or Spacedock. She was not called upon to be a part of the criminal "Search for Spock," but that's no reason why she shouldn't be involved in the pursuit of *Star Trek IV*. So, for Janice Rand's fans, the future is bright. After all, *someone* has to run Starfleet while the boys are away.

(Christine) Chapel
First appearance: "The Naked Time"
Rank and post: lieutenant, chief nurse, with a doctorate in bio-research
Rank and post in *The Search for Spock*: unknown; in *STTMP*, lieutenant commander, ship's surgeon

Christine Chapel was the only minor character who did not enter the service for its career opportunities. She has never wanted to be anything other than a wife or mother. To her, Starfleet is neither thrilling nor burdensome—it's just a way to make a living until the right man comes along. Her problem is that she cannot seem to select good men. Having lost the dangerous Roger Korby, she then found another marriage prospect in the unwilling Mr. Spock. This was quite a contrast to Majel Barrett's original role as the career-oriented and practical Number One. However, Christine has potential— more than one would suspect from the one-dimensional treatment given her.

She is indeed a good nurse, but her primary job is to assist the doctors. She does little work on her own.

Her degree in bio-research is rarely employed. Probably she was in charge of the frantic study of a neurological disease in "The Tholian Web." She also uses this knowledge for some autopsies, as in "Operation: Annihilate." Having discovered the parasites could be killed by light radiation, Kirk and McCoy were too impatient to wait for her results. She is apparently in charge of (or has access to) the psychological files. She observes that something is wrong with Kirk ("Obsession") and Spock ("Amok Time") as quickly as McCoy does. This is probably a more interesting part of the job, although the subjects usually say that it's none of her business.

Christine must find medicine in the military a peculiar thing. For McCoy, bluffing is often the only out of a dangerous situation. But he might at least warn her. Christine rarely fibs; she finds it distasteful, especially when it is pulled on her. But not all the lessons are lost on this sometimes very confused nurse. The "applied psychology" used against the brooding Ensign Garrovick in "Obsession" is not a bad imitation. It didn't actually work, but it was the thought that counted.

So, Christine has virtually no place in the series as a professional. Even Uhura's switchboard affairs and Sulu's bus-driving had more screen time than Nurse Chapel's work. She was born to be in love, and most of her appearances emphasize her failure to find a man who wants her.

Why is it so hard for Christine Chapel to be realistic? She seems to make her poor choices deliberately, as if punishing herself. She certainly would have a harder time finding a good husband in Starfleet, because most people would not accept an assignment to deep space unless they preferred to be alone.

Roger Korby certainly preferred it that way. One can admire Christine's devoted search for him before he was introduced. He was once a good man, and they had a sincere, if undramatic, love. However, she could not seem to separate the man she remembered from the one who threatened her captain now. Once he has been shown to be unstable and dangerous, it becomes much harder to respect her.

One thing she did not notice or act upon was that Roger did not love her anymore. He made no effort to communicate with or return to society, although the technology of Exo III made that quite possible. He had built a female android which somehow knew how to kiss and dress in skimpy clothing. When Christine finally did catch up to him, his androids attacked the guards and her captain. He also stole military documents and planted an impostor on the *Enterprise*. He lied to her repeatedly and showed contempt for or at least indifference toward her work, and the effort which she had taken to find him did not impress him. The sad thing is that she tolerates all this.

The android Kirk was the first to question her loyalty to Starfleet. And Korby was no doubt pleased by her answer: "Please, don't make me choose. I'd rather that you kill me." Perhaps she was merely saying this to confirm her suspicion that the room was bugged. By pretending to continue her devotion to dear old Roger, she might be able to stop him at his weakest point when he was occupied with Kirk.

From the evidence, though, it would seem that Christine really could not choose. She did not explode at Andrea, or at Korby. Her most bitter response was a mere "I am disappointed in you." A good approach for a sane man, but not against an irrational android. The more he hurts her and her company, the more numbed she becomes. This is her way of handling stress. If she had not prevented Ruk from killing Kirk, Korby would have gotten away with his dangerous infiltrations. It is a great shame that the androids destroyed themselves, thus depriving Christine of the responsibility of facing her problem.

Once Korby was gone, so was the lesson. Christine soon fell in love with Spock, another unrealistic choice. It was not a bad idea at first; Spock could certainly do worse, and Christine was the nicest woman who had ever chased him. However, as it became apparent that Spock would not permit himself to take any woman, Christine, realistically, should have backed off.

Humans and Vulcans marry for different reasons. Christine, of course, would marry for love, which is the primary basis for most Western marriages. Vulcans, and some non-Western cultures, have prearranged marriages which are based on logic. Cross-culture marriages can work, as Sarek and

Amanda have shown. The modifications are that the marriage will happen only if both parties are convinced that they can remain happily (human) together for life (Vulcan).

Sarek and Amanda made their marriage work because "it was the logical thing" for both of them. Amanda could adopt her husband's culture without being a burden to him. Neither did she sacrifice her own personality—if Sarek had wanted a doormat, there were available Vulcan women. She did not nag or try to change him, as he did not try to change her. In both work and relaxation she was a support and a benefit to him. Altogether, she was an asset to him, and he was wise to find her. Amanda had the man she loved, and he made her happy. By the standards of either culture, they have a good marriage.

In like manner, if Christine intends to catch Spock, she must convince him that he is better off with her than without her. Spock already has a successful career and a few friends, and he will remain single as long as he can. Unless she can improve on that, he will not accept her.

If Spock did have to marry tomorrow, Christine would not be a bad choice. All his girlfriends have a selfish streak; none seems particularly concerned with the wants and needs of the other person.

Leila Kalomi (in addition to her deceit) would not be a supportive woman. Her major interest in Spock is to expose his emotions. She is rather upset when he declines her invitations, saying, "I can't bear to lose you again!" The fact that he has also been hurt is secondary to her own loss.

T'Pring was much worse. Her anticipation of receiving Spock's name and property while keeping a lover is more typical of human behavior than Vulcan. She scorned the law and was not interested in the possibility that people might be killed to preserve her scheme. Fans can understand why Spock avoided her previously.

The Romulan commander is sometimes called Spock's only "true love." This is not the case, as the woman only wanted a way to control the *Enterprise*, which was the catch of a lifetime. If she could bring the Federation warship home without much bloodshed, the Romulans would have valuable officers as well. Spock goes along with her plotting to buy time for the espionage efforts, and he is more of an actor than a participant. Further contact between them might be interesting, but would also be treasonous and so would not occur.

Droxine had a crush on Spock's looks, and he had learned by then the polite human reciprocations. His main interest here is to procure the needed cargo and convince Droxine that the political and class structures were wrong.

Zarabeth was an intelligent woman, but not a truthful one. She would do what she could to keep Spock with her, but in the end there was nothing she could do. He was also not himself, and even if he had become fond of her in time, he would not have cared for her in the present.

All these women had some selfish motivation for obtaining his friendship. Christine, on the other hand, is so selfless that she cannot stand up for herself. She would adopt his culture, abandon her career, and go anyplace to be with him. The phrase "separate vacations" is probably not in her vocabulary. If Spock wants a devoted shadow, Christine is the woman for him.

However, a selfless woman frightens Spock as much as a selfish one. Christine's emotions could really grate, since they are all concentrated upon him. He is always a little unsure of himself, and he would shrink from the overwhelming attention. True love is the desire to benefit another person, not the expectation of something in return. So, Spock would find her devotion just another form of the fault-finding magnifying glass that humans use on everything except themselves.

There are legitimate strikes against him. For one, Spock had much difficulty breaking the apron strings. A man who has not come to terms with his parents is not mature enough to begin a permanent relationship. So, Christine waited until the feud with Sarek was healed, and she tried again.

Another point is that Spock has become distrustful of human emotions and motivations. Leila (and T'Pring as well) entered his life without his permission, and the scars were not yet healed (he would deny having them). Why should he trust Christine, who after all invades his privacy by entering his cabin unasked, checking his files, and "accidentally" eavesdropping on him? She does these things because she is concerned about people; she means no harm. As humans go, she is not a loud or indiscreet person, but he will be cautious around her. He does not disbelieve that she only wants to please him, but he doubts that her fragile, emotional approach could be binding or lasting in a Vulcan sense. It is easy for her to follow the Vulcan ideal when times are good, but even Amanda finds it painful when the situation demands too great a sacrifice. Spock would rather avoid that stress and just not marry. Too, he understands what it is to be without a name and culture, and he would not wish such pain on his own children, which Christine would insist upon having.

If not for the Vulcan mating cycle, one can rest assured that the Spock of the series would never marry. In "Amok Time" he finally tells Christine to get lost: "If I want anything from you, I'll ask for it!" When he realizes that he will not go to Vulcan, he figures that it is time to ask. Fortunately for Spock, Christine is not one to notice rejection. From him, "It is illogical for us to deny our separate natures" is a seduction. Christine must have kicked herself to find that she had told Spock he was going home to his wife. However, the marriage was not necessary, and Spock went free.

If *pon farr* is fatal, why did Spock survive without a wife? One, it could have been "all in his head"—that is, the body reacted to his mental health with the Vulcan equivalent of a stress-induced ulcer. This seems the likely theory, as Spock would otherwise have married by *Wrath of Khan*, and he apparently had not. Two, it could have been a "false start," which would be followed by the real thing. The human influence probably spared him this. Altogether, Spock simply could not be "got." He would not yield to emotion, and he had no physical need for a wife.

(However, if the incidents of *The Search for Spock* are to be accepted, the Genesis Experiment has disrupted Spock's biology. If he recovers, his mutant physiology may require a Vulcan married life-style after all.)

However, it would seem that Christine has finally snapped out of her trance and given up on him. In *Star Trek: The Motion Picture*, she has proudly taken her post as the new ship's surgeon, which is an admirable advancement. She has evidently come to take satisfaction in her career and become a self-respecting woman. Her goal to be a wife and mother was a good one, but she set about finding it in the wrong way and with the wrong men. It was unhealthy for her to live only for other people and not develop a sound personality of her own. Now she seems a happier and more likable person. She has not been seen since *STTMP*, but she probably has new duties and hobbies (maybe new men) on which to spend her time. In addition to her abilities in practical medicine, she may be studying the many cures and devices she discovered on her first trip into space and introducing them to the scientific community. It is possible that she will turn up as Sulu's ship's doctor, although that remains to be seen. However, now that she has broken free of the flat stereotype originally given her, she can go nowhere but up.

(In the second half of this article, we will examine the other part of the "neglected whole," the gentlemen of the *Enterprise*.)

THE STAR TREK FILMS:
VARIATIONS AND VEXATIONS

Mark Alfred

Did you ever turn to the person watching a movie on TV next to you and say, "I don't remember that part!" Well, sometimes a faulty memory can fool you, but if such a mystery scene popped up during a Star Trek movie, then maybe it wasn't really there when you saw the film in the theater. In the following article, Mark Alfred explains how and why missing scenes suddenly appear in network and videotape prints of some Star Trek films; and, for those of you who missed them, he outlines exactly where and what those scenes were.

Thanks to an unsung hero at the ABC television network, Trekkers have been able to see more of their favorite universe: the universe of the twenty-third century, the universe of Star Trek. New footage was added to both *Star Trek: The Motion Picture* and *Star Trek II: The Wrath of Khan* when they aired on ABC TV. This article's purpose is to describe those additions (and minor exclusions), and along the way point out some flaws in continuity and some technical errors that made it onscreen.

Before we begin our discussion of the films, however, we must realize that *STTMP* and *Wrath of Khan* were not the first Star Trek to exist in differing versions.

Differing Versions of Episodes

After a ten-year wait, the original version of Star Trek's first pilot, "The Cage," was finally shown at a New York City Star Trek convention in January 1985, as reported in *USA Today*. There are a number of differences between this original version and the version existing as part of "The Menagerie." The major differences are a striking special effect in which the *Enterprise* became semitransparent during warp drive, and the original ending which showed Chris Pike watching Vina return underground with his illusory double.

As described by Allan Asherman in his excellent book *The Star Trek Compendium* (Wallaby/Pocket Books, 1981), the second pilot, "Where No Man Has Gone Before," exists in two versions.

The untelevised version included William Shatner's familiar "Space, the final frontier" voiceover, included more footage in the show's first minutes, and was divided into four acts like such Quinn Martin series as *The Invaders* and *The Fugitive*.

Observant viewers will note that Kirk's tombstone reads, "James R. Kirk. C 1277.1 to 1313.7." The mistake concerning Kirk's middle initial was made by someone at Paramount who had not paid attention to format (or, to be charitable, is perhaps an indication that Gary Mitchell's memory, at least, is not godlike). The dates are stardates, as shown by Kirk's final Captain's Log entry, dated Stardate 1313.8.

Star Trek: The Motion Picture

Star Trek: The Motion Picture was released on December 7, 1979, and was shown on commercial television by ABC on February 20, 1983. The film as broadcast ran two hours and twenty-three minutes, or thirteen minutes later than in theaters and on cable TV. The response of fans, as described later in this section, demonstrated that the longer version was vastly preferred to the original. Paramount, to its everlasting credit, re-released *STTMP* in its longer version on video.

Interestingly enough, the versions shown by ABC and re-released on video, while containing the same added footage, are not identical. ABC's copy was very dark and dingy, to the extent that Kirk's and the crew's light blue uniforms appeared light gray.

ABC's broadcast version of *STTMP* also differed in the panning-and-scanning techniques used to prepare it for telecast. [Because the television image is much smaller than the film image, the camera must be focused on whatever part of the movie image is deemed most important. This technique is called scanning. —Ed.] Some of the most obvious examples follow:

On Epsilon 9, ABC showed the English readout of the

Klingon transmission, whereas the video version shows the Klingon's face.

ABC cut to the far right side of the frame to include the black crewman saying, "I have an exterior visual."

In Kirk's beaming to spacedock, ABC showed the transporter operator; the video version shows Scotty, who stands beside her, instead.

After the wormhole debacle, ABC cut to the right and eliminated McCoy's face as he tells Kirk that his wits were casualties.

In a few places, ABC chose to show close-ups of characters as opposed to original wide-angle shots, as when Sulu says, "Thrusters at stationkeeping," in drydock, and when Chekov and Spock meet at the primary hull's docking port.

However, ABC's pan-and-scan techniques are not our main topic. Here are the additions and changes made in *Star Trek: The Motion Picture* to create "the complete version," as well as some of the "bloopers" that made it onscreen:

The first item is a possible continuity error. When Scott and Kirk arrive on the *Enterprise* via travel pod, they debark from an airlock numbered 5. Then a computer voice announces that a travel pod is available at "cargo six." This appears to refer to airlock five, the one Kirk and Scotty entered through.

The first instance of new material occurs while the *Enterprise* is still in drydock. After Kirk has ordered Chekov to assemble the crew on the rec deck and disappeared into the turbolift, Sulu states, "He wanted her back; he got her." Actor Billy Van Zandt, playing a high-pated Rhaandarite, asks about Decker's status. Uhura retorts, "Ensign, our chances of returning from this mission may have just doubled!"

In the rec room sequence, more shots of the assembled crew have been added, so that some of the 125 Star Trek fans used as extras can be identified. Among those visible in the ranks are Bjo Trimble, David Gerrold, Millicent Wise (the director's wife), Susan Sackett (Roddenberry's secretary), and Marcy Lafferty (Shatner's wife, playing Chief DiFalco, who later takes over Ilia's post).

The next addition occurs on the bridge after Kirk leaves to meet McCoy in the transporter room. Decker instructs Sulu to "take Lieutenant Ilia in hand," and our suave swashbuckler is transformed into a klutz by Deltan pheromones. Ilia makes a verbal jab at Decker concerning "sexually immature species."

Meanwhile, new footage in the transporter room shows

how McCoy won't beam up until, according to an ensign, he sees "how it scrambles our molecules."

When the *Enterprise* leaves drydock, the navigational deflector at the fore of the secondary hull is shown as red. Throughout the film (and in Wrath of Khan as well), it alternates between red and blue, for no apparent reason. Since it is self-lit, the color variations are not due to reflections of exterior light sources.

A continuity error may be seen in the moments after the *Enterprise* escape from the wormhole. In a wide-angled shot we see the bridge leveling off. Across from the camera, Decker and Chekov are at the weapons console. The next shot, a closeup of the two, shows Decker's hand still firmly resting on the console.

After Kirk, Decker, and McCoy depart for Kirk's quarters, on the bridge Sulu gives an order to Ilia which she does not at first notice; it is obvious she is concerned for Decker. This is new.

Also added is more discussion in Kirk's cabin between him and McCoy after Decker departs. McCoy gets Kirk's attention by telling him that he is "now discussin' command fitness."

More insight into McCoy's concern for Kirk is shown in the officer's lounge after Spock has left them. Kirk has said he can't believe Spock would put personal interests above the ship. McCoy retorts, "How can we be sure about any of us?"—meaning Kirk's selfish obsession with "his" ship.

When V'Ger's first energy blast is on its way toward the *Enterprise*, its transit time is extended while new dialogue is added concerning such things as evasive action, notifying Starfleet, and yaw and pitch.

After Chekov is zapped by the effects of the first plasma bolt, Dr. Chapel and a medtech are shown entering; Uhura directs them to Chekov. Ilia rises from her chair and informs them, "I can stop his pain." She does so: Chekov thanks her fervently.

A few sentences concerning the attributes of V'Ger's transmissions are added.

Then comes a major continuity error, to the effect that Ilia is two places at once. While Spock is speaking of sending *Enterprise*'s friendship message at the proper rate of speed, a camera angle from his point of view to Kirk shows Ilia's bald head at the navigator's console, while she is still fifteen feet away at the weapons console with Chekov. Indeed, the very next shot shows her getting up to return to her chair.

After Spock's message has been received, Spock speculates on the intruder: "It has a highly advanced mentality, yet it has no idea of who we are." Its plasma bolts were not a warning, for that would presuppose an emotion, which Spock senses no indication of.

More reactions of the crew to the V'Ger flyover are added. Uhura speculates, "It would hold a crew of tens of thousands," McCoy, returning to the bridge with Chekov, replies, "Or a crew of a thousand, ten miles tall." Spock observes that V'Ger's forcefield is "greater than that of Earth's sun."

A major mistake included in the film is the final version of the energy probe sent by V'Ger onto *Enterprise*'s bridge. This is one of the few special effects designed by Robert Abel and Associates that remained in the finished film.

The probe, according to Walter Koenig, consisted of an eight-foot-high tube of neon gas with handles on one side. An effects person would carry it vertically as it glowed, thus simulating the probe's movements about the bridge. Originally, the effects man wore white, so as to be "washed out" by the tube's brilliance. This didn't work, so it was tried with him wearing black clothing. He was still visible. The final course taken is painfully obvious, especially in one wide-angle, left-to-right pan. With the effects man standing to the right of the probe, a take was filmed as the probe crossed in the foreground. Then the scene was reshot with the effects man standing on the probe's left. Then the film was sliced in half vertically, and the halves without the technician were married to produce, theoretically, a perfect illusion. Unfortunately, the takes do not match: Kirk in his command chair is suddenly about six inches narrower and eight inches taller after the probe passed "in front" of him. A much cheaper and more effective means of achieving the effect would have been simple animation, as was used for the probe's "tendrils." This sequence is almost painful to watch because of their definitely substandard special effect.

An interesting slight error can be seen as the probe reads out the *Enterprise*'s memory banks. Instead of blueprints of the uprated *Enterprise*, the viewscreen shows the six-year-old blueprints of the television *Enterprise*! (By the way, look at these blueprints closely. They are the only place we'll ever see a bathroom in Star Trek.)

More additional footage shows McCoy coming onto the bridge after DiFalco arrives; Decker instructs Uhura concerning sending a message beacon to Starfleet.

A major sequence was added after Spock is discovered to have taken a thruster suit. Kirk suits up, follows him, and actually has him in sight before Spock ignites his thrusters. It is also interesting to note that Kirk moves forward by using thrusters at the front of his suit, thereby violating the laws of motion and action and reaction.

Some playful special-effects workers were no doubt responsible for the two fantastic characters encountered by Spock in his journey to V'Ger's heart. If you will watch carefully while Spock is saying the line "I am witnessing a dimensional image," a reflection at the left of the screen on Spock's visiplate looks remarkably like the helmeted visage of Darth Vader! Further, immediately upon Spock's line "But who or what we are dealing with?" the attentive viewer will note the face of the Muppet Miss Piggy rapidly appearing, rolling down and out of the picture at the bottom center of the screen.

The scene in Ilia's cabin concerning the Deltan headband is expanded. The Ilia-probe states that V'Ger knows the Creator is on the third planet. It then asks why carbon units have entered V'Ger and what their purpose is. McCoy retorts, "Their purpose is to survive!" The probe responds that V'Ger will survive by joining with the Creator.

It will be noted that this scene, located at this same point, also in Roddenberry's novelization, was inserted in *STTMP*'s original release between Spock's neck pinch at airlock four and Spock's first speech on his suit recorder. The new dialogue indicates that the correct place for this scene in Ilia's cabin is here, not in its earlier position.

A rather noticeable error in continuity is apparent in sickbay after Spock's return. We see Spock's right profile as he lies in a diagnostic bed with Kirk on his right side. Spock's sideburns are distinctly squared at the bottom, yet, minutes later, when Kirk orders the bridge cleared, Spock's sideburns are back to their regulation pointed shape. (Perhaps a quick shave?)

At the same time, the Ilia-probe is stating that only V'Ger and similar life forms are "true." Then, McCoy deduces, V'Ger's god might be a machine.

After Kirk instructs the bridge crew to resume duty stations, he tells Scott to prepare to execute Starfleet Order 2005, the self-destruct order. An engineering crewman asks if they will thus destroy V'Ger too; Scott replies, "When that much matter and antimatter get together—oh, yes, we will indeed."

More activity by the bridge crew is shown concerning crew status, remaining time to V'Ger's orbital devices' equidistant orbits, and the fact that the ship is seventeen kilometers (ten and a half miles) inside the alien vessel.

Kirk asks Spock for an evaluation, and the most affecting addition to the original film is seen: Spock swivels in his chair to expose tear-stained cheeks. He is weeping not for their plight, but for the waste of V'Ger's vast potentialities. "As I was, V'Ger is now," he says. "Logic and knowledge are not enough." McCoy asks, "Are you saying you've found what you needed?" Spock nods and continues talking about each person's search for the meaning of life. This brief scene and Spock's conversation with Kirk in sickbay are the keys to Spock's final integration of his personality as evidenced in *Star Trek II: The Wrath of Khan.*

However, we journey from the sublime to the ridiculous when Kirk and company ride an elevator to the personnel hatch atop the *Enterprise*'s primary hull. Imagine the top surface of the primary hull's saucer shape to be composed of three levels: The top level is that of the bridge; the middle level contains the officer's lounge; the third level is the vast sloping shape of the saucer itself. Yet, when the Ilia-probe and followers emerge into the oxygen-gravity envelope surrounding the ship, the special-effects modelers omitted the second level, and the large lower level of the hull is forced inward at a sharp ascending angle to meet the bridge level. Many viewers noted that the saucer looked "funny" here; this is why. The primary hull is not the same model seen through the travel pod's windshield during Kirk's trip to the *Enterprise* at the beginning of the film.

Another mistake is put into the mouth of Commander Decker, when he states that Voyager VI was launched "more than three hundred years ago." Moments later, Kirk states that Voyager VI was "a late-twentieth-century space probe." This places *STTMP* in the late twenty-third century. This conflicts with the carefully researched and Paramount-approved *Starflight Chronology* of Stan and Fred Goldstein (Wallaby/ Pocket Books, 1980). This meticulously worked-out timeline places the action of *STTMP* at A.D. 2215, toward the beginning of the twenty-third century. We must assume that in the excitement Commander Decker became a bit tongue-tied, and that he meant two hundred, not three hundred, years.

A final change in the expanded version of *Star Trek: The Motion Picture* is a minor one: The background music heard as Kirk, McCoy, and Spock return to the bridge at story's end continues throughout their ensuing discussion; it originally faded out until Kirk's final lines.

Almost immediately, the fans responded positively to the new incarnation of *Star Trek: The Motion Picture*. A letter to *TV Guide* stated, ''A terrible disservice was done to the movie when it was originally edited. . . . This was the first time that it all really made sense. And Mr. Spock with a tear on his cheek! Paramount left *that* on the cutting-room floor!''

Writers to *Starlog* also expressed general approval. One wrote, ''It seemed as though all the scenes deleted from the movie's initial release contained just those little touches of humor, character development, and plot explication that the film was originally criticized for lacking.'' Another correspondent said, ''Thank you, ABC, for treating all the Trekkers in the nation to extra footage. Thanks also to Paramount Pictures for releasing the extra footage. . . .''

Happily, Paramount re-released *Star Trek: The Motion Picture* on video with all the added footage. This is the version ''now available at stores everywhere,'' for as low as $24.95—definitely a bargain.

Star Trek II: The Wrath of Khan

Star Trek II: The Wrath of Khan was broadcast on the ABC network on the evening of Sunday, February 24, 1985. Some Trekkers, having read all ABC's advertising and finding no mention of added material, were caught off-guard at the sight of the words ''Edited for Television'' that appeared onscreen. Usually, this phrase means that something has been cut out. It transpired that only two brief sections were excised, amounting to perhaps five seconds of screen time (the two bits actually showing the Ceti eels entering and exiting Chekov's ear); but some anonymous Santa Clauses at ABC and Paramount had also added three or four minutes of new footage.

Sadly, however, ABC followed its own *Star Trek: The Motion Picture* precedent and broadcast an extremely dark and muddy print. Further, from the point where Kirk's shuttle heads for the *Enterprise* until the point where Khan states the

Klingon proverb concerning revenge, the broadcast sound was shaky and draggy, as if a tape reel was dragging.

The first incident of note in *Wrath of Khan* is not an addition, but an obvious boo-boo. In the *Enterprise* bridge simulator, as on the real *Enterprise*, there are two turbolifts. As Saavik orders the simulator into the Neutral Zone, over her shoulder we see that the starboard door's turbolift insignia is covered by a large, rectangular section of what looks like duct tape. This patch is about eight by ten inches and quite visible in the background. Yet, seconds later, when Kirk has entered and walks behind Saavik, the same insignia is now completely visible, and the gray mask is gone. This sort of maintenance does not take place in battle.

When Kirk reads the label of the Romulan ale, he reads the date, 2283, aloud, and McCoy comments that "it takes the stuff a while to ferment." Since our characters are living toward the beginning, not the end, of the twenty-third century, we can only assume that 2283 is a date of Romulan reckoning. This only makes sense, since it is illogical to assume that Romulans would label their product with the Federation's *lingua franca*, Standard English.

Immediately following is the first addition of new material. McCoy tells Kirk that the glasses are "more than four hundred years old. It's hard to find any with the lenses still intact." He has to tell Kirk, "They're for your eyes." McCoy's statement concerning the glasses' age would place their manufacture at around 1800.

Due to some odd value judgment concerning the relative offensiveness of profanity, ABC allowed McCoy's various "damns" to remain in this scene, but looped out a preceding "God" when McCoy is describing Kirk's relations with a computer console.

The next technical slipup is one familiar to the hearts of all fans of the TV series. On Ceti Alpha V, which is shown processing only one sun, Chekov and Terrell cast multiple shadows. This is caused, of course, by Nick Meyer's policy of filming these scenes on a Paramount soundstage, not at some desert location. The multiple shadows are most noticeable when Chekov and Terrell ascend the final ridge before seeing Khan's cargo-hold containers.

An incident upon Chekov's and Terrell's capture by Khan has caused much speculation. How did Khan recognize Chekov? In William Rotsler's highly recommended *Star Trek II Biographies* (Wanderer/Pocket Books, 1982), Chekov, in a

Starfleet debriefing, says, "He recognized me! I have no explanation for that, as I came aboard the *Enterprise* after the contact with the *Botany Bay*. I recognized him from ship's records and from historical photographs. But he is a kind of superman and . . . he might have memorized the face of the entire Starfleet." Vonda McIntyre, in her uneven novelization of Star Trek II: The Wrath of Khan (Pocket Books, 1982), states only that Chekov "remembered the incident itself with terrible clarity," thus contradicting Rotsler.

Exactly how Khan recognized Chekov must remain a mystery, since two different and contradictory Paramount-authorized accounts exist.

Khan states, "On Earth, two hundred years ago, I was a prince with power over millions." Since Khan is referring to the 1990s, before his exile in 1996, this conflicts with Commander Decker's statement in *Star Trek: The Motion Picture* that Voyager VI, a late-twentieth-century space probe, was launched "more than three hundred years ago." Again the Goldsteins' *Spaceflight Chronology*'s dates—that the events of *STTMP* and its sequels takes place in the first third of the twenty-third century—are more acceptable.

After Ricardo Montalban has, with the aid of an unseen hoist, lifted Walter Koenig off the floor, it is obvious that he has to pull Koenig down. This does not go along with the law of gravity. Better for the off-camera technician to have simply let Koenig down on cue, and Montalban to have followed that lead.

Scotty's nephew, Peter Preston, is finally identified onscreen, and the added scene where Kirk baits him with the statement that the *Enterprise* is "a flying deathtrap" is a wonderfully warm moment. We can imagine a young Midshipman Kirk reacting in just such gung-ho fashion on his first voyage—you will recall that Kirk described himself in "Shore Leave" as an "absolutely grim" student.

A few seconds are added to the possessed Chekov's first communication with Dr. Carol Marcus. Chekov attributes *Reliant*'s new orders to "Starfleet General Staff"; then, pinned down by Dr. David Marcus, he admits, "The order came from Admiral James T. Kirk."

The next change in *Wrath of Khan* is not the inclusion of additional material, but the inclusion instead of a variation on an original scene. You will recall that the "joke" scene in the turbolift between Kirk and Saavik was all of one take: Saavik stood at the left of the screen and Kirk was on the right. This single-take procedure was to show off the different corridor seen when the doors reopened, enhancing the illusion that the turbolift had actually moved vertically. The video release of the film cut right and left to show Kirk and Saavik. The ABC version, on the other hand, used a different take featuring full-face camera angles. Saavik's apparent come-hither looks at Kirk are nowhere more prominent than here.

The "pawns of the military" scene on Regula I now ends with Carol Marcus telling her workmates to pack what they can. "Where are we going?" someone asks. "That's for us to know and *Reliant* to find out," she replies.

More welcomed dialogue appears in Kirk's cabin after the three friends have watched the Genesis proposal. Spock agrees that Genesis, in the wrong hands— "Whose are the right hands?" McCoy breaks in. A few more moments of argument are added before the scene returns to familiar material.

Upon Khan's sneak attack, added material in engineering makes it more obvious that Preston has gone out of his way to save a crewmate's life. Scott's voice is heard crying, "Get back to your posts!"

In sickbay, after Peter Preston's death, McCoy asks how Khan knew about Genesis. Still, he tells Kirk, the *Enterprise* gave as good as she got. No, Kirk replies in frustration, they are only alive "because I knew something about these ships he didn't." Scott states that the main engines will have to be taken down for repairs.

A noticeable continuity error has its inception in Preston's death scene. The bloody handprint the young man leaves on Kirk's uniform blouse is roughly halfway up the exposed portion. Immediately thereafter, when Kirk steps onto the Bridge, the handprint has moved six inches higher, is smaller, and is much lighter in color!

Another slight error is only evident when the film is shown on a wide screen. When Kirk and Co. are in the anteroom to the Genesis Cave and David Marcus says, "We can't just sit here," Kirk is shown putting on his glasses to look at his wrist chronometer. Then, seconds later, we cut to a wide-angle shot. Kirk's glasses have disappeared from his face, and he is still sitting in the same position with no movements to indicate he has replaced them in a pocket.

The next insertion of new material is a brief scene back on the *Enterprise* after Spock has informed Kirk that the turbolifts are inoperative below C deck. They ascend through the same vertical access tube later used by Spock in his descent to engineering. Kirk says, "That young man—he's my son!" Spock replies, to our delight, "Fascinating."

When the ship goes to Red Alert status, various crewmen are shown at their Red Alert tasks. One is carrying the same vacuum-cleaner backpack seen used at the film's beginning in the background while Kirk and Spock discuss the *Kobayashi Maru* scenario. I find it hard to believe that a vacuum cleaner is a Starfleet-authorized piece of emergency battle equipment.

The final bit of extra material is added as the *Enterprise* is trying to lure the *Reliant* into the Mutara Nebula. Saavik asks, "What if the *Reliant* does not follow?" Spock replies. "Remind me to discuss with you the human ego."

As you can see, some of these changes and additions are more noticeable and important than others. Still, all are nice touches, whose exclusion from the original release print I, for one, cannot explain. The total time taken up by the additions amounts to but three minutes; surely no one could argue that such a small amount of footage, spread over a 113-minute film, could slow the action.

Further, since the total running time of *Star Trek II: The Wrath of Khan* was only extended by a small amount, it is virtually certain that Paramount will not run the large expense of re-releasing the film on video in an expanded version. However, it will likely be repeated as a rerun, and, now forewarned, more Trekkers can see for themselves Scotty's nephew call Admiral Kirk blind as a Tiberian bat.

Star Trek III: The Search for Spock

Star Trek III: The Search for Spock has only recently been released on video. Paramount has, according to the April 1984 issue of *Video* magazine, an exclusive contract with the Showtime and The Movie Channel cable networks for the film's first TV showing, scheduled for July 1985. As with the previous films, at that time it will probably appear in its originally released form. However, when it appears on network television in a couple of years, we can only hope that more "outtakes" will be reinstated.

It would be fruitless to speculate at this time what material might be added to *The Search for Spock* at some point years away, but this viewer for one noted a few mistakes and continuity errors that are interesting to point out.

The alert viewer will note that the layout shown on Chekov's security scan, indicating a life form in Spock's quarters, is from the TV blueprints, not the updated blueprints issued after *Star Trek: The Motion Picture*.

After Kirk's unsuccessful discussion with Starfleet Commander Morrow, he enters a turboshaft with Chekov and Sulu. Chekov is told to inform Dr. McCoy of their plans. Yet, when they arrive to rescue McCoy, he acts completely surprised, not forewarned.

Once more, the "exterior" shots on Genesis provide cast members with multiple shadows, evidence of soundstage "on location" shooting.

Another Genesis question: All views of Genesis show only the plant itself and its sun. It has no moon, and the flaming gas sheets of the ex-Mutara Nebula were condensed to form the matter of the planet and its sun. So where, then, does the nocturnal illumination, bright as that of Earth's full moon, come from?

When Saavik is awakened by the eruptive falling of a tree just before she notes that Spock's *pon farr* has come, a sloppy film editor inserted a momentary glimpse, from the rear, of a Klingon warrior being buried under a treefall. This brief clip belongs much later in the action.

In "Amok Time," the first incidence of *pon farr* in Spock, we can safely assert that he is at least thirty to thirty-five years Terran years old. Yet, a young actor playing Spock at the age of seventeen (according to *The Search for Spock*'s credits) undergoes the throes of *pon farr*. How can we resolve the one with the other?

When Kirk and company depart the *Enterprise* for the last time, the quick-eyed viewer will note that the transporter room walls have been changed, again. In the first film, the walls were a dull gray color. Nicholas Meyer's passion for little blinking lights caused the transporter room walls as shown in the second film to be covered with tiny panels, each flickering madly. Now, in *The Search for Spock*, the transporter room is back to its original appearance as seen in *Star Trek: The Motion Picture*.

As you will also recall from *Star Trek: The Motion Picture*, the self-destruct contingency of the *Enterprise* involves the uncontrolled conjunction of matter and antimatter. The very detailed and useful "cutaway" painting of the *Enterprise* by David Kimble, released as a poster after the release of the first film, clearly indicates that the antimatter pods and the matter/antimatter mix chamber are located on the lowest levels at the very front of the secondary hull. Since this would be the source of an explosive reaction, that is of course the first place where damage would become apparent to an outside observer. Yet in *The Search for Spock*, it is the primary hull which explodes in separate detonations; as the *Enterprise* plunges toward Genesis's atmosphere and begins to heat up, the secondary hull, the location of the matter/antimatter pods and the very heart of the self-destruct system, is shown to be completely intact. Once again, *The Search for Spock* has violated established (and Paramount-approved) continuity.

My final observation is but a minor quibble. A scene present in both DC's comics adaptation and McIntyre's novelization is the brief appearance of a Vulcan child who says, "Live long and prosper," to Spock's empty body while it is being carried up to Mount Seleya. It is not present in the film. Even so, the girl, Katherine Blum, is given credit in the cast list.

Many of the continuity difficulties of *Star Trek III: The Search for Spock*—the use of TV blueprints; the age of Spock at *pon farr*; the source of the *Enterprise*'s self-destruct explosions—could have been resolved had someone simply intended to check everything with what had gone before. Other errors, in all three films—moving handprints to multiple shadows to nonexistent moonlight—must have their origin in sloppy filmmaking.

There is so very much to love and thrill to in the (so far) three Star Trek films: characters old and new, costumes, spaceships, triumphs and tragedy. It's a shame that errors, large and small, detract from the fantasy that what's up on that screen is possible and real. My hope is that Paramount, the producers, writers, and directors will find it necessary to budget the time and expense to get it right. Further, it is a shame that Paramount, with so much money and materials invested in the Star Trek property, does not consider it worth its while to police the various products it licenses to make sure they are consistent with each other.

Nobody can get it right the first time. Now that Paramount has had twenty years of practice, this Star Trek fan is hoping that some of the obvious blunders and conflicts such as those listed above will be very rare (dare I hope nonexistent?) in *Star Trek IV* and beyond.

STAR TREK CHRONOLOGY, PART II

Jeffrey W. Mason

Fans have been clamoring for years for a continuation of Jeff Mason's "Star Trek Chronology" as originally presented in Best of Trek #3, and also for an explanation of how he reconciled his chronology with those assembled by others and published elsewhere. Now that the Star Trek universe has "advanced" fifteen years or so, there has been enough new "history" for Jeffrey to update his chronology. We think you'll find it both entertaining and enlightening.

Since the second and third Star Trek motion pictures were released (in the summers of 1982 and 1984, respectively) many fans have wondered what events have occurred between the first film and the last two (which can be viewed as a single two-part episode, since *The Search for Spock* picks up exactly where *Wrath of Khan* leaves off).

Many questions were left unanswered, such as: How long has it been since the first five-year voyage of the *Enterprise*? How did the *Enterprise* become a training vessel? When was Spock promoted to captain? Did Kirk command the *Enterprise* through another five-year mission after the death of Will Decker in the first film?

In order to answer these and other questions, we must start our analysis with a review of the dating scheme set out in the article "A Star Trek Chronology" (*Best of Trek #6*, pp. 89-106), and then look at evidence provided by the Star Trek films and their respective novelizations.

Based on the excellent timeline provided by Stan and Fred Goldstein's *Star Trek Spaceflight Chronology* and other sources, a chronology was established setting the date of the USS

Enterprise's first five-year voyage (commanded by James Kirk) as occurring between the years 2207 and 2212.

In this chronology the events of the first Star Trek film (*Star Trek: The Motion Picture*) are established as occurring in the year 2215. The span of time between the last year of the five-year mission of the *Enterprise* and the V'Ger incident can be ascertained from information provided in Gene Roddenberry's novelization of the first film. Here it is suggested that Kirk hadn't commanded a starship for almost three years. For instance, on page 109 of the *STTMP* novelization, Willard Decker, in defiance of the admiral's intention to resume command of the *Enterprise*, states that Kirk "hadn't logged a single star hour in over two and a half years." Kirk himself indicates that he spent two and a half years as chief of Starship Operations.

In order to establish a timeline for the second and third films we need only consult pages 51-52 of the novelization of *Star Trek II: The Wrath of Khan* (by Vonda N. McIntyre) to discover that Khan had been marooned on Ceti Alpha V for fifteen years. Having determined (in the article "A Star Trek Chronology") that the date of the "Space Seed" episode is 2208 (the use of this date, rather than 2207, is justified by the fact that this episode was one of the last aired in Star Trek's initial season), a quick mathematical computation allows us to establish 2223 as the date for the events of the second and third films.

This guesstimate can be enhanced by the supposition that in the film *Wrath of Khan*, Admiral Kirk is celebrating not just any birthday, but his fiftieth. By analyzing verbatim dialogue from various Star Trek episodes (including "The Deadly Years," where Kirk testifies that his age is thirty-four), we are able to ascertain that around the time of the events of the episode "Space Seed," Kirk was in his mid-thirties. Adding the fifteen years that Khan was marooned on Ceti Alpha V onto Kirk's age at the time of his first encounter with the eugenic superman gives us a figure of approximately fifty years.

This supposition is consistent with Kirk's attitude about feeling old and the unusual attention given to this day by his friends McCoy and Spock in the early moments of *Star Trek II: The Wrath of Khan*. And thus there is agreement with the birthdate established for Kirk in "A Star Trek Chronology." If Kirk was born in 2173, his fiftieth birthday would occur in 2223.

Thus it would appear that the events of *The Search for Spock* also occur in the year 2223.

But what events occurred in the Star Trek universe between 2215 and 2223 (the dates established for the first and last two films)?

The most logical guess is that Kirk and some of the crew of the "old" *Enterprise* combined with Willard Decker's hand-picked group to serve for another five-year mission. This mission lasted from 2215 to 2220. It is possible that Kirk had to accept a temporary reduction in command in order to captain the *Enterprise* on his second five-year mission, but because there is no evidence of this occurrence in any of the films or their novelizations, we may assume that Kirk remained an admiral during this time period and thereafter.

After this mission, Starfleet Command probably decided to relegate the *Enterprise* to an auxiliary status, considering its age and length of service (which was more than thirty years according to information provided in the Goldsteins' book, which fixed the date of the *Enterprise*'s construction as 2188).

With an auxiliary status, the *Enterprise* would have served as a ceremonial and nonpriority patrol vessel, sometimes doubling as a training ship.

Perhaps Starfleet recognized the value of the great experience of the team of Kirk, Spock, and McCoy, and allowed them to serve together again as a training unit for the newly educated cadets.

In this scenario, Kirk and a much smaller number of his former crew would serve on short training cruises of the *Enterprise* from 2220 to 2223. In addition, Kirk, Spock, and McCoy might serve as part-time instructors at Starfleet Academy Command School.

But before we proceed with a continuation of the chronology established in this author's first article, let us examine some of the other sources for such speculation besides the Star Trek television and film episodes.

The most valuable sourcebooks for compiling a relatively consistent and effective Star Trek chronology deserve mention here. Bjo Trimble's *Star Trek Concordance* (1975), Stan and Fred Goldstein's *Star Trek Spaceflight Chronology* (1980), and John Upton's *Introduction to Navigation* manual in Bantam Books' *Star Trek Maps* (1980) are extremely important source materials. Of course, the *Best of Trek* series has also provided necessary background information and speculations.

One of the most recent books of interest in this area is

William Rotsler's *Star Trek II Biographies*. Rotsler's work provides interesting personal information ("garnered" from the characters' personal correspondence, memoirs, diaries, communications, "official" Starfleet documents, and "published" articles and books) on the life histories of the most famous of the *Enterprise*'s crew.

Despite the errors in his work (including his placing Star Trek in the twenty-second century), Rotsler does a credible and informative job of cataloguing the biographies of Kirk, Spock, McCoy, Chekov, Scott, Sulu, and Uhura.

Now we can continue with our chronology of the voyages of the *USS Enterprise* for the time period 2215 to 2223:

APRIL 2215

After successfully ending the V'Ger threat, Admiral Kirk resumes command of the *Enterprise* for his second five-year mission.

APRIL 2220

The fifth five-year mission of the Constitution II Class Starship *Enterprise* is completed successfully. Starfleet Command plans to permanently retire the ship from first-line duty and establish it as an auxiliary Academy Training Vessel and UFP Headquarters Quadrant Patrol Ship.

MAY 2220

The *Enterprise* returns to Earth for refitting as Academy Training Vessel. All crew members are scheduled for six months' leave, with most being reassigned thereafter.

JUNE 2220

Admiral James T. Kirk accepts the position of Starfleet Academy Command School Commandant, stepping down from active starship exploration duty. Spock of Vulcan is promoted to captain of the training vessel *Enterprise*. Spock is also appointed assistant dean of the Academy of Starfleet Sciences.

NOVEMBER 2220

The USS *Enterprise* begins its first of many monthly training cruises in the UFP Headquarters Quadrant of interstellar space.

NOVEMBER 2223

While answering a distress call from the Regula I space station, the USS *Enterprise*, under the temporary command of Admiral James T. Kirk, comes under fire from the USS *Reliant*, whose command was wrested from Captain Clark Terrell by the renegade Earthling Khan Noonian Singh. The *Enterprise* is damaged extensively in its successful engagement with the *Reliant*, but it limps back to a nearby Starbase for repairs. The Federation suffers the loss of Captain Spock, who perished in a valiantly successful effort to save the *Enterprise* from destruction.

DECEMBER 2223

On what began as an unauthorized mission, the USS *Enterprise* (running under an automatic helm) engages a Klingon spy vessel near the doomed Genesis Planet. Admiral Kirk orders the destruction of the *Enterprise* (which self-destructs and burns up in the atmosphere of the planet) to thwart the capture of his ship by the Klingon captain, Kruge. After the defeat of Kruge, Kirk and his crew escape the Genesis nova in the captured Klingon fighter.

A continuation of the chronology of the larger Star Strek universe can now be established for the same time frame:

2215

The first "Dyson sphere" (a solar-sized artificial planet that encloses and traps the energy of a dwarf star and provides a Class M environment on the interior surface of the sphere) is discovered by a Federation vessel on a routine patrol near the Milky Way's galactic core (see *The Starless World* by Gordon Eklund). The civilization which constructed the artifact was discovered to have been extinct for millennia.

2216

The Second Dissolution Crisis of the United Federation of Planets is precipitated by the Voran Hegemony Bloc of delegates at the annual Babel Conference. The alien Omne fuels the debate with his alleged "immortality" offer. A dissolution motion is defeated, thanks to the assistance of Admiral

Kirk, in the closest vote ever. The Directive of Noninterference is overwhelmingly upheld during a challenge vote. (See *The Fate of the Phoenix* by Sondra Marshak and Myrna Culbreath.)

2216

A Federation building program begins for the new Galaxy Class of intergalactic scoutships.

2216

The Napoleon series of "suicide" probes are sent into the Galactic Maelstrom (also known as the Shapley Center Zone of Intense Radiation), a gigantic black hole located in the center of the Milky Way Galaxy.

2217

Aleph Prime, a mining colony, becomes the 700th member of the United Federation of Planets (see *The Entropy Effect* by Vonda N. McIntyre). The UFP colonization sphere now encompasses over 2,000 Class M planets (including UFP member worlds, colonies, outposts, and experimental stations).

2217

Merfez Enarhcoc, a mysterious physicist, reveals the theory of transwarp drive. Within months of the theory's publication, a UFP scientific colloquium recommends a crash program to design and build a transwarp drive vessel by the year 2225.

2218

On the tenth anniversary of the Organian Peace Treaty, the joint UFP-Klingon Treaty Review Conference proves unable to summon the Organians to attend the annual meetings they originally proposed.

2218

Subspace radio is uprated to Warp 40 efficiency.

2219

The first contact with the Naoli occurs. The Naoli represent a peaceful solar-based humanoid culture that traverse interplanetary distances using solar sails. They claim they were seeded on their planet 75,000 years ago by the "Preservers."

2220

Starfleet Academy retires its previous training vessel, the USS *Potemkin*, commanded by Admiral Mendez, and assigns the USS *Enterprise* as the new Academy Training Vessel and UFP Headquarters Patrol Ship.

2220

The first experimental transwarp vessel is tested successfully in Quadrant Alpha, a space desert. A prototype ship is built and tested one year later.

2221

An unmanned transwarp drive "contact" ship leaves Federation space bound for the home planet of the Kelvan Empire in the Andromeda Galaxy. An earlier warp drive probe to Kelva disappeared in an uncharted region of extragalactic space.

2222

Naoli becomes the 716th member of the United Federation of Planets.

2222

The first phase of the ultrasecret Genesis Project is successful in creating a life matrix pattern where none existed previously.

2223

The first of the Galaxy Class scout vessels, the USS *Magellan*, leaves on an exploratory manned mission to the Andromeda Galaxy. A second and third vessel (the *Andromeda* and *M-31*) are tested in Quadrant Alpha.

2223

The unplanned discharge of the Genesis Device results in the birth of a new Class M planet in the Mutara Nebula. However, within days of its birth, the unstable star and its companion—the Genesis Planet—explodes.

2223

The USS *Magellan* reaches Andromeda and completes the first close-range observation of a supernova. The USS *Andromeda* leaves the Milky Way Galaxy en route to Andromeda via the Galactic core.

2223

UFP membership reaches 725 members with the admission of Fabrina-Yonada (Daran V-A).

2223

The transwarp drive vessel USS *Excelsior* becomes the first such ship to patrol Federation space.

And now another look at some important individuals in the Star Trek universe:

Commander Kruge (?–2223)

Commander of the Klingon fighter that undertook an espionage mission to steal the secret of Genesis. Kruge perished on the Genesis Planet.

Star Fleet Commander Harry Morrow (2170–   )

Hero of the Battle of Kzan in 2205. Served as captain of the USS *John F. Kennedy* for ten years; promoted to commander of Starfleet in 2221.

Captain J.T. Esteban (2183–2223)

Commander of the scientific survey ship *Grissom*, which was destroyed by a rogue Klingon vessel near the doomed Genesis Planet; formerly served as science officer on the USS *Exeter*.

Captain Mandala Flynn (2185–   )

Commander of the first manned extragalactic mission; she captained the *Magellan* on the first historic exploration of the Andromeda Galaxy. Previously she served as head security officer on the *USS Enterprise* (see *The Entropy Effect* by Vonda N. McIntyre). Flynn represents the rare minority of Starfleet officers who did not attend the Academy but who rose up the ranks via the Federation Border Patrol.

Lieutenant Marla McGivers (2183–2209?)

Ship historian on the USS *Enterprise*; participated in the awakening of Khan Noonian Singh in 2208 and was exiled from the Federation for her complicity in Khan's attempt to steal the *Enterprise*. She died of madness and the accompanying physical effects of the parasitic Ceti Eel, not long after the explosion of Ceti Alpha VI.

Captain Clark Terrell (2177–2223)

Captain of the uprated starship USS *Reliant* for three and a half years; formerly served as captain of the scoutship *Battlemaster* and destroyer *Singapore*; he sacrificed his life to thwart Khan Noonian Singh's plan to kill Admiral Kirk during the Genesis incident.

David Marcus (2203–2223)

A genius in the fields of astrobiology and chemisty; educated at the universities of Delft and New Harvard. Marcus, along with his mother and his late colleagues Jedda Adzhin-Dall, Vance Madison, Delwin March, and Zinaida Chitirih-Ra-Payjh, developed the failed Genesis Effect of Life Matrix Creation. He perished on the Genesis Planet hours before it exploded.

Carol Marcus (2179–   )

Formerly director of the Project Genesis team at Regula I Spacelab and a biological engineer/physicist by profession, Marcus and her son—David Marcus—headed a team of Earth and Deltan scientists that invented the Genesis Effect. The project failed and was abandoned in 2223. She is now working on another classified project on Earth.

Khan Noonian Singh (1962–1996; 2208–2223)

An infamous twentieth-century dictator who escaped Earth (see the Tokyo Tribunal of War Crimes, 1966–1998) in 1996 and was awakened two centuries later aboard the sleeper ship *Botany Bay*. Khan and the remnants of his followers escaped banishment from Ceti Alpha V when they commandeered the USS *Reliant* from Captain Terrell. The *Reliant* was defeated in battle by the *Enterprise* and Khan and his followers all perished.

Merfez Enarhcoc (2171?–   )

Inventor of the theory of transwarp propulsion; hails from the Gamma Canaris system. Little is known about this mysterious theoretical physicist whose physical features have never been revealed to the public. Enarhcoc, in his early fifties and married, is a throwback to a school of theoretical physicists who lived over 150 years ago and called Alpha Centauri their home.

Omni (?)

Also known as "Black Omne." The true identity of this individual is shielded but it is known that he is the last survivor of an extinct alien race of humanoids and is an expert linguist and a brilliant scientist. Before his mysterious disappearance, he ruled a loose confederation of alien enclaves on the so-called Black Hole Planet. (See *The Price of the Phoenix* by Sondra Marshak and Myrna Culbreath.)

Lieutenant Saavik (2202–   )

Of unique mixed parentage, Vulcan and Romulan, she was rescued from the savage Romulan colony world Hellguard at an early age by a Federation relief team. She completed her studies at Starfleet Academy, graduating with honors, and attended Starfleet Command School. After a brief tour of duty aboard the training vessel *Enterprise* (for which she received a special commendation for her role in the Genesis incident),

Saavik was assigned to the USS *Grissom* as ship's science officer.

Commander Pavel Chekov (2184–   )

First officer aboard the USS *Reliant* and formerly weapons/ security officer aboard the USS *Enterprise*; received commendations for his participation in the defeat of Khan Noonian Singh, despite suffering a serious injury.

Lieutenant Commander Winston Matthew Kyle (2170–   )

Communications officer aboard the *Reliant*; formerly served as transporter chief aboard the *Enterprise*. Previous assignments include security officer on the USS *Paul Revere* and assistant security chief aboard the *Queen Victoria*.

Cadet Peter Preston (2209–2223)

Training cadet who participated in a short training mission aboard the USS *Enterprise*. His valor during the Genesis incident helped the *Enterprise* fend off the renegade Khan's attacks; he won posthumous commendations for his bravery. Nephew of Commander Montgomery Scott.

Commander Hikaru Walter Sulu (2179–   )

Chief helmsman and Assistant Professor of Star Navigation and Aeronautics aboard the training vessel *Enterprise*; his promotion to a starship captaincy is imminent. Formerly he served as chief helmsman aboard the USS *Enterprise* and *Hua C'hing*.

Commander Montgomery Scott (2160–   )

Chief engineer of the USS *Enterprise* and assistant professor of Engineering Sciences on the training tour of the same vessel. Formerly he served with James Kirk aboard the *Enterprise*, *Hua C'hing*, and *Starstalker*.

Commander Penda Uhura (2179–   )

Communications officer and assistant professor of Signal Command Sciences aboard the *Enterprise* training vessel. Her past assignments included tours of duty aboard the *Atlantica* and *Adad*.

Commander Leonard "Bones" McCoy (2158–   )

Ship's surgeon and chief of Medical Science aboard the *Enterprise*; served as assistant dean of the Starfleet School of Medicine and medical officer during the training tour of the same vessel.

Captain Spock of Vulcan (2166–2223?)

Captain of the training vessel *Enterprise* and assistant dean of the Starfleet Academy of Sciences; formerly he served as first officer and science officer during three tours of duty aboard the same vessel. He was awarded the UFP Golden Medal of Honor and Star of Sirius (posthumous) in commendation of his valiant sacrifice during the Genesis incident. (See Star Trek II Biographies by William Rotsler.)

Admiral James Tiberius Kirk (2173–   )

Captain of the USS *Enterprise* through two five-year missions; promoted to admiral in 2212; stepped down as captain to serve as chief of Starfleet Operations (2212–2215) and commandant of the Starfleet Command School (2220–2223). He commanded the *Enterprise* on its last voyage soon after his defeat of Khan during the Genesis incident.

A LETTER FROM
TERENCE BOWDEN

Here is another in our continuing series of letters which have proved to be interesting and lengthy enough to qualify as articles. We found Terence Bowden's thoughts to be quite stimulating, and we're sorry that space limitations forced us to edit many of his remarks. Never fear, though. Terence presented us with several article ideas, and we feel confident you'll be seeing much more of him in future Best of Trek *volumes.*

Bonjour mes amis!

Greetings and felicitations from the Great White North! (Actually, in my part of the country it's only white about six months a year; right now it's 23 degrees Celsius, or, for you metrically tardy Americanos, about 80 degrees Fahrenheit!)

Hot or not I had to take this opportunity to say hello and offer you my sincere gratitude for what has been a most enjoyable two weeks of reading. . . . Yeah, I just discovered in my local book supermarket ("The World's Biggest Bookstore," which is a huge operation the size of a department store but filled entirely with books) your marvelous *Best of Trek* series. . . .

Now let me explain, gentlebeings. . . . I've been a science fiction fanatic for most of my earthly existence (at least, in this particular incarnation, anyhow . . . !). I started reading the stuff shortly after Yuri Gagarin blasted into history and I found our next-door neighbor tossing out a box full of paperbacks. Being a precocious child (my father taught me to read at age three) and by then (age seven) in love with space (remember those wonderful Willy Ley books about space-

175

flight with the classic Chesley Bonestell art masterpieces?), I instantaneously snatched up the box and beat a fast retreat into my room, promptly losing myself in extrapolative space-time! After reading my first SF book, the plot of which I remember clearly to this day twenty-four years later (Alan E. Nourse; "Scavengers in Space"), I was hooked for life.

To the televised accompaniment of Mercury-Atlas and Vostok liftoffs, I was voyaging with Heinlein, Asimov, Clarke, and company. Along with real-life heroes like Glenn and Leonov, Carpenter and Tereshkova, I had fictional paragons like Kim Kinnison and John Carter. While Gemini-Titan demonstrated docking and rendezvous in space, my horizons were being expanded by esoteric future sciences like psycho-history and warp drive physics. And of course, during the Great Lunar Bonanza Race, well, naturally, I became a fan of a certain new TV series, from day one.

I needn't say *which* series!

Oh yeah, there had been SF films and TV series before Star Trek, but, with the exceptions of a very, very few movies (like *Forbidden Planet*, the direct precursor of Star Trek in my view, *The Day the Earth Stood Still*, *War of the Worlds*, *Destination Moon*, and two or three others) and those classic anthology TV series *Twilight Zone* and *Outer Limits*, all of it was utterly intolerable trash. Television producers just didn't understand the science fiction premise: believability, scientific accuracy, intelligent speculation, and thought-provoking themes in a consistent future setting. And actors forced to work with silly scripts, no matter how talented they themselves were, always came off as cardboard characters in TV SF.

But then, swooping into American network conformity, from the heart of our galaxy, came a Great Bird.

And TV finally found fulfillment in futuristic fiction of the first caliber!

It has been said, quite accurately, that there are no really new stories to be told, no new heroes to be created. All stories have their roots deep in the primeval mists, in myths. But it is equally true that every civilization, great or small, generates its own myths and heroes from this root material. First there is fiction and fictional characters, designed by a writer to state a point of view important, in his opinion, to society at large. At some point, if the message is recognized as valid by a sector or subculture of society, if the characters are memorable and typical of the highest aspirations of that subgroup, the status is upgraded to folktales and folk heroes. And finally, more rarely, if the message is taken to heart by the whole of a society, and the characters become symbolic of the very highest values, the story enters the rarefied realm of mythology.

It is given to very few artists to create a myth, but Gene Roddenberry has done it. I suspect a thousand years hence men will look upon Star Trek in the same light as they look upon the story of the Argosy or the Odyssey. James T. Kirk will be seen as another face of what the mythological scholar Campbell calls "The Hero with a Thousand Faces," along with Jason, Odysseus, Gilgamesh, Noah, and all the rest.

And what Roddenberry has done is perhaps even more important—he has created the first truly *global* myth. All previous myths were regional or national, from the ancient tales of Sumer to the American myth of Superman. While reflecting certain elements of import to all humanity, they were based firmly in a national-cultural ground and sprang from that soil to reinforce local value systems. Star Trek, however, springs from an internationalist-planetary consciousness, a One World consciousness, if you will, and reinforces the values important to the achievement of that sort of unification: understanding, love, brother/sisterhood, respect for diversity.

While I am certain many American fans think of the Federation as a direct descendant of the U.S.A., a capitalist Christian society, Roddenberry was always careful not to state that. Indeed, he implied instead that it was more of a historical product of the United Nations and of many political systems and religious traditions. The presence of Chekov onboard certainly implies that the convergence of capitalism and communism is one of the key roots of twenty-third-century civilization (and let us hope it takes place in reality before it's too late for us all, amen!).

By taking such care in building the structure of his fictional universe, by his sensitive selection of actors with talent and the creative capability of portraying humanity's highest values, Gene Roddenberry has given the whole world one of the most valuable gifts conceivable: a sense of hope for the future, a better future, for our children's children's children. And for all of us in these times of turmoil, a banner and a torch to hold aloft, inspiration to keep on keeping on.

He is the Homer of late-twentieth-century civilization.

And, oh, how we needed him!

Here we stand on the edge of infinity with our right foot stuck deep in the mire of history, or tradition, of custom, of social conformism, of fear and war and hatred; while our left foot swings boldly into the yawning chasm of uncertainty, change, evolution, and interplanetary space. This is an age unlike any other since the dawn of civilization and the invention of writing itself, perhaps humanity's greatest previous step forward. Indeed, in a grander sense, today we face a challenge like the one the first amphibious fish faced when evolution's imperative, the urge to survive, drove them to lay their eggs on land away from aquatic predators.

The urge to survive.

Yes, we are driven creatures. Still very much animals, striving to survive against antilife pressures and ecological imbalances. Oh yeah, we are *proud* animals. So we rationalize it all. We say we are venturing forth into the cosmos for scientific reasons. Or for industrial reasons. Or for philosophical reasons. But at the root of each of these rationalizations lies that primal imperative.

It is oh so clear and oh so simple, and, being complex creatures who are hypnotized by complexity, we often do not see what is before our eyes: Life is growth. When growth ceases, death inevitably follows sooner or later. Growth involves physical, intellectual, psychological, and spiritual expansion on the human plane. While there is virtually infinite room for expansion in the human mind and its organized extension, society, for the last three forms of growth, physical expansion remains a key element. And a planet has only so much room for physical expansion. In a short time, cosmologically speaking, sentient creatures with a high survival imperative and capability, especially society-building sentients, will reach the limits of physical growth; social organization will clash more and more repeatedly for limited resources . . . many will be lost in the shuffle; no matter how much they may wish to interact cooperatively for mutual benefit, it is the very nature of individualized consciousness to perceive differences, some of which will inevitably be irreconcilable. Freedom and slavery, for instance, are concepts which simply cannot coexist for long. Social clashes, wars, population pressure, need for resources . . . all of these are driving us to the planets, and eventually the stars.

The Human Adventure was always inevitable, despite the skeptics of the past, the scientists who even in the early 1950s said lunar travel was "impossible." (Yes, even scientists can be unscientific. Many today swear up and down that faster-than-light travel is "impossible." Yet the Einsteinian principle they base their argument on only says it is "impossible" to travel *at* the speed of light, or more correctly, infinite energy is required to travel *at* that speed.) It was always a foregone conclusion, despite the diligent efforts of antitech fanatics in the 1970s to halt the U.S. space program (where are they now, one wonders?). And in spite of the fact that the smaller planets and the larger moons look like pretty bleak places, we *will* colonize them. The survival imperative demands it of us. With planetary colonies, even a total war on Terra will not destroy humanity. Our colonies will be the guarantee of racial survival in the face of the apocalypse.

You know, the ancient rabbinical scholars of Judah had an interesting paradox. It went, "We *have* to use our *free will*, we have *no choice* in the matter." Given a capability, you must use it to survive. Life itself demands this of you.

So the human adventure is indeed just beginning, and, yes, somewhere down the line there will be a Federation or a Union or a Polity or an Empire of planets. And at some point in elsewhen there will be starships and heroes. Almost certainly there *will* be a starship named *Enterprise*; do we not use mythological and historical names for our own vessels?

Legend, myth, and history often have converged, creating real puzzles for the scholar. For ages historians believed the city of Troy in Homer's *Iliad* was merely a legend; that is, until the late nineteenth century when a dedicated German amateur archaeologist dug up the city in Asia Minor! The same is true of many Biblical stories. Whole empires previously thought to be the creations of religiously inspired Jewish writers have been uncovered from the sands of Time. The whole story of the man Yesu ben Yosef, the Nazarene, Jesus Christ, is an awesomely tangled compendium of myth, legend, and reality. He must have been a brilliant man, whatever else he was, for he literally created himself, constructed and planned his own life and death, out of a dozen religious and mythical traditions.

And such puzzles may plague future historians if, say, many of our records are lost in wars. Consider the shuttle program for a moment.

There's a shuttle named *Columbia*. This was also the name of the command shuttle module of Apollo 11, man's first voyage to the lunar surface. *Columbiad* was the name of the spaceship shot out of a giant cannon from Florida in Jules Verne's *From the Earth to the Moon*!

There's a shuttle named *Discovery*. This was also the name of Captain Cook's historic exploration vessel. And it was also the name of the Bowman-Poole vessel which went to Jupiter in Arthur C. Clarke's *2001: A Space Odyssey*!

The prototype shuttle was, of course, named *Enterprise*, also the name of a U.S. aircraft carrier, and of Stephen Decatur's ship which went up against those Mediterranean terrorists of the past, the Barbary pirates. And, of course, it is the name of a certain starship created by a Great Bird!

Myth, history, and science fiction are all converging here and now. It is strangely appropriate, is it not? We, like the Nazarene, are creating ourselves anew each day, combining all the streams from ancient sources to nourish and sustain our spirit. Roddenberry's vision gives us hope. It shows many people otherwise uninterested in science the *meaning* of the space programs humanity pays its tax dollars for—and this singular service in itself is another reason to value Star Trek and science fiction in general.

We *can* build that future, that Federation. All is not hopeless, despite news headlines. The individual is *not* powerless. We do not need to wallow in despair. If we are enterprising, willing to risk, trust, and believe, if we keep our eyes, hearts and minds open, if we vote for those who *will* work toward those values, toward space colonization, toward that future, we *will* achieve the dream.

That's the message in Star Trek.

Life is replete with encouraging phenomena. While our media tend to emphasize the negative aspects of prebimillennial life like wars, hijackings, natural disasters, starvation, religious strife, new diseases, and so on, we virtually ignore the positive things happening all around us. Smallpox, that ancient killer of millions upon millions, has been almost eradicated worldwide thanks to modern medicine. Technology has brought us computer power accessible to any middle-class family—which promises vast educational benefits for our children. The media themselves are being demassified and rendered accessible to average folk through cable TV. There is more creative energy in global society than ever before. One needs just listen to 1980s music in all its marvelous diversity to see that. Love and compassion are on the rise. The aid to famine victims in Africa by average people, governments, youth, churches, women's groups—all proves this.

And then there's the space program, once again gearing up to full bore in the U.S. with plans for a permanent space station, with the Space Telescope and the Galileo Jupiter probe to be launched next year, with the unending Soviet Salyut missions, with next year's triple-header, missions to Halley's Comet by the U.S.S.R., by the European Space Agency, and by Japan, and with the durable U.S. probe Voyager II reaching Uranus in January '86.

Yes, the signs of hope surround us.

About *Best of Trek*:

I do recommend that you consult with someone scientifically literate to advise you on which speculations are worthy of publication and which are not. It is the one weak area I see in your otherwise great books, and I for one would like to see more science and sociopolitical articles and less movie reviews—most of which are extremely redundant. Lately there also seems to be a distinct imbalance of character-analysis articles and religiophilosophical essays. Some of these have been very good indeed.

I think the best writer you have is Joyce Tullock, who is quite insightful and a talented wordsmith. If she has a fault it is in not taking her argument to its logical conclusion. While reading her articles I find myself sort of cheerleading her on—she sees things more or less clearly and I keep hoping she will take the next step, but she never does. There are levels of meaning to all the concepts she deals with, and while she is on a higher level than the rest of your writers, she seems unable to take the next step. A prime example is in her latest article on *The Search for Spock* where she concludes that "the needs of the one outweigh the needs of the many." Needless to say, this is as bad, accepted as an absolute, as the reverse statement. And it is certainly not the theme of either *The Search for Spock* or Star Trek as a whole, a series which time and again showed characters willing to sacrifice self for the many. The message of *The Search for Spock* was that there are no absolute moral truths, no laws which are perfect, no duties higher than life and love. Sometimes the one outweighs the many. It depends on circumstance.

An area to which you should devote more effort is the sociopolitical, the "future history" and "future society" scenario. I for one would really enjoy reading speculations about these areas. Houston's and Mason's efforts were interesting. Mason in particular did his research well, though I've spotted a number of inconsistencies. I also enjoyed Rebecca Hoffman's and Pamela Rose's work. But so much more could be done! Just what kind of society is the Federation? How does it work? What sort of political system does it have? How are elections managed? What kind of governmental mechanism does it have? What, exactly, is Starfleet? Is it military or paramilitary? How does it work? How does one rise through the ranks? What about the Academy? It is elitist? You had the one brief article on Starfleet security and marines. What about intelligence agencies and counterespionage? What about the army?

Then there are the other societies in the Star Trek universe. I have to discount Leslie Thompson's articles on the Klingons and the Romulans, which were extremely superficial examples of political bias and historical ignorance. While Leslie seems a very pleasant person, she isn't much of a thinker. What about the Andorians, the Tellarites, Vulcan, the Orions, the Gorns, the First Federation, etc., etc.? So much exists for you to print articles on, yet you seem to ignore all these areas in favor of endless reviews and trivia. Is the problem simply that no one submits quality articles in the areas I have suggested?

Thanks very much for listening to all this and thanks even more for *Best of Trek*, which has convinced me there are lots of worthwhile people left in the world. You guys down there deep in the heart of the Lone Star State do a great job. Keep it up, y'all hear? Till later then, *au revoir* and *hasta la vista*!

THE SECOND STAR TREK
FAN POLL RESULTS

compiled by G. B. Love

Literally thousands of you were kind enough to respond to our second fan poll. It took longer than we anticipated to open, read, and tabulate your votes—we didn't know so many of you would write! Thanks, and look forward to our next poll, coming soon!

We expected a flood of mail in response to this poll, but we had no idea so many of you would take the time and effort to participate. Frankly, we were amazed as the pile of responses just kept growing, day after day. We received so many, in fact, that we were somewhat daunted by the thought of having to open, read, and compile each and every one of them.

But we got it done. Statistically, these results are going to be off a bit. A number of responses just plain arrived too late to be included. (They're *still* arriving, even as this is written, and we expect they'll keep coming in for quite a while. Heck, we occasionally get a response to our *first* fan poll!) We did (and do) read these responses as well, so no one needs to feel left out.

As with our "fan on the street" poll, the percentages are rounded off—for example, 56.34% became 56%, 34.74% became 35%—and any response totaling less than 1% was dropped. So none of the categories add up to exactly 100%; some noticeably less. "Favorite" and "least favorite" episodes were given weighted values, and are presented in resulting order.

Before getting on to the poll results, we'd like to say that we were pleased to see that virtually everyone included name and address, as well as the other personal information we asked for in question #1. (Several fans even sent photos; one sent a lovely shot of an entire menagerie of animals, all named for *Enterprise* crewmembers!) We take this as a sign of your confidence, and we'll use the information only in the way you'd want us to: to make our *Best of Trek* series more interesting and entertaining for our readers.

We received a larger percentage of responses from male readers than we expected: 46%. (This percentage *does* add up to 100%—54% were female.) Response to our earlier poll and mail to Trek Roundtable, etc., has always indicated a larger female readership, upward of 65%. Apparently you guys just weren't writing. Seriously, it looks as if fandom is beginning to balance out a little bit, which can only be for the better.

Most of our readers are single (73%) and under thirty (55%). The oldest respondent was seventy-three, the youngest eleven. The profession most listed was "student," followed by medical services and nursing, teacher, librarian, housewife, engineer, and secretary. The most unusual occupation was that of a fan who lives and works on the Ringling Bros. Barnum & Bailey Circus train!

Most of our respondents live in the U.S., of course; we think we detected a larger number of rural dwellers than would be expected in a general sampling of this size. We received a goodly number of foreign responses: a whole bunch from Canada, of course, always staunch Star Trek fans, several from Australia and New Zealand, a smattering from the Netherlands, Belgium, and England. A couple came in from Japan, two from India, one from Hong Kong, and one from Nepal. We received our first letter from Malaysia, and our second from the U.S.S.R. Other countries we heard from included Mexico, Brazil, Ireland, France, Italy, Spain, Monaco, and Yugoslavia. We've yet to receive our first from mainland China, but we're hoping!

(Unfortunately, before we could write this article—but, thank goodness, *after* compiling results for the poll—all of our foreign responses, which were together, were accidentally discarded. So while the votes of our foreign friends counted, we aren't able to share any quotations from their letters with you. We apologize to you and to each and every one of them.)

Okay, here goes:

2. Please, list, in order of preference, your ten favorite episodes.

1. "City on the Edge of Forever."
2. "Amok Time"
3. "Balance of Terror"
4. "All Our Yesterdays"
5. "The Menagerie"
6. "The Enemy Within"
7. "The Trouble with Tribbles"
8. "A Piece of the Action"
9. "Shore Leave"
10. "Space Seed"

(Quote: "City" is a solid drama, with excellent use of the characters, and a nice dramatic "punch." Ellison's original script was, as he has contended, better drama, but the episode as aired was better Star Trek." Wendy Worthington, Huntingdon Valley, Pa.)

There are two major surprises here:

Not only did "A Piece of the Action" rank above two episodes which placed in both our first fan poll and our "street" poll, but it was not even in the running in either of those polls. We can't explain this, except to guess that fans are beginning to more fully recognize and appreciate the fine comedic performances of Shatner and Nimoy, as well as the rest of the cast, in this episode. As one fan put it, "even though Fizzbin isn't *anywhere* in Hoyle."

"All Our Yesterdays" also didn't appear in the top ten of either poll, but its presence here is somewhat less surprising. We feel that the popularity of A. C. Crispin's wonderful novel *Yesterday's Son* increased awareness and appreciation of the episode.

Runners-up included (in order) "Mirror, Mirror," "Assignment: Earth," "Arena," "The Enterprise Incident," "The Empath," "Friday's Child," "The Devil in the Dark," and "This Side of Paradise."

3. Please list, in order of dislike, your five least-favorite episodes.

1. "And the Children Shall Lead"
2. "Spock's Brain"
3. "The Way to Eden"
4. "Let That Be Your Last Battlefield"
5. "The Apple"

Finishing up, in order, were "Miri," "The Savage Curtain," "Who Mourns for Adonais," "Plato's Stepchildren,"

"The Omega Glory," and "Charlie X." Things certainly have changed. Our original poll indicated that "Omega Glory" was one of the most-disliked episodes. Now several others finished even lower, many of them generally considered to be superior episodes. "Charlie X," for example, made a decent showing in the "favorite episode," category; "The Savage Curtain" was listed by a number as being their very favorite show.

(Quote: "Unfortunately this list was all too easy to make; however, I could only have added about three or four more to it." Rob Haycock, Carbondale, Ill.)

4. Who is your favorite Star Trek character?

The voting in this category was split quite a bit more than we've seen in the past. Captain Kirk won this with 39% of the vote. Second place, as would be expected, was captured by Mr. Spock, with 32%; Dr. McCoy came his perennial third with 18%. Newcomer Saavik vaulted her way over the "old crew" with 9%; a number of readers indicated that they would have voted for her had Kirstie Alley continued in the role.

Uhura came in fifth with about 1%, followed by Scotty, Sulu, Chekov, and Christine Chapel, all (somewhat surprisingly) with less than 1%. A few votes went to the *Enterprise*; others listed as favorites were Sarek, Janice Rand, David Marcus, Kevin Riley, Lieutenant Kyle, and Amanda. One adamant and unapologetic reader cast a ballot for "Mr. Adventure"!

5. Who is your favorite Star Trek actor?

William Shatner won this handily, with 40% of the ballots. Leonard Nimoy and DeForest Kelley finished almost dead even with about 22% each. Nichelle Nichols came fourth with 6%; Kirstie Alley fifth with 5%; James Doohan, George Takei, Walter Koenig, and Majel Barrett all fared better than their characters, getting approximately 1% each. Garnering just a little bit less, but about enough to round out the hundred, was Mark Lenard. Also named were Grace Lee Whitney, Merritt Butrick, Robin Curtis, and Roger C. Carmel.

6. Which character do you feel is most important to Star Trek?

Captain Kirk won this one going away (54%). Spock finished second with a respectable 39%. Dr. McCoy came in a distant third with 5%. A surprising fourth-place finisher, with almost 1% of the total, was the *Enterprise*. Among the crewmembers, only Scotty got enough votes to mention.

(Quote: "I have to say Captain Kirk. As shown in the movies, it is only his presence that brings them all together. He is the one that is closest to the hearts of the crew. Even though they were all willing to sacrifice for Spock in *The Search for Spock*, I don't think that it could have happened without Kirk's leadership." Betty Anne Wright, Sugar City, Ida.)

7. *Which actor do you feel contributed the most to Star Trek?*

William Shatner and Leonard Nimoy finished much closer together in this category than in "favorite actor": Shatner led by only one percentage point, 43% to Nimoy's 42%. DeForest Kelly came third with 12%. Several readers insisted upon listing all three men as one entry, contending that their ensemble was so effective that it became an integral part of Star Trek's success. Nichelle Nichols earned mention in this category, as well.

(Quote: "I don't think that you can really put a "price tag" on what actor contributes the most to Star Trek. I think that *all* the actors together form Star Trek and you can't take away from or add to that." Janet Andrews, Seattle, Wash.)

8. *Who is your favorite villain?*

Lots and lots of votes were cast in this category, and although we can list leaders, there's no clear, outright winner. Khan Noonian Singh led with 21%, far below his runaway lead in our "fan on the street poll," but considerably higher than his lowly finish in our first poll. His manic performance in *Wrath of Khan* obviously still remains vivid in fans' minds, but not to the point of driving out everyone else.

In order, the next favorites were: Harry Mudd (18%); the female Romulan commander (12%); Kor (11%); Trelane, the "Squire of Gothos" (9%); Mark Lenard's Romulan commander (8%); Kruge (4%—a somewhat surprisingly poor showing for the killer of David Marcus); T'Pring (2%); the Gorn (2%); Kang (2%); and a whole slew of others with less than 1% each: Elaan of Troyius, Dr. Simon Adams, Joachim, Captain Koloth, the Horta, and Ruk.

9. *Who is your favorite male guest star?*

Mark Lenard won this category with a hefty 53%. He has always been the favorite of many for his performance as the sympathetic Romulan commander, but it was probably his return as Sarek in *The Search for Spock* which boosted his popularity almost twenty points over his first-place finish in our original poll.

William Campbell, who appeared twice as the immature Trelane and as Kirk's nemesis Koloth, again finished second, this time with 14%. Third place was captured by Merritt Butrick (11%); fourth place was a tie between Robert Lansing and Roger C. Carmel (8% each). No one else did nearly as well: William Windom, who finished in a tie for third in our original poll, didn't even get a full percent this time around; also finishing surprisingly low was Ricardo Montalban, whose Khan topped the favorite-villain list. Also getting enough votes to be mentioned were Jeffrey Hunter, John Colicos, Christopher Lloyd, David Soul, Paul Winfield, and Gary Lockwood (who also finished considerably higher in our first poll).

10. Who is your favorite female guest star?

The voting in this category was much closer than in the male guest star contest. Mariette Hartley won this category with 21%; she is much more visible now than several years ago and the popularity of *Yesterday's Son* probably helped her out considerably. Finishing second was Jane Wyatt (19%), proving that the fans haven't forgotten her even if Paramount seemingly has. Third place was captured by Joan Collins with a meager 10%. Miss Collins finished first in our first poll; obviously fans have a hard time reconciling her current super-bitch image with the goodness of Edith Keeler. Joanne Linville was fourth with 6%; Bibi Besch a close fifth with 5%; Teri Garr sixth with 2%. Rounding out the list with less than 1% each were Sabrina Scharf, Susan Oliver, France Nuyuen, Arlene Martel, Celia Lovsky, Dame Judith Anderson, Sandra Smith, and Kathryn Hays.

11. Which do you think is the most believable piece of equipment aboard the Enterprise?

The computer won hands down with 34% of the vote. The communicator came in second with 25%; the phaser third with 20%; and the transporter fourth with 13%. Getting about or less than 1% each were the ship's communications network, the Spacedock, McCoy's instruments, the shuttlecraft, and faster-than-light warp drive.

(Quote: "In line with my experience with "high tech" gadgetry in police work, I'll believe anything as long as it breaks down when it's most needed." Dolores Wolan, Jacksonville Beach, Fla.)

12. Whom do you consider the best writer of televised episodes?

D. C. (Dorothy) Fontana was the runaway winner in this

category, with a whopping 54% of the vote! Coming in second was Theodore Sturgeon (17%), and the Great Bird himself, Gene Roddenberry, was third (15%). Fans seem to have warmed up a little bit more to Harlan Ellison, giving him fifth place with 9% of the vote. David Gerrold (2%) was followed by Gene L. Coon, Samuel A. Peeples, Richard Matheson, Jerome Bixby, and Paul Schneider.

(Quote: "D. C. Fontana seemed to have a real feel for the characters, a dedication to continuity, and an ability to make even the most ludicrous plots seem credible." Lynda Cohn, Palmdale, Calif.)

13. Do you prefer "action" shows or "think" shows?

As was expected, "think" shows won this by a wide margin—68% to 32%. Most people, however, pointed out that a mixture of both is the way to go, and that Star Trek as a series did an exceptionally good job in that area.

(Quote: "Star Trek is a dramatic adventure series, period. Action should be the predominant mode of entertainment. "Thinking" should reflect the action and remain consistent throughout the framework of the series. However, Star Trek as an allegory has brought it to its current cult status. Some people have come to "believe" that symbol manipulation, no matter how "logical" can be an adequate substitute for reality. It is an artifact that is held in high regard as possessing some sort of magical power. Star Trek should tell a story, but its premise should not be a way of life for Mankind—it is a *military* mission! Most certainly, even from this, favorable resolutions will occur, but they should not be blown out of proportion to the original event." John M. Farion, Los Angeles, Calif.)

14. Do you think that the major characters should die, marry, or otherwise undergo major changes?

It's virtually impossible to state the answers to this question in percentages. The majority—the vast majority, in fact—of those responding said that change is both inevitable and necessary, and that Star Trek's major characters *should* change.

Marriage seemed to be an acceptable character development for just about everybody except Spock. But very few readers said they would like to see any (more) deaths, no matter how dramatically valid.

Most readers felt that the best kind of change would result from the characters reacting naturally to age, reassignment, death (of others), etc., and agree that some of this is developing in the movie series.

15. Would you prefer to have Paramount keep making Star Trek movies, or would you prefer to have Star Trek return to television (commercial or cable) as a regular series?

A dual set of percentages on this one: Fans favoring a new series over movies, 67% . . . *but* fans preferring movies if there is no guarantee of maintaining a series' quality, 87%!

In other words, fans are more than willing to wait the two years or so between films to ensure that they will have a well-made and entertaining Star Trek "episode." Since no one can guarantee that a series will always be first-rate (we know that the nature of television works against such success), this is virtually a landslide in favor of films versus TV.

16. Woul you go to a Star Trek movie or watch a television series if new actors played the parts of Kirk, Spock, etc.?

For a yes-or-no question, we sure got a lot of answers on this one. Some fans said maybe, depending on how and why the original actors were replaced. A goodly number (39%) said a flat-out no, and insisted that a Star Trek without the original cast would not be Star Trek at all. A somewhat lesser number (23%) said yes, maintaining that Star Trek as a concept is so strong and viable that new actors would only present new and exciting facets of it. Yet a fourth contingent (as with the "maybes" above) said that they'd give it a chance, but that the new people had better be "damned good."

(Quote: "It would break my heart, but I'd go. With all due respect to the actors' other roles, they *are* my twenty-third-century friends. . . . The smile in Kirk's eyes, the slight cock of Spock's head, the cat-who's-swallowed-the-canary look on McCoy's ["Your mother says you had a teddy bear . . ."] face. The actors have added the dimensions to the one-dimensional stick heroes. They breathed life into the parts, and each hesitation, each gesture, each quiet word is Kirk, is McCoy, is Spock. . . . These are people I knew very well, and that is what makes Star Trek what it is." Kathryn Jones, Rice Lake, Wis.)

17. Do you think that the producers should start bringing in new, younger actors, playing new characters, who can take over when the original cast members retire or move on to other things?

A resounding 89% of our readers said that, yes, new characters should be introduced and developed.

(Quote: "Look at *M*A*S*H*. They were very successful at bringing in new characters. They did so well in some cases the new characters were better liked than those they replaced." Karen Kujala, Taylor, Mich.)

18. If you could change any one thing about Star Trek, what would it be?

Somewhat surprisingly, a large number of readers (35%) said they wouldn't change anything, even if they could. We were also somewhat disconcerted by a lot of the answers to this question, as most fans apparently saw it as an opportunity to mention either their "pet peeve" or "secret wish." Responses ranged from "Get rid of Robin Curtis's hair style" to "Let's see Kirk and Spock come out of the closet!" Other changes mentioned were: "Bring back the original uniforms"; "Use Kirk less"; "Use Spock less"; "Use Kirk more"; "Use Spock more"; "Bring back the original *Enterprise*"; "Keep politics out of the movies"; and so on.

It's interesting to mention that about 20% of the respondents mentioned the Star Trek books, either to wish that they were more like the series or to hope that they will appear more often.

(Quote: "I'd bring on the rest of Kirk's children. Lord knows David wasn't the only one!" Kelly Fitzgerald, McAllen, Tex.)

19. Who is your favorite Star Trek writer?

Some fans were confused by this question; we wanted fans to consider *all* Star Trek writers—television, movies, novels, fan fiction. Until our next poll, when we can state the questions more clearly, we'll have to settle for these results, which may or may not be exactly what fans think: D.C. Fontana (25%), James Blish (22%), Diane Duane (19%), Gene Roddenberry (11%), A.C. Crispin (9%), Harlan Ellison (6%), David Gerrold (3%), Jean Lorrah (3%), Theodore Sturgeon (1%). Many, many others were mentioned.

20. Which is your single favorite episode?

Because the results in this category were not weighed as they were in the "ten best episodes" question, the favorite turned out to be one of which did not even make the top ten: "Journey to Babel" (26%). It was followed closely by "City on the Edge of Forever," with 23%. No other episode even got close to these two. A distant third was the two-part "The Menagerie" with 9%. It was followed by "Shore Leave" (5%), "Amok Time" (4%), "The Enemy Within" (4%), and "Balance of Terror," "The Trouble with Tribbles," "All Our Yesterdays," "Miri," "A Piece of the Action," and "For the World Is Hollow and I Have Touched the Sky," all with 2%. Getting approximately 1% were "Arena," "Mudd's Women," "The Deadly Years," "Assignment Earth," "The Galileo Seven," "The Devil in the Dark," "The Tholian Web," "Charlie X," "Errand of Mercy." Virtually every episode was named in this category; we'll let you guess which three or four weren't.

21. *Which is your favorite Star Trek movie?*

This finished up a dead heat. *Star Trek III: The Search for Spock* got 45% of the vote and *Star Trek II: The Wrath of Khan* got 43%. *Star Trek: The Motion Picture* got the remaining 12%.

22. *In which episode do you think each of the major actors gives his or her best performance?*

We decided to include the movies in this category as well, as many fans obviously consider them "episodes" in the ongoing Star Trek saga. Because each star much be listed, we're only including the top vote-getters for each.

William Shatner—"Turnabout Intruder" (25%), *The Search for Spock* (20%), "City on the Edge of Forever" (18%), "The Enemy Within" (11%).

Leonard Nimoy—"Amok Time" (22%), "The Enterprise Incident" (15%), "All Our Yesterdays" (14%), "This Side of Paradise" (11%).

DeForest Kelly—"For the World Is Hollow and I Have Touched the Sky" (30%), "The Empath" (24%), "The Tholian Web (19%).

James Doohan—"Who Mourns for Adonais" (21%), *Wrath of Khan* (20%), "Lights of Zetar" (19%).

Nichelle Nichols—"Charlie X" (35%), "Mirror, Mirror" (23%), "Plato's Stepchildren" (14%).

George Takei—"The Naked Time" (65%), *The Search for Spock* (23%).

Walter Koenig—*Wrath of Khan* (31%), "The Deadly Years" (22%), "The Way to Eden (11%).

Majel Barrett—"What Are Little Girls Made Of?" (43%), "Amok Time" (36%), "Return to Tomorrow" (15%).

23. *Which episode do you consider to be the best-written?*

"City on the Edge of Forever" won going away with 33% of the vote. It was a tie for second place, with "Amok Time" and "The Trouble with Tribbles" each getting 17% of the vote. Fourth was "Requiem for Methuselah" with 10%, fifth was "Journey to Babel" with 9%, sixth was "The Enemy Within" with 6%, seventh was "The Menagerie" with 4%, and "The Tholian Web" was eighth with 3%. All other titles mentioned got less than 1%.

24. Which episode was the very first you saw?

This, admittedly, was a pretty subjective question. Most fans, especially the younger ones, don't have a clear memory of watching their first Star Trek episode. But we included it so that fans who wished to do so could make a distinction between their *first* episode and the one that made them a fan (next question). Surprisingly, not one, but *two* episodes got a substantial number of votes here: "Devil in the Dark" (11%) and "The Man Trap" (16%).

"The Man Trap," of course, was the first episode aired, and therefore the first episode those of us lucky enough to be watching that night back in 1966 ever saw. As to "Devil in the Dark," we feel that it is probably the unique combination of characterization and a "monster" that made this episode one that was memorable for quite a few readers. Once hooked by the "thriller" aspect of the show, one couldn't help but be impressed by the humanistic resolution.

Naturally, many other episodes were also named.

25. Which episode so interested you that you became a Star Trek fan?

Judging by the responses, this was perhaps the most frustrating question we asked. A goodly number of fans were able to simply list a title: "Journey to Babel," "City on the Edge of Forever," "Devil in the Dark," "Amok Time," and "The Doomsday Machine" were among a number which cropped up regularly. But the most common answer was "All of them," followed by "I don't remember."

26. Which Star Trek novel is your favorite?

Hot competition here, folks. First place was captured by Ann Crispin's *Yesterday's Son* (24%), followed closely by Sonni Cooper's *Black Fire* (20%), Diane Duane's *The Wounded Sky* (18%), Linda Kagan's *Uhura's Song* (15%), and Jean Lorrah's *The Vulcan Academy Murders* (11%). Vonda McIntyre's novelization of *Star Trek II: The Wrath of Khan* finished sixth with 6%, and her *The Entropy Effect* was seventh with 2%. No other novel got more than 1%.

27. Who is your favorite Star Trek fiction writer?

Even though her books finished sixth and seventh in the above query, Vonda McIntyre easily won this category with 28% of the vote. A. C. Crispin came in second with 19%, James Blish was third with 11%, and the team of Sondra Marshak and Myra Culbreath finished fourth with 10%. Alan

Dean Foster got 3% of the vote (we suspect from longtime but loyal fans) to tie with Diane Duane. Sonni Cooper, Janet Kagan, Melinda Snodgrass, and Jean Lorrah each got 1% of the vote.

Responses to the preceding two questions indicate that except for the Blish and Foster series, it is the more recent titles which come to mind when fans think of novels and writers.

28. What is your favorite Star Trek merchandising tie-in?

The winner, by a landslide, is novels (65%). Posters and photographs (invariably mentioned together) also got a good vote (20%), followed by magazines (11%), patches and buttons (8%), and model kits (5%). Also mentioned were bumper stickers, blueprints, dolls, phasers, bubblegum cards, and "those things with Kirk or Spock's face that fit in your car's back window and wave."

29. Give a brief description of your "dream episode"—the Star Trek show you'd *make if you had the chance.*

We're very, very limited on how much space we can devote to detailing the "dream episodes," so we played a little unfair, pulled a bunch at random, and kept the ones we felt were either entertaining, interesting, offbeat, or particularly representative of a majority of readers.

Surely, the most often mentioned "dream" was to have an episode or movie in which all of the stars had featured roles. A good script, excitement, action, etc. were secondary to letting each member of the "family" participate.

It occurs to us that some folks might be embarrassed by seeing their fantasies in print, benign and common though they may be, so we're deleting the names from the "dream episodes" quoted below. The fun in this case is in seeing what our fellow fans think, not particularly in knowing who they are.

"Spock falls in love (as Sarek must've done with Amanda) without any contrivance in the plot, and has to choose between his bond-mate and Kirk/Starfleet."

"A blend of exciting action and thoughtful plot, all regular characters used to their full potential, charismatic guest stars (especially villains), interesting, well-integrated special effects."

"Where Dr. McCoy meets the woman of his dreams. Come on, give the poor guy a break! He's been so neglected all these years that it would only be fair!"

"The Star Trek episode I would most like to see would be one in which all the characters are shown having flashbacks into their earlier lives. I realize this would take some time (not to mention the difficulties of making the actors look younger or having other actors portray them), but if possible, it could be a series of episodes on television in which each character is spotlighted thinking of his or her past life and having this tied in with the present situation. In this way, new actors could be introduced without changing the characters in any way. I realize this may well pose a problem for future episodes, but once the public is indoctrinated to new faces, it may be easier for them to accept other characters in the future when the actors or actresses move on or retire."

"At least two hours in length, written by Gene Roddenberry and D. C. Fontana, produced by Gene Roddenberry and directed by Leonard Nimoy. Minor regulars (Uhura, Chekov, Sulu, etc.) get good parts; major story."

"*Star Trek II: The Wrath of Khan* was the perfect Star Trek episode. It can't be improved upon."

"My 'dream episode' would have all the characters present. There would have to be a tragedy/sorrow storyline. One of the characters would have some tragic experience and the rest would try and help him cope with the problem. The storyline would probably center around Kirk, Spock, and McCoy, emphasizing the friendship of the three of them. It might have a sad ending, as in 'City,' because that would emphasize the friendship more than a happy ending would."

"I've always wanted to see more of Spock's family and culture. The Vulcans are such an interesting group of people that a series could probably be done with them as the main characters."

"My dream episode would include a brief romance between Kirk and Rand. One that is mutually ended, but does not present a future problem with them working together. (For instance, having them stranded in a dangerous situation together and they turn to each other for comfort.)"

"I would like to see them do a series of Star Treks that would show the backgrounds and childhoods and teenage years of the main characters. Such as show Spock growing up on Vulcan; how Spock related to everyone, then show him in Starfleet Academy and on pre-*Enterprise* space missions. I wish they could do this with each main character.''

"I would like to see Kirk and Uhura get married. It seems he always had a soft spot in his heart for her. I would also like to see McCoy reunited with his daughter Joanna.''

"Well, since I am one of those females who is hopelessly infatuated with Spock, it is one in which he gives in to that worst of emotions, love. He is trapped on the surface of an inhospitable planet with Christine Chapel (well, she's been waiting a long time for it, and I think she deserves Spock) —the *Enterprise* has been forced to flee from a Romulan surprise attack—Chris and Spock have to fight off Romulans and the elements—Spock realizes that Chapel is an extraordinary person and that he likes her very much—they end up in bed together (after all, Spock is only half Vulcan; let's not forget the other half is *human*)—the *Enterprise* returns to rescue them—Spock and Chapel return to their former relationship, although perhaps friendlier.''

"I would like to see a serious episode where Uhura is in charge of the ship while her superiors are elsewhere or unable to command, or she could be in charge of a large landing party, trying to survive in a hostile environment. I bet she'd make a good diplomat, too. I would like to see more interaction between Uhura and Spock (not romantic).''

"The Gorns come back to help the Federation beat back a Romulan invasion of both the Federation and the Gorns' empire.''

"Kirk gets suspicious of particular crew members, and decides to do some quiet checking. He discovers that there might be a quiet conspiracy, i.e., spies aboard the ship who might have a connection with spies aboard other Constitution Class ships. The only thing he could do would be, with Spock's expert help, to find out who the mastermind is and expose the plot.''

"The Federation sends Kirk and crew with Sarek on a diplomatic mission into the Romulan Empire. Once there,

Saavik learns that she has a sister who was raised as a Romulan! A sister who looks suspiciously like Kirstie Alley.''

"Saavik, who is discovered to be a blood relative to Spock, gives birth to a daughter by David Marcus. The girl grows up and marries the grandson of Leonard McCoy. The couple produce a set of twins, genetically merging our beloved triad into the ideal combination of Vulcan-human hybrid."

"Kirk and Spock are stranded on a hostile planet while the *Enterprise* is off warning Starfleet of impending doom. The captain and his first officer become very close in their relationship/friendship. They are never together long enough or often enough to suit me."

"I would like to see Uhura and McCoy travel to the deep South of the mid-1800s via the Guardian of Forever. Let's see them enlighten some attitudes in *that* era."

"I'd really like to see a good treatment of the character of Montgomery Scott . . . all we hear is that he has a brogue and drinks a lot (which would get him bounced out of the present-day military). I am sure that with his Celtic heritage there would be a lot of poetry in his soul and more than engineering in his career, as more than one "biography" would have us believe."

"I never thought about this except that I'd like to see Uhura, Sulu, etc. get more to do, and I get tired of Kirk chasing every skirt in sight. I would like to see more minorities, females, and aliens in the crew/Starfleet. (I'm not a minority, but the predominance of Caucasians is ridiculous.) It would be a 'think' show."

"I'd write an episode where the *Enterprise* and crew discover the *Star Wars* galaxy, and they join forces with Luke, Han, and Leia to fight some more evil that has sprung up in the galaxy."

"An episode where all the characters get a chance to display their style with an adventure to bring this out. *Star Trek III: The Search for Spock* was nearly perfect if Spock was in it more."

*   *   *

"Civilians, mystery in the 'Courtmartial' style, a bit less Kirk so I can have more of the rest of the group, and a value/moral dilemma that is well stated to provoke thought without hitting me over the head. Plus it would have to have comedy. Chekov couldn't scream, Uhura could open only one hailing frequency, Chapel couldn't pine over Spock (perhaps a torrid affair with a younger man like Kevin Riley?), and Kirk couldn't go to bed with anyone (maybe his teddy bear). It would have to have Klingons (Kor! Koloth!) and Romulans and Vulcans; and I insist on some Andorians—to include at least one female. Uhura would have to sing several times and Spock would have to play his harp. Security could see a 'job action' because of the hazardous duty—I'd like to see some faces remain the same from week to week. And younger crew people to be integrated in some way—I'd like to resurrect Scotty's nephew. Of course this description comes under Uhura's classification, 'This is fantasy.' "

"Put me in it! (That brief enough for you?)"

That's all we have room for. Perhaps if enough of you request it, we'll run a special article in a future volume featuring more of the "dream episodes."

We'd like to thank each and every one of you who so kindly—and enthusiastically!—responded to our poll. We now have a better grasp of what we feel the majority of our fans would like to see in forthcoming *Best of Trek* volumes, and we're already making plans to run another poll sometime in the near future. (Not too near, however . . . we're still recovering from counting this one!)

Thanks again, and we hope you enjoyed seeing how your fellow fans feel about Star Trek. Most of all, we hope that these results will make you take the time to think *why* some answers were the same as your votes, or more likely, different from yours. We don't want anybody to change their opinions to reflect a perceived majority, but knowing what others think (and a little bit of why they think that way) is the first step to understanding and acceptance. And isn't that what Star Trek is all about?

BEST OF TREK
AUTHOR INDEX, VOLUMES 1–10

compiled by Deanna Rafferty

ABOUT THE EDITORS

Although largely unknown to readers not involved in Star Trek fandom before the publication of *The Best of Trek #1*, WALTER IRWIN and G. B. LOVE have been actively editing and publishing magazines for many years. Before they teamed up to create TREK® in 1975, Irwin worked in newspapers, advertising, and free-lance writing, while Love published *The Rocket's Blast—Comiccollector* from 1960 to 1974, as well as hundreds of other magazines, books, and collectables. Both together and separately, they are currently planning several new books and magazines, as well as continuing to publish TREK.